Deadly Silent

Ann Girdharry

Published May 2023

Chapter 1

Some days were good and some were bad. It was like that when you were a survivor. Emma was glad there were getting to be more of the good ones. But it didn't change how some days were still so bad they felt like a living hell and well shit, today had been one of them.

Emma sat on the edge of her sofa bed and sank her face into her hands. Fifteen years since the trauma and it still had the power to drag her down. She grabbed a bunch of her hair, tugging hard enough to bring tears to her eyes. Dark days like this were a test of her determination to never go back to Moorlands Psychiatric Hospital.

She'd dealt with post-traumatic stress disorder from a child aged six all the way through to the young woman she was now. She knew that if the day had been bad, the night would be worse. She still had the hours of darkness to get through.

You can make it. You're stronger. You can handle this.

But could she?

The light was fading, as a long summer day came to an end. It meant the darkness would be short, which was a blessing.

Closing her eyes, she took deep breaths. Then braced herself.

Don't be afraid. Your hands are going to be normal. And there will be no noises, I promise. If there are, you know it's not real.

Her breath was ragged as she cracked open her eyelids. Her palms were shaking. But they weren't red. They weren't slick with her sister's blood. There were no sounds. No rasping and bubbling as her sister struggled to hang on to life.

As Emma sagged, a muffled sob escaped her lips.

A while later she crossed to the window and gazed down at the street. Her apartment was in the shabby part of Himlands Heath, where only groups of young people ventured out at night. The area was deserted. She let down the blind with a *clack*.

She must do her best not to fall asleep and then she could keep away the recurring nightmare of the day her mother and sister died. Tomorrow would be a better day.

Her tried and tested method was to watch her favourite sci-fi series and curl up waiting for daylight. A giant bag of potato crisps was what she needed. She was a no-alcohol and no-drugs kind of gal, but comfort food could be a lifesaver.

Emma was rummaging in the kitchen cupboard when her phone rang. Shit. She hadn't turned up for her evening shift at the fast-food place and she hadn't bothered to call in sick either. She needed the job and she really needed the money but what could she say? That she couldn't toss burgers because she was having a bad day and would end up burning the food or herself, or both? That she had to stay inside until she felt better?

It was the first time she'd skipped a shift since she started work a month ago but hey, they'd be bound to give her a hard time. It was too much to deal with right now. Grabbing the bag of crisps, she was about to toss her phone onto the sofa when she saw who it really was – her best friend – Phoebe.

'Hey,' Emma said.

'Hey,' Phoebe replied.

Emma had met Phoebe when they were both fourteen and doing a therapy week at Moorlands. Back then, they'd both been in the children's part of the hospital. Emma had been going there off and on since she was six, but it was Phoebe's first visit. Right from the beginning there had been a bond between them, which was strange because Emma was used to being a loner. They had a special connection and knowing Phoebe had made Emma's life so much more bearable.

There had followed several years when they were both in and out of treatment. They had progressed to adult services and Phoebe was staying at Moorlands at the moment, whereas Emma had not been there for months.

She knew Phoebe's trauma well enough to not ask inane questions like, how are you doing? Instead, she waited.

'I went into town today,' Phoebe said.

Phoebe's voice was flat. The monotone was one of the side effects of medication.

'Okay,' Emma said.

'Kate wanted to see how I'd manage when I come out.'

Kate was one of the occupational therapists and her taking Phoebe on a home visit to her apartment would have been a way for her to assess if Phoebe would be able to cope on the outside.

'Kate's nice,' Emma said.

Kate was a motherly kind and she had a caring nature. Patients liked her.

'I know, but I can't come out. I'm not ready.'

Emma frowned. The last time they'd spoken, Phoebe had been hoping to leave Moorlands as soon as possible. What had changed?

'I saw *him*,' Phoebe said, and her voice broke.

A cold hand squeezed Emma's heart. 'No!'

'It was horrible.'

'How can that be possible? I'm so sorry.'

'They don't believe me but I swear it was him. He was standing outside the post office. I couldn't stop screaming.'

'Shit.'

Phoebe could only be talking about one person – the perpetrator who'd sexually assaulted her when she was a teenager. He was the reason Phoebe had ended up in hospital in the first place after she had taken an overdose. He was the one responsible for Phoebe's self-harming and her panic attacks.

Emma growled. 'The bastard. What the hell's he doing in Himlands Heath!'

The piece of shit had been released from prison recently. Phoebe's father was supposed to be keeping track of him and he'd said the bastard was hundreds of miles north in Birmingham. How dare he cross paths with her friend. He deserved to be dead.

'No one believes me,' Phoebe said. 'But I *know* it was him.'

'I believe you.'

She heard Phoebe take a shuddering breath. 'Thank you.'

'Don't be stupid, you don't need to thank me. Why are these people so dumb, why can't they believe you?'

'I don't know.'

'Kate didn't see him?'

'No, and she had to call the cops to help get me back to hospital.'

'Ah.'

Having a breakdown in public was horrible. Bystanders could get frightened. Sometimes onlookers were abusive. The police could be heavy-handed and especially with someone like Phoebe who kicked out and bit people when she panicked.

'I know it was him. Which means it isn't safe for me to leave Moorlands.'

'Do you want me to come?'

'I know you can't stand it here, even as a visitor. And, they won't let you see me this late.'

No, they wouldn't. The only way she'd be able to see Phoebe would be if Emma were admitted herself and she didn't want that to happen. Ever. She had promised herself, *never again*. She was building a life for herself and Moorlands wasn't part of it.

'Listen to me, he can't get to you.'

Phoebe didn't respond. The thing was they both knew it wasn't true. He could get to Phoebe in Phoebe's head and that was where he did the damage because Phoebe couldn't get him out.

'You're safe,' Emma said. 'You're in control and he can't hurt you.'

'Yeah.'

'Can you keep yourself okay tonight?'

This was a high-risk event. Emma knew enough about psychology and had been around enough patients and doctors to know the danger inside out. Meeting your perpetrator in a surprise situation would be a massive trigger for the original trauma. Phoebe would have been plunged into her own living hell. Would she be able to control her urge to self-harm?

'They didn't put you in Secure?'

'No.'

Emma already realised they hadn't because phones weren't allowed in Secure except in the afternoons, and then it was only under supervision. In Secure, there were no objects people might use to harm themselves or hurt other people, liberties were limited, and you were watched by staff or by cameras. Whereas the inpatient unit, where Phoebe was now, was much more relaxed.

'I'll be all right,' Phoebe said.

'You promise me you'll keep yourself safe? You can call me anytime. I'm not going to be sleeping tonight anyway. Even if I were, I wouldn't care.'

'I know.'

'Say it then.'

'I promise.'

There was a long silence. Emma could imagine the terror her friend had experienced in the high street. She could sense Phoebe's disintegration. The anguish as well, at how years of therapy and work on her self-worth and confidence had been dashed to splinters in an instant. It would take a mammoth effort for Phoebe to stay well and keep her grip on the here and now.

'You can do it. I know you can. You've got this,' Emma said.

'Uh huh.'

'He can't win.'

'I won't let him.'

'That's good. Keep thinking it. Repeat it like a mantra.'

'I'll try.'

'Which nurse is on duty tonight?' Emma asked.

'Lin.'

'That's good. You know you can talk to her.'

'Yeah.'

Lin was the kindest nurse of the whole lot and everyone's favourite.

'I'm on extra medication so I should be okay.'

There was another long silence.

'Hang on to the good things. Think of the picture you painted with the sea and the sky. That's where you're headed,' Emma said.

'I've got it in my room.'

Emma was pleased. 'Are you looking at it now?'

'How did you know? Yes. Lin put it at the end of my bed.'

Emma sent her silent appreciations to the nurse. That had been a very good idea.

'Keep looking at your dream. Remember, that's where you're going and nothing and no one is going to get in your way.'

Another long silence.

'I love you, Phoebe. I'm here for you.'

'Thank you.'

Phoebe sounded utterly broken. Anger and protectiveness made Emma clench her fists. She knew if she ever came face to face with Phoebe's perpetrator she would kill him with her bare hands.

There was a *click,* as Phoebe hung up.

Chapter 2

Emma's phone was on her knee with the volume right up. She kept glancing at the screen, to make sure she didn't miss a message from Phoebe. Phoebe was like family and she was all the family Emma had left.

She let Star Trek run on the television and the episodes went past one by one. It was an anchor and she'd used it many times over the years to while away the night hours. She had picked up the idea from another patient, who had used James Bond films in the same way.

Emma knew the Star Trek storylines, she'd watched them so often. That was the beauty of it and she got satisfaction out of lip-syncing with the actors and saying aloud the key lines of dialogue.

She hoped her friend was safe in bed, knocked out by medication. Sometimes drugs were the only thing to take the pain away. The problem was, you couldn't stay drugged out of your mind forever.

How could the perp be walking free after what he'd done? It was so wrong. And what the hell was he doing in Himlands Heath?

Poor Phoebe. It didn't matter how much Emma hated Moorlands, tomorrow she would go there to comfort her friend and give her strength. Phoebe might not be able to do it alone but they could do it together.

She sent a message.

I'm coming tomorrow. See you then.

Phoebe did not reply.

Emma fought off the drowsiness. She finally fell asleep a short while before dawn, but there had been no point in struggling because the nightmare she had desperately been trying to stave off, finally caught up with her.

I'm standing in my living room at home. The carpet is fluffy beneath my feet. I'm a little girl again, and my sister is here with me.

'Get a move on, Emma, or Dad'll be here before we're ready,' Juliette says.

Though she sounds exasperated, I know Juliette's not mad at me. She's nineteen and she's my big sister and she understands how excited I am and that's why I'm not helping much – it's not because I don't want to but because I'm jittery and my mind is jumping all over the place. We're supposed to be tidying the living room but she's the one doing the work. My job is to put away my stepdad's magazines. He always leaves them lying about. *I glance down and I see one of them in my hand.*

We're getting ready for the party – my party. I'm six today, and because it's my special day, my dad is allowed to visit me at home. That was my birthday wish, that and a bicycle.

In my nightmare, I know my wish is not going to come true. Wake up!

Juliette is humming. She's happy too, because of Dad coming and also she's a little bit in love. She's liked the boy down the road ever since we arrived in town, and he's asked her to the end of term gala. It's her first real date and it's a huge thing. Not only that but he's also written her a song. Imagine, your very own song. She told me he plays the piano, and he wants to be a famous songwriter one day. She's so lucky. My sister played me a recording of it, and she's humming it now.

'Are you two finished in there?' my mum calls from the kitchen.

Hearing my mum's voice, it's like my heart is being ripped apart. I want to shout at her and warn her. I want to wake up. Please let me wake up.

'Almost,' Juliette shouts back.

'Good,' my mum says. 'Then you'd better hurry Emma and get changed.'

My mum is decorating my cake in the kitchen which is why I'm not allowed in there. She's made me a special one, chocolate and shaped like a hedgehog. Juliette told me.

I go closer to my sister. 'Do you know what they got me?' I whisper.

Juliette laughs. 'You keep asking and I'm not going to tell. It's a secret.'

I can smell her perfume. See the softness in her eyes as she looks down at me. Wake up!

I give her a smile. Juliette's the best sister ever. She's pretty and smart. Actually, she's everything I wish I could be and am not. Her hair is blonde and mine is dark. She has glossy tresses and I have curls which I hate. She always has loads of friends and I don't. If only I could be more like her.

Juliette looks out for me and she keeps the horrible kids off my back. I love her for that, and for the way she stands up for me when my stepdad is nasty. He doesn't like the way I go silent around him although the thing is, I can't help it. When I feel nervous I clam up and it happens a lot when he's around.

One of the worst times is when he's with us at the dinner table and the four of us sit staring at each other and all I want is for it to be over. My throat goes tight and I can hardly swallow. I wish my mum didn't stay with him.

My mum tries to calm things down by being nice to him and I go sad inside when he shouts at me, but Juliette doesn't.

She gets angry. She shouts back and tells him to leave me alone while my mum just stares at the floor. It gets Juliette into trouble although she says she doesn't care.

'Why don't you go to our room. Start getting dressed up,' Juliette says.

Juliette is already in her party outfit. It's a red tartan miniskirt, matched with her favourite t-shirt. She got the top from our dad, and it has two palm trees on the front and an orange sun. He bought it on a trip to Miami. She loves it.

I shake my head. 'I don't know which one to choose. The flower dress or the blue one?'

'Try them both on and have a good look in the mirror. I'll be there in a minute.'

'All right. Will you do my hair for me?'

'Of course I will.'

In the nightmare, I try to stop myself from leaving the living room but I can't.

I run up the stairs and into the loft room which me and my sister share. Downstairs, Juliette has put on music. It's one of her favourites and I sing along as I rip off my jeans and sweatshirt. I'm so excited as I pull on the blue dress.

We've a long mirror in the corner and I twirl in front of it, frowning at the way my curls spring out in all directions. Taking off the dress, I try the flower one. Is this prettier? I like the colours more except the sleeves are getting a bit short. Does it look bad? Will anyone notice? I can't decide.

'Are you coming?' I shout.

There's no answer. The music is loud and I sing along to the refrain. Mum will tell Juliette to turn it down soon, I'm sure. I spy Juliette's necklace on the dresser and hold it to my chest. Wouldn't this be perfect? It's a string of silver with three blue-grey freshwater pearls in the centre. The pearls are misshapen. It's what makes them so beautiful. It'd be going too far asking to borrow it, even if it is my birthday, still I might risk it.

'Hey, what's taking you so long?' I call out.

Again, no answer. The music is so loud probably Juliette can't even hear me.

I run down the stairs and into the lounge and that's when my world is destroyed forever. Everything tilts and goes dark. I open my mouth to scream but nothing comes out.

My mother is sprawled in the kitchen doorway, her eyes are open yet sightless, her skull smashed in, like an egg cracked open. My sister is lying on the floor, her favourite t-shirt stained red. A pool of blood seeps around her. She has one hand lingering at her neck, her fingertips touching the red gash which has slit her throat in two.

I run to her and fall on my knees. I touch the puckered gash and try to push it closed. My hands are too small. My sister's hot blood spills over them, making it slippery and I can't get a hold. Juliette is looking at me. She's making a horrible rasping, bubbling sound.

No! No!

Time stands still. It's just me and her. And blood. The noises gradually fade and I see the light leave her eyes.

Emma woke from the nightmare. Clutching her knees to her chest, she gasped and tried to grab onto anything real – her sheet, a cushion, the edge of the sofa bed.

It's over. You're in your noisy, dirty little apartment, and it's over.

Juliette! Don't leave me!

Emma was sobbing. She could see her hands were slick with her sister's blood. Those moments would be with her forever. The red, the bubbling. How she could do nothing to save her. How one moment Juliette was there and the next, *poof,* gone.

Inside she was screaming her sister's name.

A part of her hadn't stopped screaming it for the last fifteen years.

Chapter 3

Vermin control is what I call it. I'm on the lookout for ones who need to be culled. A flash of leg. A glimpse of cleavage. Some of them act cute while others play innocent as they plan their advances and their treachery. But I'm watching and waiting and when they come too close, I strike.

I'm the snake hiding in the grass. They don't see the danger until they step on me and then it's too late.

People have no idea how cold and calculating I am. I suppose that's why they like me.

For this evening, everything's in place. All I have to do is wait.

Chapter 4

Phoebe Markham stared at the picture propped at the end of her bed. She traced the curl of the biggest wave with the ragged white at its tip, the moody sky threatening rain and the churn of a grey, restless ocean. In the distance lay an island, a far smudge of brown and green. This painting captured her dream of moving to Ireland.

There was a *tap tap* at the door from Lin, the nurse. Phoebe was glad it was Lin tonight. She was kind and she'd been very supportive of Phoebe's plans to move from the area.

'The doctor's prescribed you sedatives for this evening,' Lin said.

Phoebe put the pills in her mouth and drank from the plastic cup. As she closed her eyes, Lin tucked the bed sheet around her shoulders and clicked off the light.

'Give me a buzz if you need anything.'

Although they had not moved her to the Secure unit, she had been marked at heightened risk, and it was a comfort to know Lin would be monitoring her carefully. Like most of the staff, Lin was a person of habit. She would check back at the end of her rounds, before she sat through the night at the nurse's station.

Phoebe clutched at the pillow as an image came to mind of the showers at her old school. Steam rose from the hot water and she was frozen rigid, knowing someone was behind her and not being able to scream. She willed the medicine to take effect and little by little the image faded.

Her mind took her to Ireland. She tasted the salty air. One year ago she'd gone there on holiday with her parents. Ever since, she dreamed of her own cottage, isolated and far away from Moorlands and the horrible memories of Himlands Heath. The question had been, how to turn the dream into reality.

She painted many landscapes after that trip because she had fallen in love with the beauty and wild winds of the west coast. It was somewhere she felt she could be free.

She had been hopeful she could make it. Painting was her passion. Perhaps she could earn a living by selling her art, rather than relying on her parents for money. But her mother and father didn't see it that way.

It had taken Phoebe seven years to recover from the assault. She had been overwhelmed and broken and she had mended herself in the best way she could. Her parents never allowed her to work and they were always so worried about her fragility but now she was an adult and she wanted to follow her own path.

A month earlier, everything changed when she learned he was getting early parole. Her father broke the terrible news. It was two years earlier than they expected because of good behaviour. Phoebe vomited with anxiety on the spot. The sick irony and injustice of it. A sexual predator getting out due to good behaviour! Her life seemed to fall apart and a while later she was back at Moorlands.

Up until that moment, whenever she closed her eyes she had been able to taste the salt from the waves, and hear the cry of birds overhead. She had been working towards her independence.

Then today, catastrophe. She had spotted him outside the post office. He had been watching her with those leering eyes of his. She wanted to run but her legs refused. She had frozen, just as she had done when she was a fourteen-year-old girl.

It didn't matter how much they told her she would recover from the shock. Or how much they quizzed her, believing she had been mistaken and it wasn't him. She knew it *was him*.

Phoebe understood how psychiatrists worked. They thought she'd been so terrified by the *prospect* of seeing him, that she'd conjured it in her own head. For them, it had been an illusion. But Phoebe knew what she'd seen.

The aftermath was more devastating than she could ever have imagined. She wasn't strong enough and she never would be. The cottage was a dream and that's all it was – unreachable for someone like her.

Ireland was fading to a grey monotone and Phoebe waited. Thanks to the drugs her limbs were becoming disconnected from her brain. Her breathing had slowed and her thoughts felt as if they were moving away but then Hunt's face leered again.

She could smell his fetid breath as his body pushed against her chest. The shower and the terror, and the post office blurred together. She would never escape him. She didn't have energy enough to try.

As sleep finally took her, all she wanted was oblivion.

Just before 9.30pm, she suddenly awoke. A shadow leaned over her. It was as if a weight were crushing into her chest.

'Get up, Phoebe.'

The voice was dark and liquid and she was powerless again. She was dragged upright, her legs pushed from the bed.

'You're coming with me.'

'I don't want to.' Did she whisper it, or was it only a thought?

The corridor was deserted, and there were no sounds as they walked side by side to the exit keypad.

She watched through a brain fog of medication. The passcode was six digits. Each time a number was pressed, the pad gave a little beep. Then, *click*, the door was open.

In a few steps they were at the stairwell and heading up. This part of the hospital was for administrative staff and she had never been here before. At the top floor, they walked along a dimly lit corridor. Right at the end was a coffee area and a photocopy machine.

None of the windows of the hospital could be opened because they were either sealed units or they were screwed shut plus they had a security lock. She hoped it would keep her safe.

But no, for one of the windows, the screws had been removed and the lock was undone. With one shove, the frame slid open.

She tried to run but her legs would not obey.

'Out you go, Phoebe.'

They were right behind her and she wanted to protest and push back, but there was no fight left in her. She was in her nightshirt and a cool breeze brushed her body as she stepped onto the ledge.

'No. Please.'

'You'll do as I say.'

'I want to live.'

'This is the best thing that can happen. You know you've wanted it.'

'I have things to live for. Get away from me.'

'One last video, Phoebe, before you go. How about we say it's for Mum and Dad?'

Her phone was thrust into her hand.

A wave of dizziness hit her. She stared at the phone and then down at the ground which was four floors below. Her feet were white and trembling on the grey ledge.

'Please.'

'It's too late.'

She was crying, softly and silently.

'Do what you have to, Phoebe. And do it quickly.'

They were too strong. They always had been.

Closing her eyes, Phoebe Markham stepped into the void.

Chapter 5

DCI David Grant took a sip from his mug. The coffee was cold and he grimaced as he swallowed. It was the end of a long day. His first in his new role.

Grant had been promoted to lead a new Major Incident Team covering the counties of Sussex and Surrey. This was exactly the challenge he craved for his last years before retirement. It was an opportunity to really make a difference.

'Okay, Ruby, time to go home,' he said.

Ruby Silver, their consultant criminal profiler, was the only other person in the room. She was late twenties, a few years younger than Grant's daughter.

Looking up from her laptop Ruby gave him a genuine affectionate smile. 'If you say so. It's been an odd start, hasn't it?'

It certainly had.

Grant had moved across town from Himlands Heath local police station to Sussex Headquarters. The problem was, when he arrived he discovered there'd been a huge mess-up and their new offices weren't ready. In fact, it was a blundering error. Nothing was prepared. They had no furniture, no computers. Grant had to do a tour of the corridors to scrounge a couple of tables and some old plastic chairs. It wasn't exactly the beginning he had envisioned.

'An odd start? You're telling me,' Grant said. 'We're in no shape to take a case.'

In addition to the detective sergeants and detective constables already assigned, Grant had been given free rein to bring in any detectives he wanted. He had chosen to bring the best of his old team with him – Tom Delaney and Diane Collins, who had both been promoted to detective inspector, and Ruby. It was the same make-up as Grant's old team, minus his third DS who was facing criminal charges.

With a slight build, a pale complexion and dark hair, Ruby was a quiet young woman with fierce eyes. She had struggled to understand her value to him as a profiler. As far as Grant was concerned, she was a psychologist second to none. He had discovered her when she was a research assistant for a professor who'd been stealing her work. Back then, when Grant had seconded Ruby to his team, her input had been vital in solving an impossible case.

Ruby packed away her things. 'When do you think the equipment will arrive?'

'Who knows? Your guess is as good as mine. We'll have to make do until it does. Though this chair isn't doing my back any favours.'

This was a huge step up in responsibility except so far, not a step up in comfort nor resources. He didn't care. With any luck it would only take a few days for them to become operational.

'I hope Tom'll have prepared you both a nice supper,' he said.

Ruby zipped up her backpack. 'Every time Tom invites me over he makes something different. You'd be surprised. He's pretty good in the kitchen.'

Detective Inspector Tom Delaney had left a while earlier to go for a run.

'Him? A good cook? Now you're having me on.'

Ruby laughed.

Tom was Grant's right-hand man. Grant hoped that one day Tom would follow in his footsteps and lead his own MIT. DI Delaney was a rare find and one of the few with the ability to be great. The only slight complication was that Tom and Ruby were dating.

'I don't have a problem with that, as long as it doesn't get in the way of work and professionalism,' Grant had said when they'd told him. 'If it does, one of you will have to go.'

They had assured him work would be the priority, now and always. Having seen them under pressure, Grant believed them.

Ruby was on her way out and Grant was putting on his jacket when his mobile rang. Ruby stopped and Grant saw eagerness on her face. She was ready for their first case despite it having been a long and tedious day. Ah, the freshness and vigour of youth.

Thankfully, word had not yet gone out about the MIT. Official word, that was. Still, Grant knew his new boss, the detective chief superintendent, wouldn't let them sit idle for long. Despite his forty years of service and his vast experience as a detective, Grant felt his heart accelerate. He pushed back his greying hair.

'This is David Grant.'

'David, it's John Markham. I need your help.'

Grant took a cool breath and held back the rush of memories. He and John had been at school together and though they were no longer close friends, they knew each other well. The primary school they went to had only one class at that time, everybody knew everybody, and the common tragedy they'd endured as children had brought families closer together.

'It's Phoebe, she's…' John Markham's voice broke.

'Take your time. What's happened? What do you need?'

Grant knew about John's daughter. He'd not worked on the case but he knew she had been assaulted and since then, she'd had a difficult life. John was a Member of Parliament. His constituency of Mid Sussex covered Himlands Heath and the surrounding area. John had always been very involved locally and he had plenty of contacts. If he was reaching out for help, that meant it was serious.

John cleared his throat. 'My daughter's had a terrible accident.'

The poor young woman. As if she'd not suffered enough already.

'I'm at Moorlands. They called me half an hour ago to tell me she… she jumped from the top floor.'

Grant went cold. 'I'm so sorry.'

'She's dead, David. They say it was suicide.'

'I am so so sorry.'

'Can you come? Can you help me?'

'Of course.'

Grant had been listening very carefully. Behind the pain in John's voice there was insistence and anger. Why was John calling *him*? They mostly kept away from each other for fear of awakening old wounds, and John had plenty of people to call on for help.

'Wait, you don't think she took her own life, do you.'

'Of course I bloody well don't. And no one is going to believe me. Except perhaps you.'

Grant glanced in Ruby's direction. She had put down her bag.

It's personal, he mouthed. She crossed her arms and stared at him. Ah, how he enjoyed that 'don't even try it' look of hers.

He shoved the desk chair out of his way. 'We'll be there in fifteen minutes.'

Chapter 6

Moorlands was on the edge of town. It had huge grounds and at one time the main building had been surrounded by giant cedar trees. Grant remembered the previous year when many had been cut down and local people had protested. It seemed as if a second culling had taken place recently. There was a strong scent of pine, and mounds of twigs and needles were clogging up the guttering of the car park.

An ambulance and a patrol car were parked to the side of the main building. Grant and Ruby took their time going over to the cluster of activity. Grant had explained to Ruby how this wasn't an actual case for the moment. For that to happen, they would need much more than John Markham's suspicions.

A uniformed officer was standing by Phoebe's body. He was writing in his notebook.

Grant showed him his warrant card. 'Good evening. Detective Chief Inspector David Grant and this is my colleague, criminal psychologist Ruby Silver.'

'Good evening.'

'Can you give us an update please?'

The officer chewed the end of his pen. '9.50pm the Control Room was called, and we arrived on scene 9.58pm. A young woman fell to her death from the fourth floor. Phoebe Markham aged twenty-one and she was a patient here. There's a mobile phone splintered on the concrete. It's possible it belonged to Ms Markham.'

'Any witnesses?'

'One. He's another patient. Staff had to restrain him. His psychiatrist said there was no choice but to medicate him. Apparently we can't trust a word he says. His name's Charles.'

Grant frowned. 'You couldn't get the doc to wait?'

'Charles was screaming and kicking and refusing to move away from the body. It was chaos. Unfortunately, whatever they gave him practically knocked him out and he couldn't speak afterwards. But it was probably for the best.'

'Ruby, can you find him please and let me know what's going on?'

'On it,' she said then jogged across the grass.

'What did the witness tell you?' Grant asked the officer.

'He kept yelling he heard the deceased on the top floor talking to someone. He didn't realise who the victim was until she jumped. He was a friend of hers. He couldn't tell us who she was talking to.'

'What was he doing outside?'

'I don't know.'

'Okay. Any signs of a struggle or CCTV?'

'No signs of a struggle. There's a camera at the hospital entrance and one at the building entrance but none trained on the top floor. We've secured the scene – both the area where she landed and the upstairs. The top floor can't usually be accessed by patients.'

The officer flipped through his notebook. 'The ambulance crew were on site at the same time we were, though a doctor had already arrived. He's a general practitioner and lives down the road. His name's Doctor Mike Otremba. Life pronounced extinct at 10.07pm.'

'Good. Thank you.'

Grant spotted John's tall thin outline. John was standing with the paramedics and Grant went over to offer what comfort he could. The man was barely holding it together. In the gloom, Grant put his arm around John's shoulders and he had a sudden memory of when they were young, and John had done exactly the same to him, after the disaster.

'Thank you for coming,' John said.

Grant felt his friend's shoulders heave. He tried to push his feelings to the side and concentrate on what had to be done. 'What have they told you so far?'

'That she jumped. Doctor Otremba was here within minutes and he said there was nothing to be done. There was another patient screaming and ranting. He said he heard Phoebe on the top floor.'

John gripped Grant's arm.

'Take it slowly, John. We don't need to rush this.'

'I'm okay. Otremba knew my daughter. He was one of the doctors who admitted Phoebe as an inpatient.'

'How had she been?'

'Not good. Phoebe took a downward turn a few weeks ago. She was doing fine up until we heard the bastard who assaulted her was getting out of prison early. I tried to stop the parole board agreeing to it but I failed. When I told Phoebe, she fell apart. They had to take her in. They're saying it was suicide but it can't be. Someone must have been with her!'

'You feel this wasn't a deliberate act?' Grant said it gently.

'I know it sounds crazy. Yes, she's been in and out of here for years, ever since she was assaulted. But Phoebe was building something, she was getting stronger. I spoke to her a couple of days ago and she was doing okay. She'd got over the initial shock of him being released early.'

'Okay.'

'I know they're going to tell you how sometimes patients become calmer and happier once they've decided to end their lives, but that isn't what I'm describing with my daughter. She's been gradually getting better, I swear it. They keep telling me not to listen to the other patient, but he said Phoebe was arguing with someone.'

'Then let me take a look,' Grant said.

Phoebe's arms and legs were pale under the ambulance crew's lights. Grant had seen plenty of dead bodies although it never got any easier, especially when the situation was as tragic as this. The impact had ended her life instantly. A drop from four floors onto concrete did that to a person.

Grant introduced himself to the ambulance crew members and to Doctor Mike Otremba.

'Are there any marks on her body you'd not attribute to the fall?'

'We checked for signs of life. I didn't notice anything unusual,' a paramedic said. 'But then I wasn't especially looking.'

'And you, Doctor Otremba?'

The doctor was an imposing man, with broad shoulders and a deep voice. He shook his head. 'Please, call me Mike. And no, I didn't see anything to raise an alarm bell. She was a troubled young woman. When I saw her last, she was very distressed which is why she came to Moorlands.'

'I see. And do you know the witness, Charles?'

'Charles isn't one of my patients. You'll have to speak to Doctor Hargreaves, his psychiatrist. I administered the medication to Charles on her instruction.'

'He was very distressed?'

'The man was out of control.'

'I see and do we know who was in charge of the victim this evening?'

A young woman stepped forward. She was petite, with neat, shoulder-length dark hair. She had Asian ancestry he thought, perhaps Chinese. She looked to be in a state of shock with her body movements stiff as she struggled to speak. 'That was me. I'm the nurse for the ward Phoebe was on.'

'What's your name?'

'Lin Chen.'

'You were the one looking after the victim this evening? Can you tell me about that?'

'Yes, I gave her medication and helped her to bed. Phoebe believed she saw her perpetrator in town this afternoon though the psychiatrist thought it was a delusion. The psychiatrist had prescribed sedatives for the next forty-eight hours, to help calm Phoebe down.'

'Nobody told me that,' John Markham said. 'Why wasn't I informed?'

'Phoebe's an adult,' Lin said. 'The hospital isn't obliged to tell you everything. Without her consent, it would be a breach of confidentiality.'

John gave the nurse an unpleasant look. 'Oh yes, we've been through this before, haven't we?'

The nurse lifted her chin. 'We have. You can't expect to be told everything about your daughter. She's in charge of herself and it's up to her what she shares with you and what she doesn't. She has a right to privacy. She expressly told me she didn't want you to know.'

Grant took notice of the tension between John and the nurse, but it wasn't the right moment to pursue it further.

'Don't talk to me about rights! How dare you! Who do you think you are? You're supposed to take care of her.'

Grant put a hand on his friend's arm. It wouldn't help if this unravelled into animosity. He needed everyone to be on board and working together. He raised his voice a little and took charge. 'I'd like to see the top floor. Could you take me please, Ms Chen? Did you see any sign of an intruder this evening?'

'Nothing.'

As they walked towards the building, Grant wondered how long had Lin Chen been on duty. How had an intruder entered? And if Phoebe had been under Lin's supervision, how had Phoebe and another person, as yet unidentified, found their way to the top floor?

Grant followed the nurse to a side door and John came behind. Lin's shoulders were bowed and when she tripped on the step, Grant steadied her.

As they entered the building, Ruby came alongside.

'I found Charles. Seeing her fall like that has sent him into a crisis. He kept muttering the same thing – that he should have stopped it, he should have done something. We won't be able to get more from him tonight. The doc has given him a massive dose of sedatives.'

'All right.'

On the top floor they found a woman police officer standing at the open window.

'I'm DCI David Grant. What's your name?'

'Hilary Yates. I recognise you, sir. I work from Himlands Heath station.'

'Lovely. So Hilary, your colleague downstairs has given us a briefing. We'd like to hear your take.'

She looked bright and alert and ready for anything. The type of officer Grant liked to encourage.

'All the windows on the first three floors are solid pvc units which aren't designed to be opened. I've been told they're only a few years old. Whereas the ones on the top floor weren't replaced and some of them you can theoretically open, but they've been screwed shut. Every window up here also has a security lock.'

'And you know this because?'

'I spoke to a few of the patients and staff and they filled me in, and I checked the rest on this floor. This window is the only one which has been unscrewed and unlocked.'

'Good work.'

Grant looked around the window frame. He pointed. 'We can see two screws have been removed and the security latch is undone. Do we know who has a key to unlock these windows?'

'There's one master. It's kept in the hospital manager's office which is in a different building.'

'A different building, I see. Excellent work, Hilary. Do we have any idea who was up here with our victim?'

'No one I spoke to spotted anybody leaving or coming. There's the main stairwell or the fire escape as an exit route. If they exited the building.'

If they exited the building. Oh yes, she was sharp.

Grant inspected the window more closely. Where the screws had been removed, it had left two holes. And those holes were not clean. The hair on his arms prickled.

PC Yates was peering over Grant's shoulder. He pointed and she gave one tiny nod of agreement, her eyes wide and shining. He was impressed how she understood what this meant. Yet she had given nothing away.

Ruby was standing quietly in the background, as she often did, her keen eyes trained on John Markham and Lin Chen.

'Give me a few moments with my colleague, please,' Grant said to the group. He took Ruby away from the cluster. 'What's your take?'

'I've been thinking about Charles. I know we've been told he's not a reliable witness, but on the face of it, I don't see why not. And this window,' Ruby pointed, 'It's chilling. I can't imagine what she was thinking standing on the ledge. She'd seen her perpetrator today. Her psyche would have been in fragments. Whoever was up here with her, it would have been easy for them to kill her. She wouldn't have been capable of putting up much psychological resistance.'

'No psychological resistance and she was physically compromised because of the sedatives. She didn't stand a chance.'

Physically, Phoebe had been frail too, more the build of a teenager than a young woman. It was grim. Just the sort of case that hit Grant in the gut.

Grant went back to the nurse. 'What I'd like to get clear in my mind is the sequence of events. Can you take me through it step by step, starting with the first interaction you had with Phoebe this evening, please.'

Lin swallowed. She seemed to have got even smaller in the harsh lighting.

'When I came on duty, the outgoing nurse briefed me about what happened in town this afternoon. She said Phoebe thought she saw the man who assaulted her and it resulted in Phoebe having a breakdown. So Doctor Lesley Hargreaves, she's the psychiatrist on our ward, prescribed sedatives. Phoebe had already been given one dose this afternoon and I gave her another just before lights out. Then I went back to check on her once I'd finished my ward round. She was in bed asleep.'

'What time was this?'

'Around 9pm.'

'Go on.'

'The next thing I knew, a colleague from the ground floor ward rang me. I could hear patients screaming in the background. She said a patient told her someone had fallen past their window. We both rushed outside. Charles was kneeling on the ground. And that's… when I saw… Phoebe.'

John Markham made an agonised sound.

'The security camera at the building entrance,' Grant said. 'Is it monitored?'

'The camera is trained on the front door. It shows at all the nursing desks for this building. Which meant the one I was at and the ones my colleagues were at on the other floors. I didn't see anyone come or go. The front door is locked after nine o'clock. Phoebe was asleep when I left her, I swear it.'

'And you went straight to your desk after your round?'

'Yes... well no, I went to the toilet and I made a drink.'

'And who was watching my daughter while you were in the loo?' John Markham said.

'We're allowed to go to the toilet! I was only in there two minutes.'

'What about Charles, is he a patient in this building?'

'Yes, he's the same ward as Phoebe.'

So Lin Chen had been responsible for Charles also. 'How did he get outside?'

'I've no idea. He was in bed when I did my rounds. Patients aren't allowed outside after 9pm, that's the rules. But Charles is known to like stargazing. He can't do that during the day, can he? Patients aren't prisoners.'

'How are patients prevented from coming up here? I saw you didn't use a swipe card.'

'It's a keypad system,' Lin said. 'Only staff know the code.'

PC Yates cleared her throat. 'That's not true. One of the patients told me they know the code.'

A woman's voice called from along the corridor. 'That's impossible.'

Everybody turned. A blonde-haired woman was hurrying towards them, her smart shoes tapping as she went. She was attractive and late fifties, so about Grant's age. She wore a blue skirt with a matching jacket draped over her arm and she reminded Grant of an actress, though he couldn't remember who exactly.

'I apologise it's taken me so long to get here. I was returning from a training course and there was a snarl up on the motorway and we were stuck at standstill. I'm Mrs Nicholson, the hospital manager.'

She was unusually sophisticated for a hospital manager. Grant shook her hand.

'I know what's happened,' she said. 'Mike Otremba has been keeping me up to date. I'm so sorry, Mr Markham.'

Mrs Nicholson had an air about her which suggested this was already cut and dried, which Grant didn't appreciate. Who had taken Phoebe to the top floor? How had they entered and exited the building? And most damningly of all, there was debris in the screw holes. There was no way he was going to let John Markham battle this one on his own. This case belonged to an MIT. And if Grant had anything to do with it, it would be his MIT.

'We're treating this as a suspicious death,' he said.

Mrs Nicholson swivelled towards him and she swept her hair from her face. 'I'm sorry? Mike told me you're a high-ranking detective, but I don't think you've been properly informed. Tragic though this is, Phoebe was a very disturbed young woman. Whatever you've heard from Charles is pure fiction because he's a compulsive liar. The fact a young woman took her own life is tragic. Although I'm sorry to say this, Mr Markham, it's not a surprise to those of us who knew her. It's in keeping with doctors' reports and with the struggles she has had with her mental health.'

John was dabbing at his eyes and Grant's chest constricted with compassion. Mrs Nicholson was starting to irritate him. Time to shut her up.

Nicholson carried on. 'The man who assaulted her got out of prison a few weeks ago and Phoebe believed she saw him in town today. When she was assessed this afternoon the doctor found her to be delusional and paranoid.'

'That may be the case, but until a thorough investigation eliminates all other causes, I'm afraid this will have to be treated as a suspicious unexplained death,' Grant said.

Mrs Nicholson shook her head, blonde hair swishing. 'That's a terrible waste of public money. You have no grounds for an investigation of that sort.'

All eyes turned to Grant. He took his time.

'Yes, I do. I have a witness. And I have one question. When was the last cedar tree cut down?'

The hospital manager threw her hands in the air. 'What's that got to do with it?'

'Answer the question, please.'

'Well,' Lin Chen said, 'the tree fellers were here last week, I'd say six days ago.'

'I see.'

'Why is that important?' John Markham asked.

'The screws went from the window casement into the jamb on two sides, left and right.'

John Markham nodded and everyone else stared at Grant.

'Although the screws were inside, once they were removed, there must have been a tiny gap between the casement and the jamb. Cedar dust blew in through that gap and lodged in crevices. If you look closely, you can see there's a fine dusting in the screw holes and we're four storeys up, right next to one of the trees which was cut.'

He glanced around the circle.

'This tells me the window wasn't unscrewed today. We've had hot, still weather all week. Such fine dust from the cutting wouldn't have been blowing around. No, I think it means this window was unscrewed before the trees were taken down.'

John Markham sagged and leaned against the wall. 'You're saying this was planned in advance?'

'It's a strong possibility. PC Yates, please will you stay here until Scene of Crime Officers arrive. And now if you would all please leave the area.'

Grant put in a call to his direct superior, Detective Chief Superintendent Fox. She agreed that since he was already there and had turned it into a police enquiry, his team would take it.

The crime scene manager soon arrived, though she was complaining as she got out of the van. She had jet black hair with a white streak at the front. She was young, but he had to admit that everyone looked young to him these days.

'I was told your MIT wasn't up and running yet?' she said.

'I'm David Grant, pleased to meet you. This is criminal psychologist Ruby Silver.'

The CSM glowered at them. 'Sejal Patani.'

In an ideal world, he'd have liked to meet with Sejal before they got to work together. He had been planning to invite the CSMs to Headquarters so they could meet the team. Still, it hadn't panned out like that. In this job, you had to be flexible.

'Good evening, Sejal, please call me David.'

'We're going to be working together so you'd better know I was about to go off shift. Luckily for me, I was able to sort out extended childcare with zero notice.'

'Right.'

He wasn't sure why she was telling him this. He was sympathetic about childcare issues but if it was inconvenient why had she taken the callout? Why hadn't she let the next CSM on the roster step in?

'Before you ask, I wanted to come. You're a new MIT and I don't want any screw-ups. Things have got to be done right.'

Grant didn't ruffle easily. 'We're in agreement there.'

'What are we waiting for then? Where's the crime scene?'

'We've three areas for you to examine. The site where Phoebe Markham landed, the top floor where she jumped and also her room.'

The team of Scene of Crime Officers were already getting suited up.

'Where do you want to start, Sejal?' Grant asked.

'The jump site. I've got it from here.'

Sejal was already focused on the SOCOs and was handing out instructions. It was a complex crime scene. It was good to see she was on top of it.

Ruby turned to Grant as Sejal left. 'She doesn't mess around.'

Chapter 7

As he jogged across the grass, Detective Inspector Tom Delaney felt clear headed and ready for anything. Early thirties, Tom was in black jeans and an open-neck shirt. He had dark eyes and dark hair and his six foot, athletic build and good looks tended to attract the ladies, though most of the time Tom didn't notice.

This was their first MIT case and a big deal. It was important to keep an open mind and be observant of the scene. He had learned to commit details to memory from an early age, since he had dyslexia and did not like to rely on writing.

Grant looked as impeccable as ever in his signature grey suit and tie. The boss was almost Tom's height and still in reasonable shape. While Grant might appear to be inoffensive, even amiable on first sight, Tom knew Grant had a ruthless urge for justice.

The boss also had a formidable reputation which many underestimated, especially criminals. There was a reason detectives nicknamed Grant 'The Grey Wolf', because he always got his prey. Tom hoped one day he would be as good as Grant and being recruited to the new MIT had been beyond Tom's wildest dreams.

'We've a lot to get through,' Grant said.

He gave them a quick briefing.

'Our priority is to identify the perp. Tom, you and I will do a quick search of Phoebe's room and then I want you to get all hospital security footage checked through. We're looking for an intruder, timeframe from 9pm onwards. How did they come in and out?'

'On it, guv.'

As an MIT, they had a group of detective sergeants and constables back at Force headquarters to back them up. Tom would be in charge of organising their trawl of the footage.

'Diane, get going on staff interviews. Ruby, I'd like you to find out all you can about Charles.'

It took a few moments for them to locate Mrs Nicholson, which displeased the boss a lot.

'I'd like to introduce Detective Inspectors Diane Collins and Tom Delaney,' Grant said. 'We'll be questioning staff straight away. Please tell everyone to stay on site.'

The boss was courteous, as he usually was. He would want to build a good relationship with staff because it sped things up. They needed people to trust them.

The hospital manager was polished, with careful makeup and manicure. Grant had already told his team she thought Phoebe had jumped.

'Can I get you something? Coffee perhaps,' Mrs Nicholson asked.

'No, thank you. As a priority, DI Delaney will organise a check of your surveillance footage. All of it. Can you speed up access?'

'Of course.'

'Lin Chen seemed particularly upset.'

'She is. In fact, we all are. Phoebe Markham had been known to us for many years. Lin was originally in children's services so she worked with Phoebe from the beginning. I sent Lin home. She was in no state to be here.'

That was unfortunate. Grant would have wanted to put pressure on the nurse to see if he could shake her story up. 'I understand. It's a very distressing situation,' he said. 'Would you say Nurse Chen is good at her job?'

'Very. She has an exemplary record.'

'I see. If you could take us to Phoebe's room. I'd like to take a look. Diane, I'll check in with you later.'

Patients had been asked to stay in their rooms and draw their curtains. As the group walked the corridors to the inpatient wing, Tom heard muffled sounds of sobbing and wailing. On Phoebe's ward it was the worst.

Grant turned to the manager. 'Thank you, Mrs Nicholson. We know where to find you if we need you. Only Tom and I will enter.'

She took the hint and hurried away, her heels tapping.

The two of them put on protective clothing.

'She's the kind to act cooperative while not actually wanting to help in any way,' Tom said.

'Exactly.'

Phoebe's room was small, the only furniture being a bed, a bedside cabinet, a chair and a built-in wardrobe. There was a window which gave a view of the side of another building. A large painting had been propped on the chair in a way that Phoebe would be looking at it as she lay down. It was very realistic. There were some other sketches stuck to the door of the wardrobe, some of them were of people and others were landscapes.

'I heard painting was a hobby of hers and it looks like she was damn good at it. Eyes only, Tom. Sejal and her lot will be doing the full forensics search. I just want to know if there's anything vital here.'

Tom moved carefully in the small space so he didn't disturb anything. He ran his eyes around the bed frame. 'Was it usual for the large painting to be placed in her room?'

'Lin put it there. She hoped it might help Phoebe calm down.'

There wasn't much in the wardrobe – a few clothes, some sketchbooks and art materials.

Grant was kneeling to check under the chair and then he moved to the painting.

Tom wanted to know more about the picture. When had Phoebe done it, and what did it mean to her?

Grant was bending to look at the back of the frame and Tom saw Grant go still. When the boss straightened, he was pointing. 'Take pictures, Tom.'

Taped to the back of the picture frame was a blue and silver object. A screwdriver.

'Does it mean Phoebe unscrewed the window herself before tonight?' Tom asked.

'It seems that way, doesn't it. Or did somebody want us to believe that? Don't you find it odd our witness has not only been discredited but he's also unable to answer questions?'

'It could be odd, or it could be usual at Moorlands, guv.'

Grant's steady grey eyes regarded Tom. 'And what might that mean?'

He and the boss were on the same wavelength. Tom said it aloud. 'This would be the ideal environment for a stealthy murder.'

Chapter 8

DI Diane Collins set her interview table up in a therapy room and she spent the rest of the night taking statements from members of staff.

Dressed formally in dark trousers with a pale shirt, her shoulder-length hair had signs of salt and pepper these days, though not as much as the chief, who was totally grey. It suited David and so did this job and his recent promotion. David had been the right person to set up the new MIT and she was glad to be here, though she wasn't going to let the chief take her for granted.

When David had first invited her to join the new MIT she refused. In fact, she had been considering leaving detective work altogether. Having your life put at risk did that to you. In their previous case, Diane had ended up being held at knifepoint by a madman. Only the chief's quick thinking had saved her.

In the end, she allowed David to win her round. She made it clear she was only doing this as a favour and for a couple of years until his retirement.

She'd been there for hours when David finally caught up with her.

'Any positive leads?' he asked.

'Everybody is very upset but nobody saw or heard a thing beforehand. All hell broke loose when one patient actually saw Phoebe fall by his window. He was reading in bed with the curtains open. Until then, there was nothing out of the ordinary. I've no reports of suspicious persons hanging around the hospital in the last few weeks. Visitors come to see patients and they're known by staff. The only strangers have been the tree fellers.'

'There's no one been caught entering or leaving the premises, though the camera at the building entrance was malfunctioning so we don't know shit.'

'You think it might have been tampered with?'

'It's another rather convenient obstacle in a string of them. I hope the techs'll be able to tell us.'

Moorlands was a world of its own, set on the edge of town. Diane had an aunt who had been treated there and though mental health was less of a taboo these days, Moorlands was still somewhere people didn't talk about and didn't know much about either.

John Markham was well known in town. He was their MP and as far as Diane remembered, he had been involved in the same local tragedy as David, when they were boys. How unfair Mr Markham should suffer so much. First the tragedy then his daughter had been assaulted, and now poor Phoebe was dead.

Diane could understand why the chief had rushed there. The look on David's face said it all, no matter how hard he tried to hide it. She was the one who had known the chief the longest, and she was sure he had taken this case from compassion.

'You know John Markham, don't you? How's he doing?'

'Badly.'

The problem was, personal connections and detective work should never be mixed. She hoped it wouldn't whiplash against them.

David sat on a desk. 'Ruby says Charles is a manic depressive and he's here because he's in a depressive phase. He's also described by his psychiatrist as being a compulsive liar.'

'This is going to be a minefield. And it's not great timing for you is it?'

In three weeks David's daughter, Chrissie, was getting married. It had been in the planning for a while and David's wife was taking care of the last-minute arrangements, but as the father of the bride, the timing for the start of their first case was nothing short of a disaster. That was how it was with detective work – home life often got the short straw.

The chief pursed his lips. 'I haven't told Lily we've taken a case yet.'

'Then you'd better do it quickly.' In fact, his wife would have guessed already with him out so late.

'I'm supposed to have the final fitting for the bloody suit tomorrow. That'll have to go on hold.'

'I'm sure Lily's on top of it. She'll have anticipated this might happen.'

'I know. It's Chrissie I don't want to disappoint.'

'You won't, David. Don't worry. We'll get you to that church *and* we'll solve the case. Anything from Sejal and the SOCOs?'

'She said there's no obvious signs of a tussle on the top floor. We'll have to wait for the trace evidence to know more.'

'We've got Charles, and the screwdriver.'

He nodded. 'That's what we've got and that's what we're going to work with. The phone was smashed to pieces but they've recovered the memory chip. Why did she have it with her? The chip and phone data might tell us something.'

'Are you thinking what I'm thinking?' she said.

'Why the hell don't they have decent strong coffee around here? Or – this is looking like an inside job?'

'Both.'

David ran a hand through his hair. 'My daughter's wedding is going to be the biggest day of her life and there's no way in hell I'm going to miss walking her down the aisle. But the darndest thing is, I'm still glad John called me.'

The chief didn't need to explain, because Diane knew exactly where he was coming from.

Chapter 9

Emma woke to the sound of the intercom. She groaned and pushed the cushion away from her face. As she dragged herself to sitting, her shoulders were stiff and her neck ached. Damn, this sofa bed was uncomfortable and it made it difficult to fall asleep but once it happened, sleep deprivation meant she zoned out for hours. What time was it?

Zzz. Zzz. The intercom again.

She checked her phone. 11.15am. Her mouth was dry and she went to the sink and filled a glass. Whoever it was would likely go away and very probably was calling the wrong apartment, since Emma didn't get visitors except her social worker and she had no appointment scheduled.

A message pinged on her phone and she checked to see if it was Phoebe. It wasn't, it was Brett. Brett was a counsellor and he ran a self-help group and coffee session at the church community centre. Those sessions had been a lifeline for Emma and for Phoebe.

I'm outside. Can we talk? Brett had texted.

Odd. She hadn't realised Brett knew where she lived.

What for?

I need to talk to you. It's important.

Give me five minutes and I'll be down.

May I come up?

This was definitely strange. What did he want? She liked Brett and she thought of him a bit like an uncle or earnest older brother. She trusted him although home visits had never been part of the deal.

What for? she asked again.

I'd rather we speak face-to-face.

Ok.

She pressed a button to open the downstairs door, then scooted into the bathroom to splash her face and smooth her clothes. Her dark curls were their usual mess and she hastily tried to damp them down. She stared at herself in the mirror – unruly hair, plain features and freckles. She sighed, if only she had had the same looks as her beautiful sister. There wasn't time to brush her teeth properly but she gave it a quick go for politeness sake, and then he was knocking at the door.

'Hello Emma,' Brett said. 'I'm sorry to call around unannounced.'

She shrugged. 'That's all right. Come in. How did you know where I live?'

'I checked our records and dug it out.'

Brett was more than ten years older than Emma and he was studious looking. He had once wanted to be a pianist but had changed his career ideas and become a therapist instead. The two of them weren't friends, partly due to the age gap and also because Brett was fussy about the boundaries of his work, especially with the self-help group, and he didn't like spilling into social activities with members. Which was why this was strange.

He adjusted his glasses. 'I know this is a bit unusual but I need to talk to you about something serious.'

That's when the drowsiness evaporated and a nervousness crept in. 'What do you mean?'

Why did he have such a sombre expression? She studied his eyes and the grim set of his mouth and it gave her a horrible feeling.

'What's going on?'

'Let's sit down, shall we?'

A feeling of panic started to grow. 'No, I don't want to. What is it?'

'Emma, I'm really sorry. The reason I'm here is to break bad news. Terrible news.'

Brett wasn't the type to be jolly, after all he helped them through some pretty dreadful group sessions. But this level of gravitas was heavy even for him. Her knees went weak and she clutched for something to hold on to because she had a terrible premonition of what he was about to tell her.

'Don't say another word. I want you to leave,' she said.

She tried to get to the door to open it but she couldn't make it.

'I'm so sorry, Emma.'

She pressed her hands over her ears. She didn't want bad news. Not about Phoebe. It made sense of why Brett was there and acting strangely. He knew Phoebe, and he knew Emma and Phoebe were friends.

Emma didn't want to know. Whatever had happened, she didn't want to hear it.

'Get out!'

Brett took off his glasses and rubbed at his eyes. Oh god, he was crying.

No, no, not Phoebe.

'I had a call from Moorlands. Last night Phoebe stepped from the top floor. She's gone, Emma. Phoebe has gone.'

The room collapsed in on her and she was on her knees. She moaned like a wounded animal.

No! They looked out for each other. They helped each other. It couldn't be true.

Brett knelt beside her on the carpet.

'I knew how devastating this would be for you. I didn't want you to hear it from anyone else.'

Phoebe was the only person Emma cared about. The only one she loved.

Raking her fingers across the floor, she screamed. A monstrous wave of guilt and self-loathing welled up, making the world go black. Phoebe had phoned her and what had she done? She'd gone to sleep, while the person she loved fought for their life. It was like before, when she sung happily in her bedroom, trying on party dresses, while the people she loved were murdered.

Her mother and Juliette must have cried out. If only she had come downstairs sooner she could have helped. She could have phoned the police. If she had not been so selfish she could have saved her sister's life. She had been useless, so stupid and useless. And now it had happened again.

'I'm so sorry,' Brett said.

Emma screamed. 'No!'

'We can't always protect the people we love. Phoebe had her own demons to fight.'

Why hadn't she got herself admitted to Moorlands and then she could have been by her friend's side? Why had she believed Phoebe would be all right? She wiped at the tears and the snot.

'She called me.'

'It's not your fault.'

'Yes it is.' She tried to fight the sobbing only she couldn't.

'You can't think like that. It's not true.'

'But I should have done something!'

She dug her nails into her palms. She was so pathetic and stupid – a total failure.

As she curled into a ball the self-hatred consumed her.

Once again she had let down the people she loved and left them to die.

Chapter 10

I can tell you it's a struggle fighting against your real nature. In the end you have to let go. The freedom of liberation is ecstasy. For me, it's an ecstasy in red, all shades of it – blood spurting or congealing, slippery and dark. And fear. I lap up the dark terror in their eyes.

As I press *play* on my phone, my breath comes quick and fast.

I'm shivering. The ordinary world around me fades as I relive Phoebe's final moments. This is delicious. I adore the tremor in her voice and the pleading which drips from her eyes.

When I'm finished, I store her video safely. I'll be using it later to extract the full juice from her pain.

The vermin are crawling out one by one, flirting and cavorting without shame.

Patience, patience.

Though it's difficult to get the beast within me under control, I've learned an iron discipline that few can match.

There were three on my recent list. One down, two to go. I promise myself the next will happen soon.

Chapter 11

Grant had snatched a couple of hours' sleep in the early hours of the morning. He'd sent the rest of the team home to do the same. When Grant told his wife, Lily, about the case, she had rolled her eyes.

'I should have known,' she said. 'Saturday the eleventh at 11am, David. Engrave it on your brain.'

Grant had plumped his pillow and turned out the light. 'No worries.'

'I know you and I know your bloody commitment to the job. Don't make me drag you away from it to get you there. Chrissie would never forgive you.'

'I'll have to miss the final suit fitting tomorrow. Which doesn't matter. The size is fine.'

His wife snorted. It *had* been a tad tight but nothing a few weeks of cake starvation wouldn't solve. He kissed her and went straight to sleep.

Grant's team met again early the next day at Moorlands car park and Grant was pleased when Tom arrived carrying a tray of takeaway cups. Tom handed them around.

'Coffee. Strong and black,' Tom said. 'And a tea for you, guv. Anyone for a pastry?'

Grant stopped his hand from reaching out.

'I got your favourite, boss?' Tom said, offering the bag.

Diane laughed. 'What's going on? Are you cutting back? Has that got something to do with your wedding outfit?'

'No it has not. Great tea, Tom, thanks. Right, what did you find out about the hospital manager?'

Tom blew to cool his drink and took a sip. 'Mrs Nicholson has been at Moorlands for two years, and before that she managed a psychiatric hospital in Scotland. I checked the statistics. The number of deaths at her previous hospital was in line with national norms. I didn't see anything out of the ordinary in the records.'

'Keep your eyes and ears open,' Grant said. 'With the cameras and the interviews giving us nothing concrete, it could be someone inside the hospital. Tom, you and I will interview Charles this morning and Ruby, I'd like you to sit in. Diane, please start on interviewing the patients.'

'Afterwards, I'd like to mix informally with the patients,' Ruby said. 'Some of them are going to be too fragile for formal questioning.'

'Good idea.'

In the daylight, Moorlands was a rather grubby collection of buildings, though the grounds were spacious, with grassy areas and what looked like well-kept gardens. It was meant to have a wonderful view of woodland at the back.

Their shoes crunched on gravel as they followed him to the main entrance. The four of them were ushered in by the secretary, who took them to the manager's office.

'Good morning, DCI Grant,' Mrs Nicholson said.

He knew what she said was a formality, yet it irked him because there was nothing good about the morning, was there?

'We'll be interviewing patients this morning, starting with Charles,' Grant said. 'If you could let your staff know to liaise with us. We'll do our best to cause the least upset.'

The manager's hair was piled on top of her head, making her look even more like the actress he couldn't recall the name of.

Mrs Nicholson leaned back in her chair. 'Thank you for that. It's been one hell of a night.'

'I'm going to need a list of patients who knew Phoebe well.'

'The staff can fill you in best. As far as I understood, she was a bit of a loner and preferred spending her time in our art studio. For the staff, her regular nurse was Lin. Phoebe was also supported by our occupational therapists, Kate and Viktor. It's Viktor who supervises the art sessions.'

'Who would you say knew her best?'

'Lin did. And I believe Phoebe got on well with a counsellor who works for the church. His name's Brett Sinclair and he supports patients once they leave here. I can give you his details.'

'Lovely. And did you have any more thoughts on who might have had access to the master key for the window locks?'

Grant had established the night before that the key was hanging on a hook in Mrs Nicholson's office, where it was supposed to be. She told him she was not aware it had been missing, it must have been taken and then replaced. The question was, by who?

'Like I told you, my office is locked at night. It's open during the day but if someone took the key it would have happened when neither I nor my secretary were here.'

'And how often is that?' Diane asked.

'Occasionally. At lunch time for instance. Or if I have a meeting and my secretary is called on an errand.'

Not very helpful for the investigation.

'I'll take you to see Charles,' Mrs Nicholson said. 'I hear he's awake and he's been asking to speak to you.'

As Grant exchanged a glance with Diane, he felt an ominous mood descending on him. How long had Charles been conscious? Grant had specifically asked to be informed.

'I expected to be called as soon as he regained consciousness.'

Mrs Nicholson tutted. 'No need to fret. He's only been awake a few minutes.'

'I'm not fretting. I don't expect information to be withheld from me or from my team. Are we clear?'

'Of course,' she said, as she fussed with her diary and her computer mouse. 'I'm sorry for any misunderstanding.'

As they went quickly to the inpatient wing, Tom wondered why it was so quiet.

'Where is everyone?' he asked.

Mrs Nicholson smiled in his direction. 'I asked the OTs, that's the occupational therapists, to organise an event in the garden. So your enquiries wouldn't be disturbed.'

That was interesting because it was the opposite of what Grant would want. They needed to interact with people, not push them away. Was she being obstructive in an underhand way? She'd already delayed them speaking to Charles, which had gone down very badly with the boss.

It turned out Charles had the room next to Phoebe's. Mrs Nicholson knocked on the door and went straight in. Charles was sitting on the edge of his bed, wearing pyjamas and slippers. He was about Tom's age, so early thirties. His hair was wispy and untidy and he had a bemused expression.

'Hello Charles,' Ruby said. 'Do you remember me?'

The man blinked. 'Sort of. I was a bit out of it I think.'

'These are police officers,' Mrs Nicholson said. 'They're here to talk to you about last night.'

'I know that.'

'If you wouldn't mind leaving us,' Grant said. 'I'll take it from here.'

'Good. That's got rid of her. Nobody likes her,' Charles said when Mrs Nicholson had stalked out of the room. 'Why don't you sit next to me, Ruby?'

Tom wasn't comfortable with the idea but Ruby didn't seem to mind. Grant drew up a chair for himself and Tom decided to stay standing. In case.

'This is Detective Inspector Tom Delaney and Detective Chief Inspector David Grant,' Ruby said. 'DCI Grant is in charge of the investigation into Phoebe's death.'

'Into *her murder*, you mean,' Charles said.

Ruby nodded. 'Yes.'

Charles was sitting too close to Ruby for Tom's liking. The man kept shifting his weight from one leg to another, huffing his shoulders up and down and rolling his neck, and his hands didn't stop fidgeting.

'This shit they've given me. It's really fucked me up.'

'I'm sorry to hear that,' Grant said. 'Can you tell us what you saw last night, starting from the beginning?'

'It was horrible. So horrible. I didn't realise it was her until she was on the ground. The sound when she landed. I can't get it out of my head. But yes, from the beginning, like you asked. Well, I was outside and I know I shouldn't be. The thing is, the staff turn a blind eye. They know I love the stars. It's my only comfort. I'm a manic depressive and right now I find it hard to go out during the day. But at night it's so calm and there's a little grassy knoll behind the building and I go and lie and gaze up. It can make all the shit in my head go away for a while.'

'What time did you go outside, Charles?' Grant asked.

'Just before the doors closed.'

Grant took out his notebook. 'Just before 9pm?'

'Yes.'

'And did you see anyone?'

'No. I was alone. Everyone was inside. I like it that way and the constellation of Orion was very lovely. I don't remember anything else until I heard a woman arguing. I couldn't work out where it was coming from and then I realised it was from near the roof and then a nanosecond after, I knew there was something horribly wrong.'

'What did you see?'

'Nothing. It was dark up there. I could only hear the voices.'

Charles got more agitated, flicking his feet until one of his slippers fell off. Grant retrieved it and put it back on. 'What words did you hear?'

'She was pleading. Like she was pleading for her life. I heard her say, "No, please." And "I want to live.".'

'Did she say anything else?'

'That's all I could make out.'

'And the other person, what did they say?'

'I don't know.'

'Did you see their silhouette perhaps? Was it a man or a woman?'

'I'm sorry, I don't know. They were hidden. Just voices.'

'I know this is difficult,' Ruby said. 'You're doing really well.'

'What happened next?' Grant asked.

'She fell. Just like that. So quick. So final. I rushed over and she was broken. Like a doll.'

'You didn't try to call for help?'

'I wasn't quick enough. I wanted to shout up to her, to tell her I was coming. I wanted to run inside and save her. There was no time.' Charles curled his fists, pressing them into his thighs. 'I know they say I'm making it up. They often believe I'm making things up. I'm telling the truth. Every word is the truth.'

The room fell quiet and Tom could hear Charles panting. Tom kept his eyes on the man. His body language was off, everything about him was off, and how much of that was his illness or the drugs it was impossible to tell. Yet beneath all that noise, Tom had the impression Charles was telling the truth, or at least, the man believed he was telling the truth.

Charles dashed his hands across his eyes, a look of anguish on his face.

'How well did you know Phoebe?' Ruby asked.

'She was nice. She was a kind person.'

'Did you find her attractive?' Grant asked.

Charles crunched down and put his hands over his ears. 'Don't say that. I know what you're thinking. I'm a manic depressive, I'm not a pervert.'

'It's my job to ask difficult questions.'

Charles straightened up. 'All right. Yes. Of course it is. You're the one who's going to find out who did this. She was pretty, and she was, well, too young for me. I didn't fancy her.'

'I see. And when you go outside to stargaze, how do you go out and how do you get back in?'

'Through the main door. It's locked but I have my mobile so I call and the nurse lets me in.'

'You expected Lin to let you in?'

'Yes, why shouldn't she? She thinks stargazing is good for me.'

'You said you're a manic depressive. We also understand you're a compulsive liar.'

'They would say that wouldn't they? It's to cover their own arse.'

'You'll have to explain that to me. What do you mean?'

Charles sighed. 'I have my difficulties but that doesn't mean I'm stupid. Last year I spent two weeks on the Secure ward. That's where you don't have liberties and you're considered a threat either to others or to yourself. While I was there, a patient had a convulsion which left him with lasting brain damage. I'm convinced he was given the wrong amount of drugs and that's what brought on the fit. The hospital accused me of lying but he was in the room next to me and I heard him arguing before he was given the drugs. I went to see what was going on. He questioned the dosage and he was scared and the nurse told him it had been prescribed. They were holding him down while it was injected. I don't know how they did it but the hospital covered it up. I'm sure it was an error by the doctor. That's when they started to call me a compulsive liar. We all know the drugs we're supposed to get and how much of them is normal. He knew something was wrong and the staff didn't listen to him.'

'That's a serious accusation.'

'I know. The staff member left soon afterwards. Mrs Nic did her own *investigation* and said I'd made the whole thing up. My friend was too ill to remember and too ill to protest on his own behalf. He has no family to speak out for him. That's why I did. But they didn't listen. There was something wrong with the drugs he was given and he knew it.'

Tom crossed his arms. 'Where is this man now?'

'I can see you don't believe me, DI Delaney, and I mean, why should you? I'm in a psychiatric hospital. Aren't I supposed to be mad? And I've no idea where he is.'

'Do you sometimes lie?' Tom asked.

'Now that's a good question. Not more than you do, I guess. And I'm not lying about my friend nor about Phoebe.'

Tom was starting to have a liking for this quiet man. 'It's not a question of whether I believe you or not. As the guv explained, we have to dig to get to the truth. What else can you tell us about Phoebe?'

'Art was her passion. She wanted to sell her work to make a living.'

'I saw the painting in her room. Do you know why it was significant to her?'

'It's her favourite one of Ireland. Phoebe told me that's where she was going to live.'

What possible motive could Charles have to lie? When he talked about Phoebe, he seemed genuine and like he really cared about her.

There was a sudden commotion on the other side of the door. Charles yelped and grabbed onto Ruby. Tom rushed over and he was about to physically remove Charles when Ruby instead pushed Tom away.

She patted Charles's hand. 'We're fine here, Tom.'

On the other side of the door, Mrs Nicholson was shouting. 'You're not allowed to go in there.'

Grant raised an eyebrow. 'Let's see what's happening.'

Tom was quickly by Grant's side as the boss opened the door.

Mrs Nicholson had not left. She was standing outside and she was barring the way to a young woman. The young woman wore white trainers and jeans and a rather extravagant flowery shirt. But it was the expression on her face which grabbed Tom's attention. There was only one word to describe it – *desperate.*

'I want to speak to the police,' the young woman yelled. 'Let me through.'

Working in Moorlands had been bound to bring challenges. Tom wouldn't be honest if he didn't admit to wondering if they would be accosted by patients who were unstable. When Charles had asked Ruby to sit next to him, Tom's first thought had been she might be at risk, although his common sense had prevailed because Charles was more likely seeking reassurance. People were ill and had come to hospital for treatment. The old-fashioned view of them, or Charles, being lunatics was something Tom was not proud had crossed his mind.

Grant raised his voice. 'I'm Detective Chief Inspector David Grant. Can I help you?'

Charles was still standing very close to Ruby. Tom stepped back so he came slightly between them. As he did, Charles jutted his elbow into Tom's ribs.

'Phoebe and Emma were friends,' Charles said.

Mrs Nicholson was breathless. 'Emma is an ex-patient and she's still under treatment as an outpatient. I'm sure she's very upset about what's happened but that doesn't mean she can barge in and–'

Grant interrupted. 'Let's start with your name, shall we?'

'Emma White. If they say she jumped you mustn't believe them. They're lying.'

Chapter 12

Ruby took Emma into the garden. It was a lovely day, sunny and with a clear blue sky. 'Shall we sit under a tree?'

'I can't stay still. I need to keep moving or I'll explode,' Emma said. 'I hate this place.'

'How about we take a walk? I want you to tell me everything about Phoebe.'

The hospital manager had already tried to discredit Emma and had, in Ruby's view, broken confidentiality in telling them about Emma's history. Mrs Nicholson had told them Emma's sister and mother had been murdered when Emma was a child and Emma had been a psychiatric patient for many years. According to Mrs Nic, Emma was unreliable because she had memory blackouts and flashbacks.

Grant had asked Ruby to take Emma somewhere quiet and find out more.

They walked away from the buildings and towards the woods. Underneath the flowery shirt, Emma had a slight build but she did not come across as weak, in fact the opposite – she had an air of resilience about her. For someone so young, it was unusual.

Ruby was an expert in profiling and she had also spent her own childhood being passed from foster home to foster home, with stints at the children's home in between. From those days, she knew plenty of broken souls who had gone on a long journey to repair themselves, including herself. It seemed to her Emma had suffered a lot in life. She was glad Grant had asked her to build a bridge with this young woman.

'It's not fair how Mrs Nic is trying to make me sound like an idiot. I don't know what she told you about me but Phoebe and I were friends. Phoebe phoned me last night and told me she'd seen her attacker in town. I know it was horrible, especially because no one believed her. That doesn't mean she was ready to end it. She needed time to regroup, that's all.'

Emma's voice was fierce. Her arms and her body were tense.

'Why do you think people didn't believe her?'

'I guess it's because no one else saw him and he wasn't supposed to be anywhere near Himlands Heath. The bastard got out of detention early and it's been rocky for Phoebe but he was supposed to have moved to Birmingham. That's hundreds of miles away. Phoebe's father was tracking him.'

'Okay. That doesn't completely explain why they didn't take her word for it.'

'Suppose not. Phoebe was with Kate, the OT, when it happened and Phoebe said Kate didn't see him. I said I'd come today to visit and we could talk about it. I'm telling you – she wasn't suicidal. I would have known. We've been in and out of treatment together for years. We met when we were fourteen and we go to the same self-help group and we've seen the same doctors. We've been friends from the beginning. I know her. She had ideas and plans. The psychiatrists here are always making like we're on the edge. I'm sure they told you she was paranoid and stuff like that. It wasn't true.'

It was obvious there was a strong bond between these two. It made sense how Emma felt she understood her friend's state of mind, even if the professionals didn't agree that Phoebe was stable the day before.

'Can you think of anyone who might want to kill Phoebe?'

'She was quiet and she kept herself to herself. The only person who might want her out of the way would be her attacker, don't you think? I mean, he's come to Himlands Heath, why did he do that? Maybe he had it in for her. It was Phoebe's testimony that led to his arrest.'

'Hmm.'

'What? Don't you trust me? Everything I'm telling you is true.'

'I don't mistrust your judgement. What I'm trying to do is make sense of it.'

How would Phoebe's perpetrator have entered the hospital unseen and forced the young woman to the top floor? It didn't seem likely he would risk going back to prison once he had just been released. She must look into his profile.

'Is that what you're good at, making sense of things?' Emma asked.

They were walking along a path which skirted the woods.

'Sort of. If a murder has taken place, there has to be a motive. People don't kill for no reason, even if that reason doesn't make sense to anyone else, it always has a meaning for the perpetrator. Why did they do it?'

They walked in silence for a while.

'What can you tell me about the painting?'

'It was special. One of her best and definitely her favourite. It's a place in Ireland she went to with her mum and dad. Phoebe's always been a great artist but after that trip she was totally inspired. She wanted to live there and she was working on how to make that happen. When the bastard got released, it made her even more motivated to get away. That painting meant everything to her. It was her dream and her goal in life. And I know she was going to make it.'

'Everything you're telling me is really important. It will help us build a picture of Phoebe and what was going on at the time of her death.'

'Her parents were against her leaving. Phoebe had a huge argument with them about it.'

'Can you tell me more?'

'Her mum and dad were suffocating her. Phoebe can't do anything without their approval. When she told them of her plan to move to Ireland they went berserk. Ballistic. Then Phoebe got obstinate and told them she was going to do it anyway. That was the first time she's ever stood up to them. I think it made her father back off a bit. From what I understood, he was the one who opposed Ireland the most. Do you think it might be important?'

'Like I said, everything is important at this stage.'

'I suppose. Why shouldn't Phoebe have her own dreams. We all do don't we?'

'What about you, Emma. What do you want in life?'

'You'd probably laugh if I told you. Right now I work in a fast-food place. That's probably all I'm worth anyway.'

'I won't laugh, Emma.'

'Lots of people do.'

Ruby frowned. Emma was very good at putting herself down. 'What happened to Phoebe isn't your fault.'

'Isn't it? I'm probably the last person she spoke to, apart from the person who killed her. I was supposed to be the one who was there for her.'

'You were. You trusted Phoebe and she would have known it and felt it. Which is a huge thing when you're surrounded by staff who've been taught not to trust you, but rather to trust a professional judgement. Don't be so hard on yourself.'

'I can't help it.'

Ruby remembered when she'd had a similar state of mind. How long ago that seemed and how lucky she had been to meet David Grant. 'We're going to find who did this.'

'You believe me that it can't have been suicide?'

'What I believe isn't important.'

Although, for the record, no, Ruby didn't believe it.

'What I can say is, there are too many unanswered questions.'

'What will happen next?'

'There'll be the forensics report on the crime scene and a postmortem of Phoebe's body.' She glanced at Emma. The young woman was blinking rapidly. 'Are you sure you want to know this?'

'I don't want to cry about it. I want to help.' Emma was clenching her fists. 'I'm angry. Someone killed her. They're not going to get away with it.'

'No, they're not.'

'Will you tell me how it's going and if you find out anything important?'

'As much as I can, and as long as it doesn't interfere with the investigation. You must let me know if you think of anything else which might help.'

Emma was forcing back tears. It took a huge effort, and Ruby's heart went out to her. The young woman had given an extremely interesting testimony and Ruby had a feeling it would move the case forward, though it might be difficult for the boss to hear, especially the part about the conflict between Phoebe and her father.

Chapter 13

Grant wanted to meet with Phoebe's psychiatrist, Doctor Lesley Hargreaves. The manager's secretary organised an appointment for him.

Lesley Hargreaves had an office on the ground floor of a building separate from Phoebe's block and separate from the hospital manager. With stylish, cropped hair and sparkling blue eyes, she had an intellectual air about her. She had a nice office, with a view over the grounds, and an enormous desk.

There were two comfortable chairs in the corner and a treatment couch and he wondered how many patients had laid there as part of their psychiatric assessment.

The doctor wafted a hand in that direction. Silver bracelets clinked at her wrist.

'That's more for show than actual use. Freud and analytical work have long been out of fashion. Modern psychiatric work has moved on. It's all medication and cognitive behavioural approaches and dialectical treatment plans these days.'

It didn't make much sense to him, though it didn't matter. He didn't need to understand psychology. Police work was his forte.

She came across as a clever woman yet she had a coy way of tilting her head down and then flicking her gaze back at him with those dazzling eyes of hers. He supposed it was her way of flirting, though it wasn't at all the sort of thing which interested him. The more important question was, why was she bothering? Was she trying to distract him?

'Shall we sit more comfortably?' Doctor Hargreaves suggested.

She moved to one of the nice chairs. She wore a summery dress and when she crossed her legs, Grant got a flash of thigh which he couldn't help feeling had been deliberate.

'Perhaps we could start by you telling me about Phoebe Markham.'

Lesley Hargreaves steepled her fingers and the showy bracelets clinked again. 'I know this is now a police matter, so I'll cooperate as far as I can. Though I have to tell you, my belief is nobody was involved in this except Phoebe herself.'

Grant ignored that. The evidence would be the proof of it, not people's opinions. 'How long have you been Phoebe's psychiatrist?'

'Let me start at the beginning. I've known Phoebe for five years, since she was transferred to my care from children's services at age sixteen. She was known to them from fourteen, which was when she took an overdose.'

'I see. What can you tell me about her?'

'I have her notes here.'

The doctor fetched a file from the desk and sat down again, with the same flourish of her dress as earlier. Grant kept his eyes trained on her face.

'So, Phoebe was assaulted in February of her fourteenth year and the man who assaulted her went to prison in September. It was after the trial that Phoebe took an overdose. She was admitted to Moorlands, on the children's side, at that time.'

Grant nodded. The strain on victims during trial was a known risk to their mental health. And Phoebe had been so young. It must have been a horrible time for her.

'Phoebe has been seeing doctors at Moorlands over the last seven years, with decreasing frequency, and she had a private therapist too, as I understand it, organised by her family.'

'Can you tell me why she was here?'

'As I said, she took an overdose. Since then she's been self-harming, by which I mean she cuts her arms at times of distress. She's been working on this as part of her treatment program, and she was becoming much more stable and was discharged into the community. Then she self-harmed again when she heard her perpetrator got out of prison. At that time, her parents got her readmitted as an inpatient.'

'Did Phoebe come here voluntarily?'

'Oh yes, she wasn't sectioned, she said she wanted to come in.'

'Was she, or has she ever been, suicidal?'

'That's a very difficult question to answer. I can only say, yes and no. Phoebe has certainly lived through very dark times and she has had suicidal thoughts. The overdose at the beginning was an example, but it was more a signal of distress than an attempt which was at the top of the scale.'

Ah, so psychiatrists had a scale for such things.

'You mean an overdose isn't considered serious?'

'Of course we take it seriously, but there are other means to take your own life which are more likely to succeed. Which is why I say the first event was considered more as a call for help.'

'I see.'

'The event of a perpetrator being released from prison is often a trigger for old trauma to re-emerge. So a relapse at that time would not be unexpected.'

'And the fact Phoebe believed she saw the man who assaulted her? I presume that would have been a trigger too?'

'Oh yes, a huge one. I met with Phoebe yesterday afternoon. She was agitated. Emotionally she was very fragile. Did she actually see him? She certainly believed she had except we just don't know. The fact is Kate, our OT, was with Phoebe when this happened and Kate didn't see anyone staring at Phoebe.'

Grant glanced out the window. What better victim than one who isn't believed – who is called paranoid and delusional and perhaps they have been or perhaps even they are. But what if then they see something real? Something threatening? Something dangerous?

And what about motive? Who would risk coming into a hospital and taking a patient against their will? Had Phoebe been so sedated she had not resisted? Had she been carried?

'What are you thinking, detective?'

'What dosage of sedatives was Phoebe on? Would it have been difficult to rouse her? Or impossible? Would she have been capable of putting up physical resistance?'

'The dosage I gave was to induce her to sleep. It was appropriate to her agitated state of mind. It's difficult to say precisely the depth of the effect but I'd say she would rouse if she were shaken but she might have found it difficult to stand.'

'I see. So it would render her more vulnerable to being coerced or being taken against her will.'

Doctor Hargreaves shifted in her chair. 'I suppose it might. I think you've a tough case to solve.'

'I've had much tougher. I'd also like to know about Charles.'

The doctor sighed. 'Oh yes, poor Charles. It must have been dreadful for him being outside. I'll be seeing him later. You mustn't believe his story.'

'Why not?'

'Charles has a compulsion to lie. It's a habit of his.'

'I see. Why was the diagnosis of compulsive liar added to his file? Charles told me it's not something he's always had.'

'No, I added it. Charles tried to bring a complaint against the hospital for mistreatment of another patient. An investigation showed his concerns were fabricated from beginning to end and he would not waver nor accept he was wrong. My conclusion was, he was wilfully not telling the truth. In full conscience and for his own ends. It's a symptom of being a compulsive liar.'

And it had been added to Charles's notes based on a single incident? Poor Charles. Grant had already understood that what a psychiatrist decided for a patient was close to impossible to challenge – the medication, the diagnosis, the treatment plan. As a psychiatrist Doctor Hargreaves had absolute power in this institution. What might that do to a person? Might it twist their mind towards murder?

Grant consulted his notebook. 'And I understand you know a young woman called Emma White. I believe she's a friend of Phoebe's?'

'I was Emma's psychiatrist too and that's correct, they're good friends. It's really benefitted both of them. However, I should warn you Emma has flashbacks to a very traumatic experience in her life and she also suffers from memory blackouts. People who suffer PTSD can be unreliable in their relating of current events because trauma from the past intrudes and effects how they perceive things.'

Which Mrs Nicholson had already made sure was passed on. Emma was another person who they should not believe. This really was grating on him. And if you were a murderer in hiding, how very convenient it would be.

'Emma has PTSD?'

'She does. I don't want to tell you too much because of doctor-patient confidentiality, but to give you the bare bones, Emma's mother and sister were murdered when Emma was six. Her stepfather was the one who killed them. Emma was in the house at the time and she was spared. She suffered post-traumatic stress disorder and I don't know if she will ever fully recover but she does now have a life and she lives independently. However, Emma still has occasional bad episodes.'

'Thank you, that's very helpful.'

'I have a busy schedule, Inspector, but if I can help in any way, please let me know.'

'Of course, I don't want to take up more of your valuable time. I'll see myself out.'

Grant reached to shake her hand. Yes what a wonderful environment this would be, for a clever killer to go unnoticed.

Chapter 14

Tom was sitting at the edge of the lawn and Diane was a short distance away, under the trees. Despite being in the shade, sweat trickled down his back.

Across the other side of the garden, patients were clustered in groups doing gardening. Some were picking tomatoes from the allotments and others were picking strawberries and raspberries. One by one, Tom and Diane invited patients to their tables and listened to their recounts of the night before.

Tom asked questions and probed when he could. He wanted to find out about any suspicious activity in the previous days, or visitors who had stood out. People were clearly shocked and saddened about Phoebe and it made Tom aware, one more time, of the fragility of life.

Most people described Phoebe as a quiet girl and one of her pastimes had been doing portrait sketches which she gave to people for free. She had gained a lot of affection for this.

After three hours of questioning, Tom had no concrete details to add to the investigation. No one had seen somebody take Phoebe from her room, nor had they observed any intruders or any suspect visitors. Aside from the tree felling, nobody had noted anything particularly unusual in the environment of the hospital, nor to do with the windows, in the last few weeks. Nobody recognised a photograph of the man who originally attacked Phoebe.

It was only when Tom finally stretched his legs and decided it was time to take a break he realised his special pen was missing. He kept it in his top pocket. It was a Parker pen and a gift from Ruby. It had been in his pocket all morning together with his notebook, and now it was gone. He thought back over the interviews. He'd not used it. He was sure he hadn't dropped it either.

Moving his table and chairs more into the shade, Tom rolled up his shirt sleeves. It was a very hot day. Jugs of water had been laid out on a bench by the main building and he went over. He was downing a cool cupful when the nudge in the ribs Charles had given him earlier suddenly came to mind. It had happened when Phoebe's friend wanted to speak to Grant. Charles couldn't have deliberately lifted it then, could he?

The more Tom thought about it, the surer he felt. It was a tried and tested technique for pickpocketing – a thief bumps into you to create a distraction, while they deftly swipe your valuables. But Charles? It didn't seem to fit the timid, anxious man they had met that morning.

Tom downed another cup of water and headed back inside.

He found Charles lying on his bed, hands laced behind his head. The door was open and Tom knocked. Charles's eyes darted right and left. A guilty reflex, Tom thought.

'Hello, Charles. I seem to have lost my pen. I was wondering if you'd seen it?'

'What, me? No.'

'Come on. I think you bumped into me deliberately so you could finger it from my pocket.'

'I did not.'

'I really hope you didn't do the same to Ruby. Did you steal from her too? I wouldn't like that to happen to my colleague.'

'Oh no, I didn't take anything from Ruby. She was really nice.'

'But you *did* take something from me, didn't you? Believe it or not she's the one who gave me that pen. Ruby is a special person to me.'

'Is she your girlfriend?'

No need to muddy the waters with that one and he certainly wasn't going to divulge any personal information. 'We're colleagues and we look out for each other. I'd like it back.'

Tom fixed his brown eyes on Charles and kept them there, though he made sure not to be too intimidating.

Charles sat up. 'I didn't do it on purpose. I'm a kleptomaniac. It's a sickness. I didn't mention it earlier because giving you a whole list of what the doc thinks is wrong with me you'd have been even less likely to believe me about Phoebe.'

Tom was glad he had gone in the soft way. He had come across kleptomania in a previous case so he was aware kleptomania *was* an illness. It was a compulsion to take things which didn't belong to you and it was totally different to wilful criminal behaviour. Often kleptomaniacs were attracted to small objects which caught their eye and they didn't sell the items, instead they would keep them as a collection. Tom was also aware it could be a crippling addiction, and one which filled the culprit with a lot of shame.

'I've heard of kleptomania before,' Tom said.

'Have you?'

'I'm not judging. But I do want it back.'

Charles had dropped eye contact and Tom guessed he felt bad about what he'd done.

'You won't tell anyone, will you?' Charles whispered.

'I won't. You have my word it can stay between the two of us.'

Charles stuffed his feet into his slippers and shuffled to the bedside cabinet. He moved like a man twice their age. Tom was a sportsman and he found it hard to watch. Was that the effect of medication?

Charles pulled open a drawer which was full of shiny items. Tom spotted teaspoons, several nice-looking watches, and some twinkly jewellery.

'I'm working with Doctor Hargreaves on a treatment plan. She's helping me. She said when I'm stressed it gets worse. She says it's a symptom of a deeper disturbance in my psyche. I've already returned a lot to their owners. I mean to give them back, every one of them.'

'Right.'

Tom accepted back his pen and watched as Charles swallowed several times, his Adam's apple bobbing with anxiety.

'Like I said, there's no need for me to mention it outside this room, so don't worry about it.' Tom said, as he popped the pen in his pocket.

Charles nodded his thanks. 'How's it going in the garden?'

'Slowly. There are a lot of people to talk to and they have long stories to tell.'

'I suppose so.' Charles blinked several times. 'Is Doctor Otremba there?'

'I didn't see him.'

It was a strange thing being a detective, because sometimes Tom, who considered himself a man of hard facts, got a very strange feeling. It was a feeling he had often dismissed in the past, yet he had realised as he became more experienced, that his gut, against the odds, sometimes spotted clues which his head did not. He found it perplexing. And this was one of those moments. He twirled the pen in his pocket.

'Why do you ask about Doctor Otremba?'

'Oh, no reason,' Charles said.

'He was here last night. Does he spend a lot of time here?'

'Not really.'

'I've spoken to a quite a few patients already and it's obvious you all know how this place runs. You're familiar with the quirks of different members of staff and how the routines go and who'll bend the rules and who won't. So why do I get the feeling you're hinting something important to me about Doctor Otremba?'

'I don't know.'

'Did you see him acting in any way suspiciously yesterday?'

'No.'

'You can be honest with me, Charles. It can only help us. Phoebe was your friend, wasn't she.'

Charles rubbed his hands over his face. 'Don't you think it was odd he was here so quickly last night?'

It had not been odd, given the doctor lived close to the hospital and he had been contacted in a crisis situation. 'I understand he lives down the road and he's often called in an emergency. Doctor Otremba was also Phoebe's general practitioner, so he knew her well.'

'Ah, but he wasn't *her* choice as a doctor. It was her father who chose Doctor Otremba to be her GP. But maybe that wasn't the only reason he got here so fast.'

'What do you mean? If you know something, you must tell me.'

Charles's gaze kept darting towards the door, so Tom closed it. 'What is it?'

'He can't know I told you.'

'All our interviews are confidential. No one will know what you share with me, except other members of the police team.'

Was it Tom's imagination or was Charles shaking? *Come on, Charles, trust me.*

Tom knew better than to push. He waited, and watched as the man put his hand to the back of the drawer and pulled out a silver packet of pills.

'I took these from him,' Charles whispered.

'You mean you took them from Doctor Otremba's pocket? Like you did me and the pen?'

Charles nodded.

'I need you to explain what you're saying. Why is this important?'

'They're amphetamines. He's always taking them. He's an addict. There are other patients who know about it apart from me. He tries to hide it but my ex was an addict so I know the signs. I took the pills from Otremba's pocket as evidence for Phoebe. I knew Phoebe wanted to get away from Otremba. So I told her he was an addict and I took the pills for her. Then she confronted him. She told him she knew he was a junkie and she could prove it. She didn't tell him *how*, but she told him that if he didn't leave her alone she would tell Doctor Hargreaves.'

'Wait. Lots of patients know the doctor's an addict?'

Charles shrugged. 'People with addiction problems can always spot a fellow junkie.'

'I see. And so you helped Phoebe. Why did she want Doctor Otremba to leave her alone?'

'Because Doctor Otremba was Phoebe's father's puppet. Otremba was supposed to be there for Phoebe but he wasn't. He was only interested in doing what her father wanted him to do. He colluded with her father to get her put in here again. The two of them made it impossible for her to change GP.'

'Were you there when she spoke to Doctor Otremba about the pills?'

'No, I was too frightened. But we agreed Phoebe wouldn't tell Doctor Otremba it was me who got the pills from him. I was scared he might guess and come after me but then he's not my GP so he doesn't know me. She told the doctor he dropped them on the floor and she picked them up.'

'Right.'

'I was in my room but I heard them arguing next door. He got angry and threatened her. I could hear him shouting.'

'When was this?'

'Two days ago.'

'Did Phoebe tell anyone else about the pills or about the argument?'

'She was going to tell Doctor Hargreaves about the amphetamines.'

'Can I take these with me?'

Charles passed them over so quickly it was as if they were burning. 'You promise you won't tell it was me.'

'I promise. You've been very brave sharing this. It's going to help a lot. Thank you.'

Doctor Otremba would risk being struck off the medical register if he was an addict. Was he prescribing himself prescription drugs to feed a habit? Covering it up would be sufficient motive for murder. And the doctor would know his way around the hospital.

And what about the relationship between Doctor Otremba and John Markham, which sounded very murky.

Tom closed the door softly behind him. Oh yes, they were getting somewhere at last.

Chapter 15

'Guv, I found out from Charles that Doctor Otremba argued with Phoebe two days ago.'

Grant listened carefully as Tom updated him about the amphetamines and how patients knew Doctor Otremba was an addict. Mike Otremba? That was a surprise.

'Good work. I'll question him. Can you get surveillance footage for the roads around the hospital checked through? I want to know what time Doctor Otremba arrived.'

'On it.'

'And I want to know everything about Phoebe's original attacker. Where was he and what was he doing yesterday afternoon? Where was he at the time of Phoebe's death in the evening and what was he doing in between?'

'Right,' Tom said.

'Keep working at it. I want a team briefing at the end of the day. First, I want to check in with Lin Chen to see if she has anything to add to her statement.'

And of course, to put pressure on her to reveal any discrepancies.

Nurse Chen lived in a modern apartment block in a nice neighbourhood. Outside her door, two potted plants flowered in the sun.

Lin looked even worse than she had the night before. Her face was blotchy and puffy around the eyes and Grant felt sure she had spent hours crying. Despite that, she gave off open vibes and he had the impression she was the sort of person patients would trust.

'Oh, you're that detective,' she said. 'You'd better come in.'

'You probably don't remember my name. I'm DCI David Grant.'

He was led through to the living room where a window gave a view over a children's playground. Piles of laundry were stacked on the sofa and the chairs. Lin had to move a heap to make space on an armchair. Unopened post had accumulated on the coffee table.

'I'm sorry it's a bit of a mess. I can't keep on top of things. I do the washing and ironing for my sister and it's always stacking up.' Lin shrugged. 'My place looks like an overrun laundry most of the time. My sister has a terminal illness and she needs a lot of care.'

'I'm sorry to hear that.'

'Thank you. Naomi has Motor Neurone Disease. Have you heard of it?'

'I think so. The same illness as Stephen Hawking?'

'Yes. It's dreadful and the worst is how fast it's advanced. She was diagnosed when she was twelve. We were hoping she would have the slower kind, actually, that's the type Stephen Hawking had. He lived with it for over fifty years. Naomi is much less lucky. She's got the worst type of MND possible. I need to give her and our mum and dad all the support I can. But you're not here to talk about my family.'

Grant took out his notebook. 'I already have your statement from last night. Do you have anything you want to add?'

Lin's mouth trembled before she spoke. 'I've been over it and over it in my mind. Wondering what I did wrong and what

I could have done differently. The 'what ifs' are going to haunt me forever. What if I'd gone back to check on her again? What if I'd noticed something? A sign of an intruder? Someone dragging her from her room? How could someone have done it so silently? With all the patients in bed, I was the only one who might have noticed.'

He'd met plenty of people who had tortured themselves with the 'what ifs. Grant didn't wish that on anybody. He gave a sympathetic nod as she reached for a tissue and blew her nose.

'I'm sorry. I just can't stop thinking about it.'

'Is there anything else which has come to mind about events?'

'It's like I said. I tucked Phoebe up and I gave her her medication. I checked back and she was asleep. Then the next thing I know, my colleague is calling me in hysterics.'

'Who unlocked the front door to the building?'

'My colleague and I. The emergency services gathered outside and we told patients to stay in their rooms.'

Which would mean an intruder would have needed a key to exit before then. Or perhaps they escaped through a fire exit.

'I've been so tired, splitting myself between my shifts and spending time with Naomi, but I swear I didn't cut corners. I was worried about Phoebe and that's why I went back to see her one more time. Thank god I wrote it in my nurse's notes or else the hospital trust would be crucifying me. They still might.'

He wondered too if the hospital would be offering her counselling. He hoped so. 'Have you seen anyone hanging around the hospital? Any suspect visitors?'

'No. Nothing unusual.'

Grant swiped a photograph of Phoebe's attacker, Hunt, up on his phone. 'Do you recognise this man?'

Lin shook her head.

'Let's think back to the sequence. Your colleague phoned you to say what had happened, then what?'

'I went outside. I saw Phoebe. We checked for signs of life. The other nurse had already called emergency services, and the paramedics and Mike Otremba arrived quickly.'

'Who arrived first?'

'Doctor Otremba. He lives nearby.'

'He walked to where you were? Do you remember which direction he came from?'

'No idea. Some of the patients were staring out their windows and once he arrived I went inside to ask them to close their curtains. It was pandemonium. And Charles wouldn't stop screaming.'

'You didn't find it unusual that Doctor Otremba arrived so fast?'

'Not at all. We often call him when there's an emergency.'

'All right. Let's talk about Phoebe. What I'd like to get clear in my mind is what sort of person she was. I understand you knew her well?'

'I had a lot of affection for Phoebe. I knew her longer than other members of staff because I was a nurse in the children's part of the hospital before I moved over to the adult side. I met Phoebe when she first accessed mental health services. And yes, she and I got on well. What sort of person was she? Courageous and determined.'

'Determined about what?'

'To get better and to lead an independent life. I don't have the energy to be subtle and talk around things I'm sorry, so I'm just going to be blunt. Phoebe's problems weren't only about her mental health. She wanted to get away from her mother and father. They were suffocating her.'

Grant gave no reaction, though the relationship Phoebe had with her parents was starting to worry him.

'It's difficult to appreciate from the outside. The Markhams have been supportive of their daughter, and they've been like that for years. But at some point they should have moved back and made room for Phoebe's own wishes and they didn't. You could say they've been overprotective, but it was worse. Phoebe felt stifled. Her father controlled her – where she could live, who she could see. He'd already put a stop to her career ideas. From my point of view, it seemed like they wanted her to be their little girl forever.'

'Was there open conflict between them?'

'It was going more and more that way. Phoebe wanted desperately to move to Ireland and the Markhams have the financial means to help her but they refused. I mean, how nasty is that? Phoebe always made excuses for them. She kept saying how much they cared about her. She didn't want to hurt their feelings.'

Grant took his time writing in his notebook. It was a ruse, so he could consider what was being said. Pressure from Phoebe's family was an argument which would add weight to the theory Phoebe had done this herself. And what about Lin's part? After all, she was the last person they knew had seen Phoebe. And he had witnessed tension between Lin and John Markham. He could hear a washing machine in the background as it went into the spin cycle.

'It sounds like you had strong feelings about it yourself.'

'Part of my role is to support patients to become self-sufficient. We were in agreement as a staff team that the Markhams weren't helping. They were an obstacle. So yes, I had feelings about it. But not unprofessional ones.'

It made more sense of the tension between John and Lin which Grant had picked up on the previous night. Lin did not come across as a murderer nor an accomplice, she genuinely cared for Phoebe.

Grant decided to change tack. 'It must be hard having such a demanding job and looking after your family.'

'It didn't affect my concentration or my work, if that's what you're insinuating. Sorry, I know that's snappy of me. I didn't get much sleep.'

Grant waited.

'Look, I really liked Phoebe and there's no way she did this herself. She was focused on what she wanted. Yes, seeing the perpetrator yesterday was devastating, but that's completely normal and she would have worked through it. That's another reason why the Markhams trapping Phoebe in Himlands Heath didn't make sense. In Ireland, she would never see her abuser, would she.'

'I suppose not.'

Grant shifted a little on the sofa and a mountain of folded sheets at the other end tottered and fell. 'I'm sorry, let me pick those up.'

'It's okay, leave it. You've got much more important things to do. Please catch Phoebe's killer. Which brings me to the Markhams. They were holding her back and that really isn't fair. Phoebe was an adult. She should get to live her own life her own way. And I don't care what other people say, I don't believe Phoebe did this. She was murdered.'

Chapter 16

Emma was too restless to return to her apartment. After she had walked with Ruby, Emma wandered the hospital grounds, until a member of staff asked her to leave. She felt sure it was Mrs Nic who had ordered her off the premises. The previous year, Emma had supported Charles when he made a complaint about the treatment of another patient. Since then, Mrs Nic had it in for both of them. How Emma hated that woman.

Emma went to the park. The patients had been so nice. They knew what to say better than the staff did. Even Charles had come to put his arm around her shoulders. Emma knew it had been a great effort for him. It was hard for Charles to leave his room, let alone approach another person, and she appreciated it.

She had liked that police psychologist, Ruby Silver. Ruby had been quiet and attentive, the type to know a lot and say little, but that didn't mean the police would take what Emma told them seriously. Emma wasn't fool enough to fall for that one. No, she was sure they would dismiss her. She'd do the same if she was in their shoes. She must have come across as deranged, hurtling along the corridor, screaming at Mrs Nic. People never took you seriously when they thought you were screwed up.

What could she do? It took a lot of walking for her to come up with the idea of a memorial video. She could talk to people and ask for their stories and memories of Phoebe. It would be some sort of comfort to produce something she could post online. A fitting tribute to her dear friend.

It would also stop her from going mad. How about she start straight away? She could go to the afternoon coffee session at the church. There would be members of their self-help group there. She could record video snippets on her phone and edit them into a film.

Set at the back of the church, the community annexe was a modern extension with plenty of light. It had been funded by Anne Markham. Outside, there was a little garden with benches for contemplation and the main room had a set of double doors which opened to let in the summer air.

Emma had often sat in the garden with Phoebe. Their favourite bench was flanked by lavender bushes and Phoebe had liked to pick a fragrant sprig and pop it in her pocket. Emma did the same now, crushing the little purple flowers to release their sweet scent. Tears prickled the back of her eyes.

The doors to the community room were open and Brett's voice carried across the garden. It had been kind of him to break the news to her, and she owed him an apology for her rudeness. Yelling at the person who had come to help you and ordering them to leave had not been the nicest thing to do. Her face went hot from the realisation she had made a fool of herself once again.

The hum of conversation from inside the room was subdued and morose as people came to terms with the terrible news.

Brett had been supportive over the years. It was strange to think how his own life had been derailed by Juliette's death. Brett had been Juliette's boyfriend. It was Brett who had composed the song Juliette had been humming that fateful day – Murder Day – as Emma called it.

Instead of becoming a famous songwriter, Brett had changed his ideas and instead decided to train as a counsellor. He told Emma he never composed anything else after Murder Day. The horrible events had scarred him.

Once he qualified as a counsellor, Brett worked in Brighton for years. He kept occasional contact with Emma, sending her a Christmas card each year, and then one day she had walked into the brand new community room and he had been there. Brett had been employed to set up a self-help group and a drop-in mental health resource with coffee and hobby sessions. That was five years ago. It had been such a surprise.

Everyone liked Brett. At one time Phoebe had had a crush on him. Emma liked him too although she had always been very protective of Phoebe over that crush. It would have been so easy for Brett to turn Phoebe's attention towards him during their therapy sessions together. Emma had no evidence of it happening, even so she had warned her friend and it was the reason Phoebe stopped seeing Brett for one-to-ones.

She'd felt guilty for talking bad about him behind his back. Brett was non-threatening and good at facilitating the self-help group. Why was she always so suspicious of people? Each year, Brett had laid flowers on her mother's and Juliette's graves on the anniversary of Murder Day and that made Emma feel even worse for thinking ill of him.

She fingered her phone. It had a great camera and was good for filming snippets. Editing videos was something she had been practising in the hope she could make money out of it. She would really like to have something better than her work at the burger bar. Which reminded her she needed to make her apologies for missing her shift. Would they sack her? Very likely, and then she'd be back at zero again, wasting her time at the job centre. She sighed and made the call.

To her surprise, the manager was sympathetic when she told him about Phoebe's death. It turned out he had lost his brother in a motorbike accident and he told her it had taken months for him to get back to work. He gave Emma three weeks off and told her to call again if she needed longer. His compassion made her cry.

Brett came to sit beside her.

'My manager understood,' she said, blowing her nose. 'I didn't expect him to. I thought I was going to get booted out.'

'People can surprise us in nice ways.'

Emma didn't believe it. The burger bar manager was an exception.

Doctor Hargreaves told Emma her deep pessimism was a symptom of post-traumatic stress. Perhaps it was, but when you've experienced a Murder Day, how can it ever change? Often Emma felt as if she would never heal nor lead a happy life. And when she had a glimpse things might get better, life had landed another blow and took away her best friend. She stared at the lavender bush.

'I'd like to ask people if I can record them talking about Phoebe. I want to make a memorial video with anecdotes and whatever people would like to say. Would you mind?'

'It's a lovely idea. Very healing. As long as they understand what you're doing and why, and where you'll share the final product. It could be cathartic for everyone.'

He was such a therapist, using that kind of language. She'd been around so many of them she understood – by cathartic he meant the project could help people express their grief and come to terms with what had happened. If only it were so easy – press a button and horrible feelings would go away – but Emma knew it was not like that.

Brett adjusted his glasses. 'I'm going to hold a special session for members of the self-help group. A sort of goodbye ceremony where we can express our feelings about losing Phoebe. Perhaps we could show your video?'

'Maybe. And, you know, sorry I was nasty earlier.'

'You weren't nasty, you were protecting yourself. It's fine, Emma. You don't need to apologise.'

She looked away to stop herself from tearing up. 'Can I use the small interview room at the back?'

'Of course. But are you sure you want to start today? It'll be hard on you. I don't want you to get overloaded.'

'I'm okay.'

He didn't look convinced and Emma wasn't sure she was either. But not doing anything would feel much worse.

Brett studied her over the top of his glasses. 'How about I check in later to see how you're doing?'

She was dismayed how wobbly her emotions were. Perhaps Brett was right, perhaps it was taking on too much. Pushing herself off the bench anyway she made as if she was much more in shape than she felt and she walked inside.

Emma was startled by a knock at the door. She blinked and checked around her. Where was she? Her mouth was dry and she was too hot. She recognised the room. It was the interview room behind the community hall and she was sitting in a comfortable chair with the sunlight coming in the window onto her lap.

The knock came again. Her head felt strange and her thoughts were fuzzy. What was she doing there? She licked her lips.

'Come in.' Her voice was croaky.

Brett peered around the door. 'I'm not disturbing you, am I? I didn't know if you had someone with you.'

Her mind tried to catch up. Wait, yes, she'd been doing interviews and people had been talking about Phoebe. Her hands were shaking so she put them under her thighs because she didn't want Brett to notice.

'The last person just left,' she lied.

She wondered what the time was. The sun was low. Did it mean she had been here hours? Was it late afternoon already?

'I've been busy in the office. How's it been going?' he asked.

'Pretty well.'

'I'm sure people have a lot to say. Phoebe's been an important person in the group.'

'Yeah.' She hoped he would go away so she could recover on her own. 'I'm going to finish for today. I'll come back tomorrow to do more.'

'Good idea. I'll put the word around. Are you sure everything's okay?'

She nodded and pretended to study her phone, scrolling through some old images which had nothing to do with Phoebe.

'I'll leave you then. How many interviews did you do so far?'

'A few.'

She was relieved when he didn't press as to how many exactly, because she had no idea. There were ten members of the self-help group. She scrolled some more and checked how many she had actually done.

Oh no. She had only interviewed two people and the time on her phone said 5.10pm. What the hell? A cold terror took hold. She did her best to keep the fear off her face.

'See you tomorrow then,' he said. 'Make sure you look after yourself this evening.'

'Yeah, I will. See you.'

He closed the door and she gripped the arm rests. It was hard not to panic. She knew what this meant – she had blanked out. She had come in here and she had carried out the grand total of two interviews and since then she had been sitting alone for hours, in a daze.

After Murder Day, she suffered from time lapses where she would come to her senses somewhere she didn't even remember going to, her memory a blank. The blackouts could be set off by an emotion, a scent, a sound. At the beginning, there had been many triggers. With time, she had reduced them.

She had not done it for years. *Please, please, no.* She didn't want to return to those dark days.

The triggers which had been the most difficult to master had been musical. They were parts of the songs that had been playing that day, or Juliette's song. Emma had worked hard to desensitise herself and she had no recollection of what had set her off that afternoon.

Her back was slick with sweat as she left the church. Was her mind becoming unstable?

Chapter 17

It was a hot afternoon and Grant left his jacket in the car.

Mike Otremba worked in a group practice with two other doctors. It was a modern little building on a road running into town. The receptionist was young and efficient and the waiting room was busy. As one of Mike Otremba's patients left, the receptionist ushered Grant into the doctor's office.

'There's a Detective Chief Inspector here to see you,' she said.

Otremba had a striking air about him as he sat behind his desk, with his broad shoulders and resonant voice. 'DCI Grant, please take a seat. I'll be with you in a moment.'

The doctor tapped out a few notes on his computer and then he pushed away the keyboard.

'Thank you for squeezing me in,' Grant said.

'It's my secretary you should thank, she's a one in a million and we're lucky to have her. How's it going at Moorlands?'

'I'm following up a few lines of enquiry. I understand you're Phoebe Markham's general practitioner?'

'That's right. I've been her doctor for years.'

'How many exactly?'

'Let me think. She was assaulted when she was fourteen and her GP at the time was close to retirement. She stayed with him a short while longer and then her father approached me and asked if I would care for his daughter. I was honoured.'

'You knew John Markham?'

'Yes. We'd met a few times at council functions.'

'I see. Did you know each other socially?'

'Only on the business side of things. Why are you asking?'

'We have a witness who heard you arguing with Phoebe two days before her death. Could you tell me what that was about?'

The doctor huffed in surprise. 'I don't recall an argument. We often had discussions about her care and what was best for her. I was at Moorlands for another matter and I decided to pay her a visit to see how she was getting on.'

'And?'

Otremba shrugged. 'Phoebe was doing fine and she was looking forward to coming home.'

'You don't remember shouting at her for any reason?'

'Definitely not.'

'I understand she had an ambition to move to Ireland. What was your view about that?'

'Phoebe talked about it off and on. She was a vulnerable young woman. What you have to understand is she has a comprehensive package of care set up for her here. Her parents are nearby should anything go wrong. It wouldn't be easy to ensure the same standard of care in a new place. Especially if she moved to another country.'

'I take it you were against the idea.'

'You could put it that way. Basically, I thought the risks outweighed the benefits.'

Grant was observing carefully. The man seemed calm and in control. He wasn't rushing and did not appear stressed. He didn't seem to be under the influence of amphetamines – he wasn't speedy, he wasn't sweating, he wasn't jittery.

'We've received some rather delicate information alleging you have a prescription drug addiction.'

Otremba raised his eyebrows. 'Who told you that?'

'I'm not at liberty to say.'

The doctor took a moment to push around a few papers on his desk. 'I *had* a prescription drug problem. Past tense. I'm not proud of it. I suppose it was inevitable somebody would get to hear about it, though I've tried my hardest to keep it under wraps.'

'You don't deny it then.'

'It happened six years ago and it's all on record. I underwent treatment which was supervised by the General Medical Council. If you knew the pressures of this job you might be more understanding.'

'If you could tell me as much as you can, that would be helpful.'

Otremba leaned back in his chair and recounted to Grant how he began using alcohol and amphetamines when he was a junior doctor. He had struggled with the long hours and the amphetamines seemed the only way he could get through the shifts. Then he needed the alcohol to sleep and relax. The problems began when he wanted to stop and couldn't. Apparently, he had received treatment at a rehabilitation centre and was pronounced drug free and fit for work. He had had no relapses in the last six years.

'At that time I self-referred to the GMC. They reviewed my case and agreed that for me to continue practising as a doctor I had to take sick leave and undergo treatment. When I returned to work, my blood was tested once a week for six months. After that, the GMC saw no reason to continue supervising me.'

'If you had a relapse, I doubt the GMC would be so generous. You might face losing your medical licence.'

Otremba's expression clouded with anger. 'Except I haven't had a relapse. Whoever told you that is lying.'

Grant jotted down a few notes. If Otremba had relapsed and Phoebe had confronted him about the amphetamines, it was a motive for murder. Was Otremba already at the hospital when Phoebe fell? Had he been the one to take her to the top floor?

'Why are you asking these questions? Don't tell me I'm a suspect! That's ridiculous.'

'Please don't leave Himlands Heath without informing me first.'

'Why not? Am I under arrest?'

'You are a person of interest in this investigation and it would be much better for you if you cooperate in all conceivable ways.'

Otremba was livid. His face showed it as he stood and towered over Grant. 'I *am* cooperating, Inspector. Now if you wouldn't mind, I have patients to attend to.'

'Are you willing to take a voluntary blood test?'

'Certainly not.'

Grant's grey eyes were hard as granite. 'I see. As I said, doctor, please don't travel. I'll be in touch.'

Chapter 18

By the time Emma got back to her apartment, she felt sick with anxiety. She closed the door and it felt solid and cool behind her back as she slid to the floor. Hugging her knees, she took deep breaths. *You'll be okay. You can handle this. You're stronger than you think.*

Yes, she must remember she had learned to be strong. This time it would not overwhelm her.

At the kitchen sink, she poured herself some water and went to sit on the sofa. Her hair clung to the sweat on her forehead and she pushed it back. Slowly, she felt her breathing returning to normal and the shaking ebbed. Losing Phoebe was horrible. Emma still could not believe it. But she had to hold on to the hope the police would find the truth.

As the sun glanced off the grubby walls she was reminded what a dump her apartment was. No amount of scrubbing had removed the grime of previous tenants. She'd heard from a neighbour that the previous occupant had been a drug user and all kinds of unpleasant people had stayed overnight. From the dirt Emma had found when she arrived, she could believe it.

The kitchen was a hob and a fridge in one corner of the lounge. The bathroom was a mouldy, smelly room where the hot water only worked when it felt like it.

One of Phoebe's paintings hung across from the sofa bed. It was the highlight. She remembered the day she and Phoebe had brought it across town and they'd banged a nail in the wall and hung it up. Emma took another drink and that's when she noticed a difference. Something was missing.

She checked left and right. She always kept her journal in the same place – on the little table right beside the sofa bed. But it wasn't there. It was gone.

Panic mounted, making it hard to think straight. She peered under the coffee table. Then fell to her hands and knees and searched feverishly under the sofa bed. Nothing, except dust and an old crisp packet.

The journal was precious. It was an account of her thoughts and feelings. She'd first started keeping a diary when she was at Moorlands and since then, journaling had become a way for her to keep track of her mental health. She noted the ups and the downs. The things which made her happy and the things which made her sad. Over the years, she had been able to see her progress, thanks to her writing.

Her current journal had a purple cover and a gold elastic. The binding was a spiral and Emma liked to tuck a pen there so she could jot down thoughts at any time, even in the middle of the night. She searched again in vain, crawling around the room.

There was no way it was gone. She *always* put it there, she never took it outside, and she definitely didn't take it into the smelly bathroom. She searched there anyway. She had never shown it to anyone, not even to Phoebe.

This didn't make any sense. It wasn't possible. Unless... unless she had blanked out another time and she didn't even realise. She screwed her hands into fists. No, that wasn't possible. She had to believe in herself. She was better. She knew how to handle her PTSD. Which meant what? That someone had come into her apartment and stolen it?

She sat on the floor, her mind whirling. That could not be possible either. Or could it?

The only person who had keys was her landlord. It was Emma's social worker who had found this place and when she first moved in, the social worker had told her the landlord lived overseas. He never did any maintenance and Emma's neighbours had told her she would never hear from him and not be bothered by him. And she hadn't been.

It was torture to think of someone else reading her intimate thoughts.

Think, Emma, think. What the hell's going on?

She tried to check if anything else had been moved or was missing. She didn't have much – a few bits of furniture, a railing with clothes which she had carefully selected from charity shops. There was nothing worth stealing.

What was happening? Was she becoming ill again?

Breathe, Emma, breathe. Don't fall apart.

She sat on the floor, hugging her knees.

Chapter 19

Grant hurried over to the morgue timing it so he could arrive just after the special postmortem examination had been carried out. It was the right moment for a discussion with the pathologist.

Luke Sanderson was sitting alone in his laboratory, his blond head bent over the keyboard.

'What brings you to darken my door?' Luke said, without glancing up. 'I thought we'd got rid of you.'

'No such luck.'

'Trust you to barge in. Just at the right moment to skip the protocol and get the results quicker.'

'Glad I'm not losing my touch.'

Luke smiled. 'Let me finish this. Give me a second.'

Luke had an enormous amount of talent for the job. He wasn't someone who ticked the boxes, he was invested and he cared about the victims, which was rare in a pathologist. Grant had liked him from the start.

'How's it going at headquarters? I hear you've got a plush set-up over there.'

You could never beat how fast news travelled on the grapevine.

'It's not bad, especially the incident room which is state of the art. Though we haven't got office chairs yet. Or desks.'

Luke pushed his stool away from the bench, the little wheels clacking as it went. 'Right. The report on your young woman.'

'What have you got?'

'First, there's evidence of old scarring on her arms. It's from several cuts, made by a blade, in the same area on the inner side of both arms.'

'Self-harm?'

'She was known as a self-harmer? Then that's a strong possibility. There were no fresh marks, or bruising, or signs of force on the body. All the lacerations and bruising, bone breakages and internal injuries are consistent with the blunt force trauma associated with falling from height and landing on concrete.'

'Nothing unusual?'

'Nada.'

'So you can't tell if she was carried? Or taken against her will?'

'Not from the postmortem. If she had been grasped around the wrists and she had resisted, or if her limbs had been bound, I'd expect there to be clear signs. Carrying is a different matter. If she were unconscious, carrying her would not generally incur bruising.'

'I see.'

'As for the sedatives, she had levels in her bloodstream which indicated the last ones she took were around 9pm that day.'

'What about the fall? Can you tell if she was pushed, or if she jumped?'

'There are several small indicators. However, let me caution you, they're only indicators. Nothing is conclusive here. First, when somebody is pushed from a building, they tend to land further from the base. That's because the push gives them more forwards velocity. Whereas someone who falls will land nearer. Phoebe Markham landed relatively near to the base of the building. Second, she landed face down. A victim who is pushed is more likely to land face up because they have been facing their assailant, possibly fighting them off. Finally, as I said earlier, there are no defensive marks on her body which would have indicated a struggle getting her onto the ledge. It would be more usual for her to fight back in an assailant situation, but we need to take into account she was sedated so that might not have been possible for her.'

'Basically, your findings indicate that Phoebe probably wasn't pushed.'

'That's correct, but I can only say this on a balance of probabilities.'

Grant drummed his finger on the desktop.

'Then there's the sweep of her clothing. There are fibres and some human hairs. It's a busy hospital so that's not unusual. If you can find a suspect, the lab can do comparisons for DNA and fibre matching.'

'I'll be asking the CSM to run tests against Doctor Mike Otremba and Phoebe's historic attacker, Hunt.'

'Is the Crime Scene Manager Sejal Patani?'

'Yes. We didn't exactly hit it off.'

Luke laughed. 'I heard she can be a bit prickly.'

Not only prickly, but distant and with a chip on her shoulder, were the thoughts which came to Grant's mind, though he kept those to himself. Give her time. He didn't like to judge people too early on, though a top-notch CSM could make or break an investigation and everyone knew that.

'Something tells me you're having a bad day,' Luke said.

'I can't let John Markham down. A long time ago we lived through a terrible tragedy. The kind which links you for life.'

In response to Luke's expectant look, Grant shook his head. 'I'm not going into it now.'

'You're pursuing the case. I don't see why you'd be letting anyone down.'

'So far, we've one witness whose evidence is unlikely to stand up in court. There will be professionals who will speak against him. It's hard to separate off my history with John, but I know there's a perpetrator out there. This is one I've got to crack.'

'And how's Chrissie taking it?'

'Quite well.'

'Meaning very badly.' Luke raised an eyebrow. 'Poor you. She's not getting worried she needs to find a stand-in to walk her down the aisle, is she? You can tell her I'm always available.'

'You're not helping. I've missed the suit fitting and the last meeting with the caterers. The worst thing is, Lily's invited the groom's parents over for dinner in two days. That's one I can't miss. Lily and I haven't met them properly yet.'

'Ah. Have you set a reminder on your phone?'

'Several. I think I'm going to ask Diane and Tom to make sure I leave on time.'

'Good idea.'

A woman's voice called from the doorway. 'I'm so glad I found you.'

They both turned. Sejal's dark hair was tied in a ponytail, with the white streak flopping free at the front. She was clutching a manilla file.

'Hi Luke, how are things?' she said. 'I was trying to track you down, David, and heard you were here. Thought you'd want to see this straightaway.'

'Wait, you two know each other?' Grant said.

Luke grinned. 'Didn't I mention it? Sejal and my boyfriend went to school together in Brighton. They're running buddies. Which is great because it means I get to do a little bit of–'

Sejal cut Luke a look. 'No personal talk. This information changes everything. Fingerprint and trace DNA results are in, but the real game changer is what we found from Ms Markham's mobile phone.'

The triumphant look on Sejal's face said it all. Grant had the urge to hug her, or Luke, or both of them.

'What did they find?'

'The techies used the memory chip in a new phone. Network traffic analysis tells us it was Phoebe's mobile. It also tells us the last thing she did was stream a video to the dark web.'

The dark web? How was that possible?

'She streamed it at 9.42pm.'

Grant's back went cold. What the hell was going on?

'Did we get an ID on the perpetrator? Any traces of them in the video?'

'We haven't got the actual video yet. They're trying to retrieve a copy but it's not simple. The only place it's stored is the dark web and they can't access it. They're still trying.' Sejal's voice was hard. 'What we do know is the video was being sent just before the phone became unoperational. Right before it smashed. They think it was taken as she jumped.'

Luke flinched. 'What?'

Grant felt his breath change, as if ice froze his lungs and he was breathing out pure mist. In contrast to the cold in his chest, his anger flared. To keep it under control, he exhaled long and slow.

A video was taken as she jumped? Why? By who? The dark web hid the worst kinds of criminal activity. Who had watched it? Was it a site where people were filmed being murdered? Grant had heard of those though he had never encountered it before.

Sejal wiped a hand across her brow. 'Yeah I know. It's a bad one.'

Chapter 20

Tom put down the phone. The furniture for their office had arrived but everybody was too focused on work to care. Tom had shoved the new desks into a corner.

'Was that Grant? Is he on his way? What's happened?' Ruby asked.

'He got a report from the techies. The phone belonged to Phoebe. A video was streamed when she fell. It was sent to the dark web.'

There was a silence.

'If she was trying to get her assailant on film, she wouldn't have been streaming to the dark web,' Diane said.

'You're telling me.'

The dark web was a place for sadistic voyeurs and child sex offenders. It was horrible to think of a young girl's final moments being posted there.

Diane leant against the wall. 'Leave the rest of those chairs, Ruby. Tom, before Grant gets back, can you get me up to speed? You know tech isn't my thing.'

Tom explained how the dark web was an underlayer of the internet which wasn't accessible by usual search engines. To visit it, you had to use special web software called Tor. Via sophisticated encryption, Tor gave anonymity to the user. It also allowed the location of everything a user visited to remain hidden from outside scrutiny.

'There are rumours murderers have posted videos of their acts there,' Ruby said. 'I looked into it when I was doing my research into serial killers. Those videos have never been found even though lots of researchers have looked.'

Tom poured himself some water. 'Everything is decentralised. There are no crawlers to bring together information. Even the web addresses are different from what you'd use on the rest of the internet. For instance, if you want to access a site all you need to usually do is type the URL in the address bar or search for it using a browser. On the dark web, you'd have to know the URL right down to the last decimal and character. Dark web addresses are made up of random strings of numbers and letters, they're not made up of words like the ones we're used to.'

'What else can you tell us from your research, Ruby?' Diane asked.

'A number of convicted killers said they filmed their acts but it was never proven. Henry Lee Lucas and his accomplice claimed to have filmed their crimes but both men were pathological liars. Other perpetrators, like Leonard Lake, videotaped their interactions with some of their future victims, but not the murders. No research has come up with evidence of any of it finding its way onto the dark web. Are you okay, Tom? It's got to you a bit, hasn't it?'

'When I think of her body on the ground and it being linked to the dark web it makes me angry.' Tom gulped some more water. 'I've heard about snuff movies. They're supposed to have been faked. There are anonymous chat rooms too, where you can link with other people. Who knows what goes on there.'

Ruby didn't seem to have been thrown off course. How did she manage it? She sometimes looked frail compared to him and the guv, and to Diane who was a seasoned detective.

Tom knew Ruby was an expert climber with endurance on the rock face which he struggled to match. Yet she also had a wistfulness about her, which was something he adored. And then there was her psychological knowledge and her ability to get into the minds of the most hardened criminals. He admired that about her. How lucky he was to be with her.

'What?' Ruby said.

'Oh nothing. I was just thinking about our next steps.'

When Diane gave him a knowing look, Tom felt himself go red and he turned back to his screen.

'While we've got two seconds, have either of you got an idea for Chrissie's gift?' Diane said. 'They've finished the collection over at the station and they want to know what to get.'

'No idea,' Ruby said. 'Sorry. Why not pick something from her list? She's got one of those hasn't she?'

Ruby sounded irritated. Now Tom thought about it, ever since Grant had told them the news, Ruby had been unusually quiet about Chrissie's wedding. Did she disapprove? Ruby was so independent. Maybe she didn't see the point in getting married.

Tom closed down his laptop. He and Ruby were taking their relationship slowly. So far, he hadn't felt it was the right moment to talk about moving in together. Although he was ready for it he sensed Ruby was not.

Did Ruby see marriage as old fashioned? What did that mean for their relationship? Because he'd always seen himself as getting married and settling down one day.

'Yes it'll be something from the list,' Diane said. 'I was more wondering what. Quick, before David gets here. Any ideas, Tom?'

'I haven't had time to look, sorry.'

'Me neither,' Ruby said.

'Ok, I'll choose.'

'Thanks, Diane,' Ruby said. 'Weddings aren't my thing.'

Tom felt his heart sink. 'Yeah, thanks. Let me know what you pick.'

'One other thing. He's got a dinner with the in-laws coming up. That's one he's got to go to. It's almost as critical as the actual day.'

'The in-laws, right, got you,' Tom said. 'Give me the time and date and we'll make sure he gets there.'

Chapter 21

In the video clip, Phoebe is wearing her nightgown. It makes her childlike, and I enjoy that.

She's agile climbing through the window and balancing on the little ledge.

I'm trembling and salivating.

Phoebe was so desperate to rebuild herself and to get far away.

Well, she can't get much further away than this, can she?

Her hair wafts in the breeze as she tells me her final words.

I repeat them, exaggerating the sounds, pouting and distorting my mouth to let them linger.

It's like tasting fine wine.

I lick my lips and savour her sweet desire for it to be over.

Phoebe Markham was a good kill.

Now it's time for the next one.

Chapter 22

Grant got back to headquarters and found that by some miracle, the resources department had set up the incident room.

'It's all working in here, guv,' Tom announced.

Grant closed the door behind him. It was great timing. The incident room was where it was all going to happen. The adrenalin hadn't let up all day and he knew it wouldn't until the case was solved.

This place was top of the range. Computer terminals were at every workstation, each with a giant screen. Whiteboards ran the length of two walls, from waist height to the ceiling. New desks and chairs were in place.

Four windows gave a view onto the town and a tree-lined road. It was a big step up compared to the incident room they used to have which had looked over a car park.

Diane had written key names on the boards – Doctors Hargreaves and Otremba, Mrs Nicholson the hospital manager, nurse Lin Chen, Viktor and Kate the OTs. On another board Charles, Emma, then John and Anne Markham. On a third, the name of the man who had originally attacked Phoebe – Hunt, and the therapist at the church, Brett Sinclair. There were photographs pinned up of each person.

Tom set down a tray of mugs. 'Here you go, guv.'

Ruby settled herself near the windows. 'And we bought doughnuts too.'

This was where they would generate the leads and the ideas and connections to crack the case. Grant would have preferred if their first investigation hadn't involved bad memories but there was no need for him to share those with his team now, and he hoped he would never have to. He rubbed his hands together and helped himself to a doughnut. Just one little doughnut wouldn't do much harm would it? He ignored Diane rolling her eyes.

'We're lucky this place is ready for action. Let's start with the dark web.' Grant underlined it on the board. 'First question – why was she streaming? Who to? Was Phoebe even able to use Tor? She was in a mess after seeing Hunt. She was sedated. How would she be in a state of mind to use a dark web browser, access a hidden site, and send a live video?'

Tom came to the front. 'We got the report on her call log data and internet activity. She was active on social media and in several forums for artists. She did portraits online too. I'd say she was pretty tech savvy. There was no suspect chat room activity or anything like that though.'

'I agree with the chief,' Ruby said.' I don't see how she'd be mentally stable enough to take that kind of video.'

Grant stabbed the pen at the board. 'Which circles back to a perpetrator who forced her to or a perp who set up the video with her phone.'

'There's also another possibility,' Diane said. 'Charles couldn't see what was going on. What if Phoebe wasn't with someone? Maybe she was only talking to someone?'

Tom took a slurp from his mug. 'It doesn't gel with the call logs. The last call Phoebe made was to Emma and that was before the nurse did her rounds.'

'Let's keep the ideas coming, people. Motive, motive, motive. Who would want her dead?'

'Did Hunt want to punish Phoebe?' Diane said. 'She's the one who got him convicted. But would he take the risk of going back to prison?'

'Revenge can be a strong motive,' Grant said. 'Hunt would have to have been sure he would get away with it. What've we got on him?'

Tom had taken a massive bite of doughnut and he hastily swallowed it. 'The address which was agreed for his parole was his brother in Brighton.'

'What can you tell us about the original crime?'

'Hunt was a sports teacher at Phoebe's school. He coached the girls' volleyball team, which Phoebe got a place on. Hunt was known to John Markham. Apparently, they belonged to the same golf club and played together on occasion. Phoebe had been in the volleyball team about a year when Hunt assaulted her in the changing rooms. It came out it was a pattern with him to pick a couple of girls to stay behind for extra practice.'

'Grooming,' Ruby said.

'Exactly. He'd been doing the extra practice for a while with Phoebe and one of her friends and then that night her friend couldn't stay. But Phoebe did, and that's when Hunt assaulted her.'

'He was waiting for his chance,' Ruby said. 'It's a known pattern with paedophiles. He picked her and her friend out. Then when he got the opportunity he took it.'

'When Phoebe got home she told her mother and Hunt was arrested. He was suspended by the school. One of Hunt's hairs was found on Phoebe's top and there was bruising on her but not enough to bring a prosecution. It looked as if the case was going to die but then another girl came forward. Then two more. The other three were older and had already left the school. There was a lot of similarity in their statements. The interesting thing is that Hunt pleaded not guilty. The jury thought otherwise. Nine months before his parole board hearing he changed his tune and admitted to the crimes. He started to show remorse and requested counselling. He got out four weeks ago.'

'I want you to get to the brother's and talk to Hunt.' Grant paced the room. 'Arrange for Hunt's other victims to be contacted. Has Hunt bothered any of them? Have they seen him? What about his profile, Ruby? Could this be him?'

'Okay so he's changed his tune now but after trial, Hunt professed he was innocent. He kept to the story he'd been framed and kept talking about how he hated child sex offenders. It's a classic pattern of denial. All the evidence pointed to him being guilty. He plotted his crime cold-bloodedly in advance, targeting several girls. He was careful, he made sure they were under his control before he acted. But that's different from breaking into a hospital and coercing your victim to the top floor. There was no sexual motive for killing Phoebe. I'd say the modus operandi isn't compatible.'

'Then let's find out if he has an alibi,' Grant said.

Tom nodded. 'Yes, guv.'

'Next, Charles.'

'I looked into the malpractice complaint,' Diane said. 'The patient had a seizure. Charles was present when it happened and in response to the complaint made by Charles there was an internal investigation. No fault was found in the medication or how it was administered. According to the records, it was a drug the patient had received before and the dosage was correct. It was pretty cut and dried.'

Ruby screwed up her nose. 'That's odd. Charles has a law degree and his employer says he's dedicated to his work. Why would he complain if there were no grounds for it? Charles knows his stuff.'

'And that's when he got the label of being a compulsive liar from Doctor Hargreaves?' Grant said.

Diane scanned the computer screen in front of her. 'Let me check. No, it wasn't in his notes before.'

'What exactly does that mean, anyway?' Tom asked.

'It's a habit,' Ruby said. 'Compulsive liars lie repeatedly about important and unimportant events. Often they do it for no ulterior motive, which is why it's different from pathological lying which is when people are deliberately manipulative.'

'It would be unprofessional for that diagnosis to slip into Charles's notes to undermine his testimony,' Tom said.

'Yes,' Diane said. 'But we've seen it before. Professionals close ranks and the whistle-blower is the one who gets scapegoated. Or in this case, hypothetically of course, the whistle-blower is given a label to discredit them.'

Grant underlined Charles's name on the board. 'His testimony would never stand up in court. Not with that in his file. We've also got to consider he's actually lying, which would mean nobody was on the top floor with Phoebe. Luke says there's no forensic evidence to suggest she was forced. We've no prints found on the screwdriver, not even Phoebe's. Do we know where it came from, Diane?'

'That's a blank. The OT department have screwdrivers in their craft store, although not of that brand. Ditto at the Markhams; house. I interviewed both men who cut the cedars. It's a father and son outfit. They've clean records and solid alibis.'

'What's the update on the surveillance camera at the building entrance?' Grant asked.

'The technical team say they can't tell if the surveillance camera was deliberately sabotaged or if it was malfunctioning,' Tom said.

'Damn. All right, let's move on to Mike Otremba. He admits to being an addict six years ago and he said he self-reported to the General Medical Council. He underwent treatment and kept his licence. I've a friend at the GMC who's checking it out.'

'Another bout of addiction wouldn't go down well with the Medical Council,' Diane said. 'If he thought he might be exposed, it's a motive for murder.'

Grant circled Otremba's name in red. 'Would those pills Charles took prove it? No. But it wouldn't look good for Otremba if Phoebe reported it. He'd have to take a blood test and what would they find? Would he be clean? I already asked him to take a voluntary test and he refused.'

'I've been asking around about Doctor Otremba,' Diane said. 'Staff haven't mentioned any signs of addiction.'

'He could be very good at hiding it,' Ruby said.

Grant agreed. 'Do we have an answer yet about when Mike Otremba arrived at the hospital?'

Tom clicked at his keypad. 'Let me check. They've gone through the footage. No, his car wasn't caught on camera. All this technology and resources and it's not doing us any favours, is it?'

Grant was pacing again. 'Dig about the dark web, see what it throws up, that's our main focus. Somebody out there knows the truth. Find them. Tom, your priority is Hunt. Diane, I want a detailed dive into backgrounds. Ruby, go back and speak to patients and to Emma. I want answers about that streaming. In a case like this, we keep the pressure on until something cracks.'

'What about the conflict between Phoebe and her father?' Ruby said.

Grant had been about to take another doughnut but lost the appetite for it. He had spent a career tracking murderers, serial killers and fanatics, and his stomach was never affected by cases. It looked like this was going to be a first. At least it was good news for his waistline and his wedding suit, he thought wryly.

'There are questions about Phoebe's parents too,' Ruby said quietly. 'Or at least, gaps to fill in. We need to know more about the disputes between Phoebe and her mum and dad, in case they're relevant.'

'What's our next move with the Markhams, boss?' Tom said.

Grant glanced at Tom. 'Leave them to me. Go home and rest. I want everyone back on this fresh tomorrow.'

What possible motive could the Markhams have for killing their own daughter? None, as far as Grant could see. Yet he had a horrible sinking feeling. He would have to interview John and Anne, there was no doubt about it. Why did this job always drag up skeletons from the past?

Chapter 23

Early the next day, Tom drove to Brighton. It was sunny and lovely and one of his and Ruby's favourite places for a day out. He hoped they'd find space for it again soon, though he wasn't complaining about lack of free time or being immersed in a complex investigation. The MIT could have most, if not all, of him.

Hunt's brother lived in a road of terraced houses with bay windows. It was a well-kept street in a quiet neighbourhood.

Tom rang the buzzer. While he waited, he was greeted by a neighbour who was trimming the hedge. Tom's stomach rumbled. Eating well on the job was something he'd been trying to get Grant to take seriously, since the boss had spent decades surviving on tea, coffee and pastries. Tom reminded himself he needed to listen to his own advice.

The door was answered and Tom recognised the face, thinner and older than in the mug shot – it was Hunt himself.

Tom showed his warrant card. 'I'm Detective Inspector Delaney. May I come in?'

'What's it about?'

Hunt was forty-seven and he had been a sports teacher. In the file he had been not bad looking and in good shape. The man in front of Tom was tired, with bags under his eyes and a pale complexion. Often when people came out of prison they had a haggard, ill look and Hunt was no exception.

'I'd prefer to explain inside,' Tom said. 'Or would you like your nice neighbour to hear your business?'

Hunt didn't have much fight about him. Perhaps he never had, or maybe it had been squeezed from him during his spell inside. Hunt led the way down the hallway and into the lounge.

'What's this about? I've done my time.'

'I'm investigating a suspicious death. Could you tell me where you were yesterday between the hours of 3pm and 4.30pm?'

'A suspicious death? What's that got to do with me?'

'If you'd answer the question, please.'

Hunt scratched his head. 'I went for a walk after lunch. I must have got back here around 3.30.'

'Is there someone who can corroborate that?'

'Not really. My brother was asleep, like he is today. He runs a restaurant. It's a bistro place and it's doing really well. He always takes a nap in the afternoon after he's closed up for lunch. He says it keeps him in good form for the evening shift.'

'What time did he actually see you?'

'I suppose around 5.30, when he got up.'

Phoebe's trip into Himlands Heath had taken place from 3pm to 4.30pm and the estimated time they had for Phoebe seeing Hunt in town was 4pm. It had taken Tom forty minutes to get to Hunt's house, which meant there was a window of opportunity for Hunt to have been in Himlands Heath at that time and to have returned to Brighton by 5.30pm.

'Did you interact with anyone on your walk?'

'No. I went from Brighton out to Rottingdean on the coastal path. It can be isolated when it's not the weekend.'

The team were already checking through a mass of local authority CCTV footage between Hunt and the hospital to see if they could pick him out in the right area at the right time.

'What about in the evening, from 9pm onwards, where were you then?'

Hunt shrugged. 'I was here watching some stupid quiz show. My brother had already left to go to his restaurant and before you ask, no, I didn't talk to anyone else. Are you going to tell me why you want to know?'

Tom looked Hunt straight in the face. 'Yesterday evening Phoebe Markham died.'

The man's face lit up. 'You're kidding me? The lying little bitch is dead? That's the best news I've heard in a long time. She's the one who started this nightmare. She ruined me. My name was smeared. I lost my job and my reputation. All kinds of vile accusations were thrown at me. I had to defend myself against a barrage of lies. I never touched those girls, I swear I never did.'

'That's not what you told the parole board, Mr Hunt. You were released early because you showed remorse. And now you're telling me you're happy Phoebe Markham is dead.'

Hunt wagged a finger. 'Oh no you don't. I'm not sorry, I can say that. But I didn't have anything to do with it so you can keep me out of it.'

'I'd like to speak to your brother.'

'You can't. He's asleep. He won't be up for another,' Hunt consulted his watch, 'two hours.'

'Then I'm afraid I'm going to have to wake him early.'

On his way back to Headquarters, Tom phoned in. Grant did not pick up and neither did Diane.

'I'm back at Moorlands,' Ruby said. 'Did you find Hunt?'

'I was able to interview him and his brother. You wouldn't believe it but he went back to his old story of being wrongly convicted.'

'Hmm.'

He could imagine Ruby twirling her hair around her finger. He smiled. He felt sure she was going to dive into an explanation.

'It's surprisingly common in men who commit sex offences against children. If he actually admitted properly to himself what he had done, psychologically he wouldn't be able to cope. Likely he would have a breakdown because he would then be the type of man he professes to despise. Unfortunately, it's quite easy to convince the parole board you're remorseful, even if you aren't.'

Tom would never get used to how twisted the mind could be. He was glad Ruby was the psychological expert and not him.

'He was bloody delighted poor Phoebe is dead. Didn't even try to hide it. What kind of person behaves like that?'

'One who's bitter and has distorted the facts to fit his own version of reality. Do you think he's implicated?'

'Hunt has no alibi, so it brings him into the frame.'

'Okay.'

He could tell she wasn't convinced. 'What are you thinking?'

'Like I said, Phoebe's death doesn't at all match the modus operandi of Hunt's other crimes. I can't see how the same person could have committed both. The profiles are too far apart.'

There was also the fact they had no idea how Hunt would have entered the hospital, and unlocked the window in advance, without being seen.

'Did you read that Hunt knew John Markham?' Tom asked.

'Yes.'

'The two of them were golfing buddies. Don't you think that's strange? The man knew Phoebe's father and Hunt said they were friends and he said in his statement he had been to

Markham's house for Christmas drinks. And then a few months later he assaults Markham's teenage daughter.'

'Do you mean it's strange Hunt and Markham knew each other or strange Grant hasn't specifically highlighted it yet?'

'Well, both.'

'It's not strange Hunt knew Markham. Unfortunately, predators are often friends or relatives, or they have a connection to their victim's family.'

It was true. Tom knew the statistics.

'You've known the chief much longer than I have,' Ruby said. 'If or when Grant thinks it's relevant, he'll flag it up.'

'I know.'

Hunt going back into denial had got to Tom. Hunt's open delight at Phoebe's death was unpleasant too. Although, if he had been guilty, Tom would have expected him to hide his pleasure.

Tom drummed his fingers on the steering wheel. Something told him they hadn't got to the murky bottom of this yet, by far.

Chapter 24

Ruby was glad Grant had agreed to her speaking to the patients informally. Many of them needed time and a more relaxed atmosphere to feel comfortable talking to the investigating team.

Amongst this mishmash of humanity someone might have information which the team had missed. The person with that clue might have been prevented from coming forward because of their mental health issues.

Ruby discussed with Mrs Nicholson about taking part in activities with the occupational therapists. Though Mrs Nic was sceptical, she agreed to ask the senior OT, Kate, who turned out to be open to the idea.

Kate came to collect Ruby from the manager's office and she told Ruby there was an art session scheduled that morning. It would be an ideal way to mingle.

'I saw you chatting with patients yesterday. They seem to like you,' Kate said.

Ruby had to pause before replying because she almost choked on a waft of Kate's perfume. Kate was forty at the most, though she wore a pink frilly dress which was rather dated and made her seem older. Her nails were painted a matching pink.

'I suppose I felt comfortable talking to them too,' Ruby said.

'It shows.'

Kate was much more friendly than Mrs Nic, as the patients called the hospital manager. Kate took Ruby to the art studio which was a modern extension off the main building.

'This is nice,' Ruby said. 'All these windows and natural light. It's so modern too.'

'We're lucky. Mrs Markham, Phoebe's mother, set up a charitable fund and she's made it her mission to support local mental health initiatives. It's thanks to her we got this studio. She funded the community premises at the church in town, as well as their self-help program. She's been very generous.'

Kate showed Ruby all the equipment they had and the built-in workbenches which faced a long window. 'We'd never have such wonderful resources on a health service budget.'

'It's lovely.'

'I know, and listen, I want you to know you're welcome. Just ignore Mrs Nic. She's under pressure. The hospital trust will demand an inquiry and it's a lot of extra stress for her. Anyway, it's nice of you to join us.'

'Thank you.'

Kate had a maternal air about her, fussing around Ruby. 'Here you go, dear, put on an apron. We don't want you to get your clothes dirty, do we.'

'I don't mind about that. How many patients are you expecting?'

'Impossible to say,' Kate said. 'With all the kerfuffle, we might be inundated or there might be no one. People are upset. It's been very disturbing. And then all the questioning.'

Ruby tied back her hair. 'I know and I'm sorry. We've tried to keep it low-key except that's not easy.'

'Of course it's not. We understand you've got a difficult job to do. As I said, it's nice you're here. People will be able to see you're a human being like the rest of us, and who knows, someone might open up or recall a little detail. It could make all the difference, couldn't it?'

The other OT arrived. In his late twenties, Viktor was tanned and handsome. He wore a check shirt and jeans and had a laid-back attitude and a warm smile. Kate fussed around him too, asking how his morning had been and making him a drink. He put up with it good-naturedly.

'I hope you like art,' Viktor said.

'I'm no good at it. For me, this is a practical way to spend time with people.'

'Ah.' Viktor tapped the side of his nose. 'Is that a detective trick?'

'It's not a trick. I realise it's difficult for patients to trust our team.'

'Yes yes, dear, you're right,' Kate said. 'Distrust is an issue, especially when it comes to strangers. Being alongside us will help.'

'How long have you worked here?' Ruby asked.

Kate smoothed down her dress. 'More than ten years. Viktor is my new recruit. He's the baby of the team.'

Viktor was putting out paints at each easel. 'Why don't we get you set up and then it won't be so awkward when people start coming in, you know, because you'll already be working. Let them have a good look at you and don't mind all the stares.'

Ruby nodded. 'Later on, can I go around with you and chat with people?'

She had been talking to Viktor although it was Kate who answered.

'Of course you can. Viktor's the one who gives the arty tips and I give encouragement. We both like to circulate.'

Kate seemed to be the dominant one, probably because she had seniority. As the first patient walked through the door, Ruby rolled up her sleeves.

Ruby concentrated on filling her blank paper. She ignored the stares and how the two easels on either side of her were the last to be taken. She painted a picture of the woods at the back of the hospital. She added in the little path she had walked with Emma. Really it was a splodge of green for the trees and a swathe of lighter green for the grass. For the path, she painted a yellow-brown squiggle winding across the page. It really wasn't a work of art.

The elderly man to her right was super concentrated on his creation. He said nothing to her, though his eyes often darted in her direction. She made a few nice remarks about the colours he was using, all of which were ignored. The person on her left was a woman who talked pretty much non-stop, mostly to herself, though occasionally she would shout across the room to either Viktor or Kate.

Once her page was filled, Ruby went to join Kate.

'If you've finished, how about you help me take around cool drinks?' Kate said.

They went to a small kitchen at the back and Kate delved into a cupboard for plastic beakers.

'They're very quiet today,' Kate said.

Viktor took off his painting apron as he came into the kitchen. He smoothed his hair. 'Aren't they. I've never known it so subdued. I don't think you're going to get much out of anyone. Do you want to walk around with me, Ruby, and I'll see if I can get some of them to at least interact with you?'

Classical music played in the background. They did a tour of the room, with Ruby trailing at Viktor's side. Most of the patients downed their beakers in one go, exchanged none or few words with Viktor, ignored Ruby, and then got on with their painting. Only two patients were talkative and it was about their paintings. Ruby made sure she told both of them that the investigation was ongoing and any new information would be very helpful. She knew the whole room was listening to every word she said.

When they got back to the kitchen, Viktor shrugged. 'That wasn't too successful. Perhaps no one has anything to add. They were in their rooms when it happened.'

'Phoebe was a valued member of the art group,' Kate said. 'Everyone loved her and her paintings.'

Ruby was taking off her apron when a sudden thought occurred to her. 'Where did Phoebe usually sit?'

Kate looked apologetic. 'I put you at her easel. I hope you don't mind. We wanted to put her favourite Ireland picture there but the police have kept it.'

Why had Kate seated her there? It was rather inappropriate and a strange choice, especially without discussing it with Ruby first. And why hadn't Viktor said something? The other patients would have felt her to be an intruder, and worse than that, an intruder who had taken the place of someone they cared for. What better way to stir up a lot of negative and confused emotions. Ruby couldn't help thinking it would be a very good method of putting a lid on anyone wanting to talk to her.

'Phoebe's painting will be with forensics for a while. It's procedure.'

Kate smiled. 'Yes, that's what your inspector said.'

'Are there some other activities I can join in with?'

'Sure, we've got a session in the garden,' Viktor said. He glanced at Kate. 'That would be okay wouldn't it? Ruby could join in.'

'Of course. We'd love to have you.'

'I'll be there.'

And this time she would make sure neither the OTs nor Mrs Nic threw any obstacles in her path.

Chapter 25

Anne and John Markham lived on the edge of town. Their house was set back from the road and had a driveway lined with rhododendron bushes. With a high wall and plenty of shrubbery, they were well shielded from onlookers.

In his many years as a Member of Parliament, John had had a few problems with people graffitiing his wall and one incident when his car had been vandalised, although in general, he was a popular MP. John had always been very active on behalf of his constituents and went out of his way to make sure he represented everybody.

This nice house set in its own grounds was a big change from where Grant and John had lived as children. They had grown up on a council estate which had since been demolished. Himlands Heath had changed a lot over the years. He and John had changed a lot too, though perhaps they would never truly recover from the past.

Grant pulled on the handbrake. He wasn't looking forward to this encounter. He crunched across the gravel and enjoyed the few moments of tranquillity.

Anne Markham opened the door. 'Hello David.'

She was tall and slim, like her husband. Yet unlike John she had a wariness about her, as if she were always expecting something monstrous to happen. Well it had, hadn't it – with her daughter being attacked and now… this. The agony was written in Anne Markham's eyes.

He followed her to the living room, where they found John standing looking out the window. The two of them shook hands.

'Take a seat,' John said. 'You said there have been some developments?'

Grant perched on the edge of a huge armchair, resting his hands on his knees. There was no easy way to tell them that it appeared their daughter had taken a video in her last moments and streamed it to the dark web. So, he stuck to the facts and kept his voice and his manner measured and calm.

Anne's hand clutched at her throat, as if she found it hard to breathe. John stood perfectly still, but Grant could see how the man was struggling to accept what Grant said.

'That can't be right,' John said.

'Do you know any reason she might do such a thing?'

'I was going to ask you the same. Was she trying to film her attacker?'

Anne was silent, though she seemed even paler than before.

'We don't think so, the connection to the dark web wouldn't have been a good choice for that and Phoebe would have known it. Were you aware she was using the dark web?'

'I don't even know what it is, not really. Except that it's vile and full of offenders who carry out their business there. The thought of our daughter having contact…' John's voice broke. 'Words fail me.'

Grant nodded sympathetically. But he had to push his own feelings aside and press on. 'I'm sorry. I know this is really hard. I have questions I need to ask.'

John closed his eyes for a few moments. His wife had still not said a word.

'I understand Phoebe wanted to move to Ireland?'

'Wait. Do you have a suspect? Is someone in custody?' John asked.

'Not yet. If you could please focus on my questions. Were you aware your daughter wanted to move to Ireland?'

John went to pour himself a drink from the liquor cabinet. 'She talked about it a bit. Would you like something? No, not even a soft drink? Phoebe had the idea in her head to live in Ireland ever since we went there on holiday. It wasn't serious. It was a girl's fantasy. Phoebe was immature for her age.'

'I've seen her paintings. They're very good.'

Anne still had one hand lingering at her throat. Grant was relieved when she spoke, because after the shock of the dark web, he was wondering if she might never utter a word again.

'My darling daughter was such a talented artist,' Anne said. 'We hoped one day she would set up her own studio.'

John came over and patted his wife's shoulder.

'And what did you think of Phoebe's wish to move from Himlands Heath, Mrs Markham?'

'Please, call me Anne. Well she couldn't, could she, Inspector? My daughter was dependent on mental health services. She knew the practitioners and she trusted them, and we knew them too. It wouldn't be possible or safe for her to set up somewhere strange with no support network. Why would she throw away something which has taken us years to build? She needs people she can rely on.'

'Surely she could find support in a new place?'

Anne pressed her fingers to her temples. 'It's not easy. There are plenty of *average* health care workers and *average* doctors out there. We wanted the best for Phoebe and we made sure she got the best. Here in Himlands Heath we can monitor everything. We can step in if there are problems.'

Grant turned to John. 'I understand both of you were against her moving away. That the three of you had argued about it.'

'Who the hell told you that? Oh wait. I know. It was Lin Chen wasn't it? That damn nurse was always poking her nose in.'

'Don't say that, darling,' Anne said.

'It's the truth. She was always stirring things up with Phoebe. Going on and on about Phoebe's *rights*. That nurse was a menace. I tried to get her taken off Phoebe's care and you know what happened? Phoebe refused. Let me tell you what really happened. Did you know Chen's sister has a degenerative disease? The sister wants to have assisted dying. And you know what? It's illegal. It can't be done. She's twenty-eight and it's not going to happen. The parents came to me as my constituents hoping I could help them but I couldn't. Then Nurse Chen weighed in and accused me not helping because I didn't want to and not speaking up in parliament on their behalf. It wasn't because I didn't care. It was because it's not possible.'

John was pacing and he was angry.

'Chen wouldn't stop. She wouldn't accept there was nothing that could be done for her sister. She was obsessed. She kept going on about the right to a dignified death. And then she kept stirring Phoebe up about her right to live the life she wanted to live, her rights as an adult, and on and on. Phoebe was impressionable. She was easily influenced. And Chen made the most of it. I'm not at all surprised she's trying to make out we're the bastards who stopped our own daughter. But that's not how it was.'

'Are you saying Lin Chen has a grudge against you?' Grant asked.

'I didn't think of it like that, but since you've said it, yes. Yes, she did.'

'Has she ever threatened you?'

Anne was wringing her hands. 'I don't like you talking like this, John. Lin was Phoebe's friend.'

'She was *not a friend*. She was Phoebe's nurse.'

'But she was more than that,' Anne said.

'If you say so, please don't get upset, my dear. And no, David, the Chens have never threatened me, not even that minx of a nurse.'

The right to die as you wished and an assisted death, could it be a motive? Could John's perceived refusal to help the Chen family have led to Phoebe becoming a target. It was unlikely. Lin had been on Phoebe's side and she genuinely seemed to care for the girl. Although perhaps she was a very good actress and highly practised at conning people. It was the way many of the most successful criminals had evaded justice.

'Nurse Chen was very upset about your daughter.'

'Very upset or simply an exceptionally good liar?' John said. 'At the beginning we liked her too. We even invited her here on one or two occasions for Christmas drinks and once when we had a garden party for Phoebe. It took a while for me to realise she was poisoning Phoebe's mind. She turned our own daughter against us without us even realising what was going on.'

'Is that how you see things, Anne?' Grant asked.

Anne folded her arms across her chest. 'Phoebe changed so much this last year. Some of it was growing up but there were influences on her which were negative too. I agree with my husband. Lin was one of the strong voices my daughter listened to. She put terrible ideas in Phoebe's head.'

'You think the Chen family could think so strongly they would be driven to murder?'

Anne looked forlorn and lost. 'I don't know what to think.'

'And neither do I,' John said. 'I don't like to point a finger at that family but I can't help feeling they're involved somehow. I've not slept and neither has my wife. How can we? It's a nightmare.'

As his heart twisted at their anguish, Grant murmured his sympathy.

'I can't tell you how much I appreciate you taking the lead on this. It's such a relief,' John said. 'Please find out who killed our baby. And when you find the bastard–'

Grant held up his hand. 'Let's not say things we might regret later.'

John looked like he wanted to say more and then thought better of it. He went to the mantelpiece. 'There's one other matter I wanted to mention.' He took an envelope which had been propped against a clock. 'I found a letter in Phoebe's apartment. It's quite short and not at all an official will, but Anne and I want to honour our daughter's wishes.' He handed it to Grant.

Grant had agreed with his Crime Scene Manager that both Phoebe's apartment and her car would be searched for evidence. Phoebe had not lived there for several weeks, so they had decided it would not be forensically examined.

'You didn't find anything else I might be interested in?' Grant asked.

'Nothing,' Anne said.

Grant read the short letter. It stated simply that in the event of her death, Phoebe wished Emma to be given her apartment and her car.

'Did you know about this letter?'

John shook his head. 'No, although it doesn't surprise me. Emma and Phoebe were close. And I remember a few years ago Phoebe asked me about wills and such like.'

'Where did you find it?'

'At her apartment amongst her other papers. In her desk.'

'And this is her handwriting?'

'Yes, and her signature.'

It was a curious turn of events. Had Phoebe written it recently? Was Emma aware?

'I'd like to see Phoebe's apartment for myself. Have you informed Emma White about this?'

'Not yet. I wanted to speak to you first. Naturally we want to clear out Phoebe's things before we hand the keys over to Emma. We're not prepared to do that yet. I'm sure we won't be ready for some time.'

'I think I'd like to be there when you tell Emma, if you don't mind.'

Anne was frowning. 'I hope you're not thinking badly about Emma. She's a lovely girl. They were great friends. Without Emma, Phoebe would have been lost.'

'Please don't worry. I'll do my best to handle this sensitively. I simply want to be present when you make the announcement. I think that's enough for today. I'll see myself out.'

John trailed him to the door.

'I know how hard this is. Hang on in there.'

'Thank you.' The man's voice was gruff with emotion. 'How rude of me, you must be getting excited for the big day. It'd slipped my mind. We do wish Chrissie well.'

Grant winced. Chrissie was a lot older than Phoebe because the Markhams had had their daughter late in life, but the thought of his own daughter happily moving to the next phase while theirs lay in the morgue, wrenched at Grant's heart.

'No need to talk about that now, my friend,' Grant said. 'You two take care of each other and let me do the rest.'

Chapter 26

That afternoon, Ruby was back at Moorlands. As she went across the lawn, the birds were singing and the air smelled of summer.

'Hi, Ruby,' Viktor said. He was down to a vest top which showed off his tan. 'We're going to be fruit picking.'

'Hi. I think I can smell fruits in the air.'

He smoothed his hair and smiled. 'That's the strawberries. You want to help me sort these gloves?'

'Sure. Listen, I was wondering if you have much contact with Doctor Otremba?'

'A little. He's GP to quite a few of our patients.'

'What's your take on him?'

They sorted a big pile of gardening gloves into pairs.

'This lot always get mixed up, no matter how hard we try. Er, not much to say really. Mike's a good GP, probably better than most.'

'Have you known him for a while?'

'Since I came here. Why?'

'I can't really say. Have you noticed anything unusual about his behaviour? Any inconsistencies?'

Viktor frowned. 'No. But I don't have much close contact with him.'

Kate came hurrying across the lawn, the frills of her dress bouncing. She was pushing a wheelbarrow piled with little picking baskets and a straggle of patients were following her.

'Oh there you are, Ruby. I was waiting for you at the OT office.'

'Hello, Kate. Sorry, I thought I'd come straight over.'

'No worries. You two look deep in conversation.'

'I was just asking about Doctor Otremba and whether you'd noticed anything unusual about his behaviour.'

'Mike's generally conscientious. I haven't heard any complaints if that's what you mean.'

'That's good to know, thank you. Looks like it's going to be another scorching afternoon.'

'I hope you brought a sun hat,' Kate said, and she turned to the group behind her. 'This is Ruby, everyone, she's going to be joining us and she might have some questions to ask about Phoebe. Please help the police if you can.'

There were murmurs of agreement and a couple of greetings thrown in her direction.

'We'll be doing raspberry and strawberry picking,' Kate said. 'Let's split into two groups.'

Ruby put on her sun hat.

'How about coming with me over to the raspberries, my dear?' Kate suggested.

It turned out to be very different from the silent art session because Ruby was surrounded by very talkative people. She learned a lot about Phoebe's portrait paintings. Others spoke about the night Phoebe died and how shocking it had been and how sad. One of the patients had known Phoebe in children's services and she told Ruby how Phoebe's mother had transformed the OT department with her funding of the art studio and greenhouses.

Ruby was hopeful she would learn something but no one had anything new to add about the night Phoebe died. When

Ruby asked about Lin Chen, patients were quick to defend her and say she was well liked.

A while later, Ruby dusted off her hands and straightened her back. It was hard work under the heat, though she was glad she had come because she could sense the patients being less reticent to speak to her. She finished filling up her basket with raspberries.

Kate was busy down the end of the row. She never seemed to go far away and Ruby felt Kate wanted to overhear her conversations. Was it simply so Kate could ensure they went smoothly? Or was Kate interested in what the patients had to say? Ruby felt quite comfortable speaking to people on her own. She didn't need Kate as a minder.

Viktor's group was already taking a break under the trees and Ruby decided to join them. As she wandered over, she could see those taking a break were enjoying eating the strawberries.

'It looks like there won't be many left,' she said.

Viktor laughed. 'It doesn't matter. I'm betting there will still be plenty for baking. We're planning on making fruit tarts tomorrow. Would you like to join us?'

'I'm not sure I'll have time. Will you let me know if anyone specifically wants to speak to me?'

'Of course.'

'I wanted to talk to *you* about Phoebe. We found out she was taking orders for portraits and sending them to people online. It didn't seem as if she charged for them. Did you know about that?'

'No, but it doesn't surprise me. Phoebe was very generous with her talent. She liked giving people pleasure from it.'

'Do you know much about her internet activity? Was she part of any chat rooms, for instance?'

'I think she was involved in some artists groups. Chat rooms? That doesn't sound like her thing to me.'

'What about the dark web?'

'You're kidding me, right? Phoebe? I don't think so. She was a lovely young woman although not very experienced in life. I don't think she'd even know what the dark web was. I hardly know about it myself.'

'Okay, thanks.'

'Finding out what happened is really important to all of us. And poor Lin, I feel for her.'

'People have been telling me how popular she is.'

Viktor leaned against a tree and sighed. 'She's going through hell. She's had so much to deal with and now there's this. I don't know if I should mention it but I guess you might already know about her sister being ill?'

'Yes, she told my inspector. I understand Lin helps her family.'

'She underplays it. The truth is Lin's keeping her family afloat – I mean emotionally. Naomi's very sick. Their parents can barely cope. Naomi has always been adamant she wants assisted dying. As I'm sure you know that's illegal in the UK. Lin had applied to Dignitas in Switzerland. It's very complicated and they'd gone through all the hurdles and then a few days ago Naomi was turned down at the last step.'

So Lin had not told Grant the full story.

'Do you know why the sister was turned down?'

'It's because a psychiatrist said Naomi was depressed. And Dignitas won't accept anyone who is depressed. Naomi took that hard but I think Lin took it harder. She'd made it her mission to help her sister carry out her last wishes for a dignified death.'

'What a terrible situation.'

'Isn't it. And then comes Phoebe. Lin was already on her knees. I hate to think what this has done to her.'

The concern showed on his face. Ruby felt for both sisters.

'Which doctor did the assessment?'

'That's the kicker. It was Doctor Hargreaves. Lin begged her to change it but Hargreaves refused. She said it was her professional duty.'

'That's hard. You sound as if you care about Lin very much.'

'We were together for a while. Jobs like ours put a terrible strain on relationships. And then with the demands of Lin's family on top, she and I were pretty doomed. We're still friends. I was okay with her not having time for us but she said it wasn't fair. She said she felt she was using me.'

'Oh, Viktor.'

'Who knows, perhaps we still have a chance, you know, in the future. I try to support her as best I can.'

'Mrs Nicholson told us Lin's on sick leave until the hospital investigation is over.'

'I know that might sound as if it's a positive thing. I'm not convinced. That's going to be another strain on her, I think. Being under investigation must be horrible. She's already feeling so guilty about Phoebe.'

Kate had brought her group over to the shade and she joined Viktor and Ruby. 'I'm not interrupting, am I?'

'Not at all,' Ruby said.

'Has it been a useful session for you?' Kate asked.

'Yes and no.'

'I think people are starting to see you as less of the enemy,' Kate said. 'And that's got to be a good thing.'

Ruby's mind was on Nurse Chen. Lin's family situation was troubling. In terms of the investigation, might the personal stress on Lin have caused her to make mistakes? How could someone who had just received news that her sister had been turned down by Dignitas, carry out her job to the same standard?

Grant had been convinced by the nurse's testimony but Ruby wasn't so sure.

Chapter 27

Diane received a call from Grant asking her to visit Mr and Mrs Chen and check out more about Dignitas and the Chens' requests to John Markham.

The Chens lived in a row of terraced houses close to the supermarket. Parking outside, Diane didn't waste any time. She was David's go-to officer for distressed relatives, which the Chen family would be, given Naomi Chen's state of health. As a mother of three teenagers, Diane had an uncanny ability to tune into upset parents and in return they had a tendency to trust her. She also had a nose for suspicious details.

Mrs Chen answered the door.

'We're investigating the death of Phoebe Markham and I've a few questions I'd like to ask.'

Mrs Chen had a greyish pallor and was terribly thin. She looked like she had been worn into the ground.

'My husband is resting,' Mrs Chen said. 'It might be better if you and I talk first.'

'Of course.'

They sat in a tiny dining room and Mrs Chen closed the door. 'Naomi is sleeping and I don't want to disturb her.'

Mrs Chen explained how Naomi lived in what used to be their living room. In the past, Naomi had her own apartment, but as her illness progressed, she had returned to the family home so her parents could look after her.

'How can I help you?' Mrs Chen asked.

The first issue was alibis. Diane took out her notebook as Mrs Chen checked her calendar for the night of Phoebe's death. It turned out Mr and Mrs Chen had been at the hospital late afternoon. Mr Chen had had a medical appointment and his wife had accompanied him.

'My husband has had ill health. It got so bad he had to stop work. At first they thought it was stress although now the doctors have been carrying out tests. They think he has a problem with his blood.'

'I see. And for that evening?'

'They kept him in for the night. It was unexpected so I came home to collect some things for him and then I went back to the hospital. It always takes so long on the bus and Lin was working so she couldn't help. I think I finally got back here around 9pm. My neighbour had popped in to check on Naomi and sit with her for a while. She was here when I got home. She's a good friend. She lost her husband two years ago and she helps us when she can.'

'Thank you for that, Mrs Chen. I'm sorry we have to ask so many questions but it's our procedure. I know it can feel intrusive.'

'If it helps clear Lin's name, then ask whatever you want. I know my daughter is free from blame. She's dedicated to her job.'

Diane sat back and let her notebook rest on her knee. 'I understand Naomi has applied to Dignitas? Could you tell me more about that. Whose idea was it?'

The mother plumped a cushion at her side. 'I hate talking about it. But I suppose you need to know.'

Diane waited. There was no need to push for information. Mrs Chen wasn't being obstructive, it was a heart-wrenching subject for her, of course it was.

'It was Naomi's idea. She's active on a forum for people with MND and they talk about all kinds of things. That's where she first considered Dignitas. One of her friends from the forum travelled to Switzerland. And died at the facility.'

Mrs Chen was very well informed. She explained that to be accepted for an assisted death, a person had to pass rigorous medical checks, of both their physical and mental health.

'At first, my husband and I were against the whole idea. But as Naomi got weaker and weaker, we came to understand it might be the kindest way. Much as losing her would be agonising, seeing her deteriorate has been equally agonising. She's been adamant all along that she wishes to go when she decides it, and not when she's finally incapable of drawing breath. I don't know if you can understand. I don't think I'd have been able to, if I didn't have a daughter in this situation.'

Diane nodded. She felt tears prickling her eyes. How would she react if one of her sons had a terminal illness and wished to end their own life, in their own way, on their own terms?

'I'm so sorry, Mrs Chen.'

'Don't be sorry for me. Be sorry for Naomi. It's Lin who's constantly been on Naomi's side. She's always stood up for Naomi. Lin helped with all the paperwork for Dignitas, and there's a lot of it to get through. It takes months and months.'

'She also asked for help from Mr Markham, your MP.'

'She did. My husband and I went to see him. Then Lin spoke to him.'

'He let you down?'

'Yes he did. I know he couldn't change things for Naomi but he could have put his name to something which would change things for future families. So they wouldn't need to go through this torture. But don't go thinking Lin cared for Phoebe less because of it. The opposite is true. It made Lin care for Phoebe more.'

Mrs Chen reached for a tissue. 'The dreadful thing is that to get to Switzerland Naomi has to be well enough to travel. That's the difficulty when we're so far away. The weaker she gets, the more unlikely it is we'll be able to get her there. Lin was going to accompany her sister. We've been saving towards the cost of the travel.'

'Is there any chance you can get the depression diagnosis overturned?'

'We have to find two doctors who will agree Naomi is depression free.' Mrs Chen was dabbing at her eyes. 'The chances are slim. Because, of course, if your life is draining away, how can you not become depressed. It was such a blow when we got turned down.'

'And it was Doctor Hargreaves at Moorlands who gave that diagnosis?'

'It was. Lin was furious.'

Diane jotted in her notebook and Mrs Chen insisted on offering a cup of tea. Diane sipped it slowly while Mrs Chen showed a photo album of Lin and Naomi when they were small. The pictures tugged at Diane's heartstrings. She was sorry she had to disturb this desperate family.

It was unfair and cruel that Naomi should be forced to hang on until her very last breath.

How could John Markham not have been more supportive?

She could not help thinking he must be a rather unpleasant and selfish man.

Chapter 28

Phoebe was easy. The bitch. She was ripe for the picking.

The next on my list is too. She's isolated – tick. She's cutting herself off from her friends – tick. Her inner resources are failing – tick.

I hate how she flaunts and titters and wriggles. A poisoned honey bait to trap her suitor.

I'm cleverer than that. I can smell her lies. And I can get close.

She's weak and pathetic which will make it easy for me to strike.

I see it in my mind. How stealthy and silent I'll be in my approach. How she'll crumble and beg.

I imagine her slim and delicate body as the air squeezes out of her.

Her eyes will fill with tears as I drink in those delicious final moments.

You'll have it soon, I whisper to myself.

Chapter 29

Following Diane's visit to the parents, Grant wanted to speak more to Lin about her potential grudge against the Markhams.

He slammed the car door and walked to the stairwell of Lin's residence. He could not allow himself to be merciful because of the distress of the Chen family. His only concern was finding the truth about Phoebe's death. He knocked hard on Lin's door.

Lin had certainly been crying. She ushered him to the main room where he again found mountains of washed laundry. She pushed aside a pile so he could sit on the sofa.

Her eyes were bloodshot. 'How's the investigation going?'

'John Markham has informed me you asked him to petition parliament on behalf of your sister. He said she wants the right to assisted dying.'

'He's my MP, and yes, we asked him to help. He refused to petition Parliament, even though other MPs have done exactly that in other cases.'

'I see.'

'Do you? Do you see how my father cries all the time? That my mother is close to a nervous breakdown? And John Markham couldn't even be bothered to speak out on our behalf. He was too concerned about his own standing with his political party.'

'Did that make you angry?'

'Of course it did. He's a hypocrite and he makes me sick. My sister can no longer do *anything* unaided. Her breathing is deteriorating. But you know the worst thing? Naomi is perfectly lucid in her mind. She knows exactly what's happening to her. She knows she has nowhere to go except becoming so weak that one day she'll asphyxiate on her own lung fluids. So yeah, I'm angry.'

'You didn't mention this before.'

'I told you about Naomi.' Lin gestured to the laundry. 'I explained she has a terminal illness.'

'But you didn't tell me you had a conflict with Mr Markham. Or that your sister's application to Dignitas has recently been put on hold.'

'Because it wasn't relevant. And how did you hear about Dignitas? That's personal.'

'Nothing is personal in a murder investigation. You really didn't think your hostility towards John Markham was relevant, even though you were caring for his daughter at the time of her death?'

'What? You think I killed Phoebe because I was pissed off at her father? If you believe that, then you don't know the slightest thing about me.'

She was angry, furious even, and distraught at the implied accusation.

'I cared about Phoebe!'

And Grant believed her. He sat back and took a few moments to get out his notebook and flick through the pages.

'We've been in receipt of information about Doctor Otremba and allegations concerning his potential drug usage. Have you noticed any erratic behaviour on his part? Any changes in his mood?'

Grant's friend at the GMC had got back to say Mike Otremba's story about past abuse checked out. Otremba had self-referred six years earlier. The GMC had supervised his recovery and he had kept his medical licence. Grant had also checked with the hospital manager and she had been unaware of this incident and unconcerned about it, since the GMC considered Otremba fit to practice. Mrs Nicholson had told Grant she was not aware of any current complaints against Doctor Otremba nor any concerns from members of staff.

Lin shook her head. 'I've not heard about that. You should check with Mrs Nic, although she's going to be biased on that one.'

'What do you mean?'

'Didn't anyone tell you? They keep it low key, but Mike and Mrs Nic are in a relationship. They're both separated from previous partners so it's not a scandal or anything.'

Why had neither the doctor nor Mrs Nicholson mentioned this? It made more sense of why Mike Otremba had been updating Mrs Nicholson by phone on the night of Phoebe's death. Yet if staff had come to Mrs Nicholson with concerns about Otremba might she have been tempted to brush them over? It would also make Otremba a likely person to have access to the window key.

Grant didn't like being kept in the dark. It wasted his time and much more important than that, it made him suspicious.

Chapter 30

Despite being the only one working in the office that afternoon, Diane was the last to enter the incident room for the team briefing. It was like that when you had three teenage sons and a husband working away. Organising her family from her mobile phone had been fraught. An argument had erupted over lost football kit, though Diane suspected it was less to do with a missing shirt and more to do with too much teasing of the youngest one about his recent crush.

She closed the door behind her. 'The boys,' she said with a sigh. It was explanation enough.

Tom passed her a mug. 'Fresh from the pot.'

She gave him a smile of gratitude.

David was leaning against a table at the front. 'Right, let's get to it. Ruby, how about you go first?'

'I didn't get anything new from the patients,' Ruby said. 'They wanted to talk about Phoebe but they didn't have anything concrete to add. As for the OTs, this morning I had the impression they weren't helping me as much as they could. They put on a show of going out of their way to fit me in, and then they sabotaged it by giving me Phoebe's exact seat in the art studio.'

'You think they did it deliberately?' Diane said.

'Either that, or they didn't realise how the patients would react to seeing me in Phoebe's place.'

Grant wrote 'sabotage' on the board, with a question mark. 'Perhaps they're hiding something. Or shielding someone?'

'I asked about the dark web. Viktor was closer to Phoebe than Kate. He said it would be out of character for her to have anything to do with it.'

'Her parents said about the same.' Grant turned to Tom. 'How did Charles react?'

'It didn't make any sense to him either,' Tom said.

'I spoke to Emma on the phone and she told me the same. She said there was no way Phoebe would be on there,' Ruby said.

Grant tapped the board. 'Except she was. No one knows about it. Everybody's surprised. Was she hiding something from her friends and family, even from Emma? Despite the wonders of modern science, the techies are still working on getting more for us. We still don't have the video nor who watched it. They've got their best hackers on it.'

'It's not surprising,' Tom said. 'The dark web is a minefield.'

'How did you get on with Hunt?'

'He has no alibi for the afternoon or for the evening. Thing is, he was happy Phoebe was dead and he didn't try to hide it. If he were the killer, that wouldn't be smart.'

'Yet we know he *is smart*,' Ruby said. 'Because he assaulted three girls before Phoebe without coming under suspicion. And he conveniently accepted his guilt a year before the parole review, very likely so he could get an earlier release.'

'Hunt stays on the person of interest list. What about the Chens, Diane?'

She gave the team an update. 'In theory, Naomi being turned down could be a motive for the Chens getting back at the Markhams. Although Mr and Mrs Chen have alibis and personally I just don't see Lin murdering Phoebe.'

'Me neither, except she still stays on our list. She had access. She was the last to see Phoebe. She has motive.' Grant slammed the board. 'We're not getting to the heart of this. All these people,' Grant swept his arm across the whiteboards. 'They've got grudges and drama. But where is our killer? How are they hiding? How did they carry out the crime? Think outside the box.'

'I've been digging into people's pasts,' Diane said. 'It turns out Anne Markham and Brett Sinclair, the counsellor at the church, are cousins. That's not so odd. More strangely though, when Juliette White and her mother were murdered, Brett was Juliette's boyfriend.'

Ruby leaned forward. 'That's an odd connection.'

'Wasn't Juliette nineteen when she died?' Tom said. 'How old was Brett?'

'Nineteen. He and Juliette were in the same class at school.'

'That's giving me a weird vibe,' Ruby said.

Diane poured herself more coffee. 'That's what *I* thought.'

Tom went to point at the board. 'Do you think our church counsellor could have any connection to the dark web?'

Grant underlined Brett's name. 'We need to find out. Ruby, look into the murder of the White family. Tom, I'd like you to focus on–'

Diane's phone vibrated. She hoped it wasn't another fight at home. 'It's Mrs Chen. I'd better take this.'

As she listened, a wave of sadness swept through her. It must have shown on her face because the room fell quiet.

'I'll come straight over,' she said.

When she hung up, she had to take a moment. David came to her side, concern creasing his forehead.

'What's happened?' he asked.

'Mrs Chen's distraught. She came home this afternoon to find Naomi dead. Mrs Chen's asking for help because she can't get hold of Lin, and Lin is never out of touch.'

Chapter 31

When Diane, Tom and Grant arrived at Mrs Chen's, they found a police officer in the hallway.

'Can you give us an update?' Diane asked.

'It's very sad,' the officer said, keeping his voice low. 'The daughter, Naomi Chen, had a long-term illness. Her parents came home and found her in bed. She had passed away while they were out.'

There were noises of distress coming from the far end of the hallway and Diane felt her stomach tensing.

'Where did Mr and Mrs Chen go?' she asked.

'Mrs Chen accompanied her husband to a medical appointment. He had a scan at the hospital at,' the officer consulted his notes, '2pm. They were there for almost two hours because the consultant was running behind time. They got the bus back and when they came in they found their daughter. That was 4.50pm. They phoned their GP and she came straight over.'

'All right. Anything else we should know about?' Grant asked.

'Mrs Chen is worried about her other daughter, Lin. She can't get hold of her.'

Diane moved towards the bedroom. 'That's how we got to be here. Lin is connected to one of our current cases.'

'I'll wait outside,' Tom said. He spoke softly. 'The alarm on my watch went off. It's minus one hour to your dinner guests arriving, guv.'

Grant nodded. 'Thanks for the reminder.'

The doctor was sitting with Mrs Chen who was by her daughter's bedside. The doctor gave Diane a small smile and she introduced herself. 'It's a sad day. Naomi has finally slipped away.'

'Yes. I know the family,' Diane said.

The doctor told them she had prescribed a sedative for the father, who was distraught, and Mr Chen had gone to lie down.

Naomi had not yet been moved, though the ambulance crew were ready to. It seemed Mrs Chen however wanted her daughter to stay where she was and the doctor was trying to persuade her otherwise.

'You called me, Mrs Chen. I'm sorry for your loss,' Diane said.

Mrs Chen was hunched over her daughter's body and her voice was muffled. 'Thank you for coming.'

Grant cleared his throat. 'My condolences, Mrs Chen. Doctor, do you have a cause of death?'

'I'll be noting respiratory insufficiency on the certificate,' the doctor said. 'It's what we were expecting. Her capacities have been steadily declining.'

'I see, and was it usual for Naomi to be left alone?'

The doctor pursed her lips. 'It wasn't unusual. Naomi was a very independent young woman. She could breathe independently and was medically fit to be cared for in a home environment. Naomi had already refused assistance with respiration. She didn't want to be kept alive by machines. It's all been documented correctly.'

Mrs Chen was screwing a handkerchief in her hands. 'It's Lin I'm worried about now. She's been under so much pressure. You can't imagine how guilty she felt about poor

Phoebe and she's carried an enormous burden caring for her sister. They loved each other so much. She and I are in constant contact. It's not like her to not answer my calls. Please can you help us find her?'

Diane was concerned about Lin too, although not in exactly the same way as Mrs Chen. Diane cleared her throat to try to get rid of the knot which had lodged there. 'Of course we will. Do you know when Lin last saw Naomi?'

'This morning. She called by for breakfast and fed her sister. She talked to my husband about his appointment and reassured him about the scan. He doesn't like going in those big machines. That's why I went with him. Actually, Naomi insisted I go. She was like that. She didn't want us to do so much for her that we stopped living ourselves. The truth is, I stopped living the moment we found out about Naomi's diagnosis.'

The doctor bowed her head and Diane thought of her own three sons. All healthy and filling her house with noise and dirty laundry and arguments. She took a deep breath.

'I'm so sorry, Mrs Chen. And Lin didn't come to be with Naomi while you went to the hospital?'

'No. She took the laundry this morning and she went home. Naomi accepted help from us and from her sister but she hated being babysat. Besides, Naomi's energy has been very low recently. When we left after lunch, she was resting. Likely she fell asleep and that's when…' Mrs Chen turned a tear-streaked face to Diane, '… that's when it happened. I'm so grateful it was a gentle ending. That's all we wanted.'

Despite her experience, Diane struggled for words, because you could never stop being human.

Grant put his hand on Mrs Chen's shoulder. 'We'll check with our colleagues. And we'll go to Lin's apartment now.'

Chapter 32

Once they were in the car and Tom started the engine, the alarm on both Tom's watch and Grant's phone sounded. Diane and Tom exchanged a glance.

'T minus thirty minutes, boss,' Tom said as his alarm stopped.

Grant silenced his. Half an hour until the in-laws came for dinner. He had time. 'Right. Let's get over to Lin's.'

Diane turned to him. 'This isn't hanging together. Naomi's passed away and Lin's missing – I don't like it.'

'I know. I'll call it in and see if there have been any reports from the public of women matching Lin's description, maybe distraught, or wandering, or acting strangely. What are you thinking?'

'I don't know. The parents went out and Lin didn't come to stay with Naomi? I can't help wondering if Lin was there when Naomi died. Why would she ignore urgent messages from her mother? They're in constant communication. It doesn't make sense.'

Grant agreed. A girl devoted to her sister who suddenly went missing at the same time her sister died? The parents were right to be afraid. His thoughts were grim as they drove to Lin's apartment.

Mrs Chen had given them a key and they were quickly inside. It didn't take them long to discover the worst.

'Oh my god, no,' Diane said. She knelt by the bath to check for Lin's pulse. 'Nothing.'

'No, no, no! Tom, let's get her out,' Grant said. He pointed to a mobile phone which lay underwater on Lin's lap. 'What's that doing here? As we lift her try not to touch it. I'll start compressions. Diane, call an ambulance. There might still be a chance.'

Though Grant wanted to believe it, he doubted it were true. The water was cold and so was Lin. Her lips and skin had a bluish tinge.

They kept up artificial respiration and chest compressions until the ambulance crew arrived and took over. The paramedics tried everything they could, but there was no reviving her.

A second young woman dead in as many days. No! This was so wrong. He had been taken by surprise. He'd not been expecting it. The killer, because now he was convinced they were dealing with a murderer, had sprung it on them. Blind-sided them. Fooled them. Why did he think this was murder? Because of the mobile phone. True, it could be a coincidence but Grant didn't believe in coincidences. Phoebe and Lin – two girls, two deaths and two mobile phones, and he had never known nor heard of a suicide victim taking a mobile phone into the bath with her.

It should not have been Lin. A woman who cared for her sister and who had been supporting her family, who had accepted his questioning to the best of her ability, shouldering it with a quiet good grace. Grant clenched his fists.

His clothes were soaking from when they'd lifted Lin out of the bath. He stared at his wet trousers.

'This has been made to look like a suicide.' He could hear anger in his own voice.

'Agreed,' Tom said.

'It's very convincing coming at the same time as Naomi's death. Wouldn't it seem logical for the girls to have a pact? Except I'm not buying it because what the hell is Lin's phone doing here? Just like with Phoebe. That one little detail throws the whole thing into the air.'

'You think there's a link?' Diane said. 'Something to do with the dark web?'

'I *know* there's a link. And we're going to bloody well find it.'

Grant called Sejal. He wanted a full forensics on Lin's place and he was making it a priority for the techies to get everything they could from the phone.

'This is going to finish the mother. And the father,' Diane said.

Twin alarms sounded on Tom's watch and Grant's mobile. They silenced them immediately.

'Guv, that's your guests arriving,' Tom said.

'I know,' Grant said. 'Tom, please stay here and work with Sejal on the crime scene. Don't worry, Diane, I'll break it to the parents as gently as I can.' Except of course there was no gentle way. What a devastating day. The parents had lost both their children. Words failed him.

'I can do it,' Diane said.

Grant appreciated that, he really did, except he would not let her take such a shitty task.

'No, that's down to me. I'd like you to stay with the parents after I leave. I'm sure they'll want to see Lin and you can accompany them. Find out what you can. Is there a connection between what's happened today and Phoebe's death? I think there is. What we need is evidence.'

When they returned to see Mrs Chen, the house was quiet. A neighbour let them in. She explained she would be staying for the time being. She led them through to the kitchen where Mrs Chen was sitting at the table, staring into space.

'They've taken Naomi,' Mrs Chen said. 'Did you find Lin?'

Diane looked as stricken as Grant felt.

He sat opposite the poor woman and Diane sat beside her. Grant took a breath as the kitchen clock ticked in the background. He made sure to keep his voice calm and even.

'I'm sorry, Mrs Chen, I have some terrible news. I'm afraid I must ask you to prepare yourself.'

When Grant said the awful words Mrs Chen wailed as if she were mortally wounded. Grant sincerely hoped the shock did not give her a heart attack. He put his hand on her arm and waited for the worst of it to subside.

'Diane is going to stay with you. My sincere condolences to you and to your husband.'

Grant had faced some dreadful situations but this one ranked amongst the worst. As he sat in his car, he had to take a few minutes to regroup. Then he refocused. He sent an apology text to his wife to say he was on his way. Lily messaged saying he'd better hurry or he'd miss dessert too.

Grant pulled into the traffic. Two victims and two mobile phones. Had the killer just made their first mistake?

Chapter 33

The next morning, Tom came in extra early and found Ruby and Diane already in the office. They were each impatient to get started on the briefing.

'How are you holding up, Diane?' Tom asked.

'I'm okay. I stayed late with the Chens. They're devastated.'

'I can imagine. Did the boss make it home on time?'

Diane snorted. 'What do you think?'

'Ah, so he didn't.'

'By my estimation he probably got back in time to join them for coffee.'

'Yikes. We did our best. You know what he's like.'

'Don't I just.'

'Maybe Chrissie didn't mind as much as you imagine she did,' Ruby said. 'It was only a dinner. Grant can meet the new in-laws any old time.'

Diane pulled a rueful face. 'The thing is, these things get to be significant. Believe me, my lot at home can list in detail the times I've been doing police stuff when I should have been doing family stuff – important sports matches they were in, great goals they scored, school plays. I even missed my middle son's seventh birthday party.'

'Did he care?' Ruby asked.

'Very much. He's sixteen and still reminds me of it when he wants something.'

Grant walked in. 'Thanks for turning up early. A six o'clock briefing isn't easy, I know.'

Tom cleared his throat. 'How'd it go at home, guv?'

'Lily did a wonderful job in my absence like I knew she would. The groom and his parents were very understanding.'

'And Chrissie?' Diane asked.

'Still not talking to me.'

Tom groaned.

'I totally understand,' Grant said. 'This is her big thing and I wasn't there. Besides, she's been very emotional the last few weeks, what with the stress of the arrangements, and wanting it all to be perfect. She'll come round. I think my mistake was not sending her a message to let her know I was delayed.'

'What! But David, when we arrived at Mrs Chen's I reminded you to do that,' Diane said.

'Did you? It must have slipped my mind. I was already focused on the killer. Right, let's get to it.'

Diane rolled her eyes at Tom as Grant wrote on the whiteboard. Tom shrugged. Nothing was going to change the way Grant gave everything to his work.

The hairs on Tom's arms prickled as they revisited the details about the deaths of Naomi and Lin Chen. This was starting to feel personal.

'Anything new from the parents, Diane?' Grant asked.

'Nothing.'

'Right,' Grant said. 'I'm trying to keep Naomi out of this because the last thing that family needs is a postmortem into Naomi's death. We'll be focusing on Lin, and for good reason.'

Grant meant in case Naomi had been given medication, which would naturally implicate Lin and perhaps her parents too.

'We got a positive from the technical team,' Tom said. 'They've worked overnight with Lin's memory chip. They confirm it was Lin's phone we found in the bath and they confirm a video was streamed to the dark web, one hour before we found her and one hour after the estimated time of death of Naomi. You were right, boss.'

Grant's grey eyes were intense. 'That's our link to Phoebe's death. We'll have to wait for toxicology and forensics results on Lin and her house. It doesn't matter. Now we know they're connected.'

'Another murder made to look like a suicide,' Diane said.

Grant placed his hand close to Lin's photo. 'Exactly. With this same twisted link to the dark web. There were no signs of an intruder at Lin's and the neighbours didn't see anyone come or go.'

Tom scratched his forehead. 'The perp seems to be a ghost. We can't find a trace of them.'

Grant nodded and turned towards the board. 'A ghost? Exactly.' He picked up a marker pen and the moments ticked past. 'And if we think outside the box, what about Charles? He didn't see the perp either. That's why we wondered if Phoebe had been talking to someone on the phone.' He murmured Charles's words. '*No please. I want to live.* That's what he heard her say. Charles wasn't supposed to be outside. The killer didn't mean Charles to overhear Phoebe but if the killer wasn't seen either, were they really there that night? What if they actually were as you say, Tom, like a ghost – not present. What if Phoebe was alone?'

After entertaining the groom's family, had the boss spent the night awake, pondering the case. Maybe it was a method Tom should try himself because he had fallen asleep as soon as his head hit the pillow. He had awoken raring to get back with the team but he would have loved to have pulled together an idea like this one.

'You're wondering if Phoebe was talking to herself?' Tom said.

'Right,' Grant said. 'Because we know she didn't make a call at that time. She took the video, but there was no call log.'

Diane wasn't convinced. 'We considered that before. What she said though, that's not what you say if you're talking to yourself. It was like she was talking to another person.'

'Like she was talking to another person. Yet that person may not have physically been present,' Grant said. 'So far, Tom, does the footage from the surveillance cameras around Lin's house show any of our suspects?'

'No and they've already checked back three weeks.'

Grant paused his scribbling on the board. 'Is it possible to manipulate someone to the degree that they'd argue with you as if you were there, even if you're not? Could this have been what was happening with Phoebe?'

Ruby tucked her hair behind her ear. 'You mean, what if the person wasn't standing with her, what if they were in her own head?'

'Is that possible?' Grant asked.

'Perfectly possible,' Ruby said. 'Psychology is used in hospitals to build people up and help them overcome difficulties. It can just as easily be used to break people down. Mental interrogation techniques have been used for decades on terrorists and spies. There've been well-documented cases of mistreatment of wartime prisoners which has resulted in people literally going mad. There are plenty of examples where psychology has been used to meddle with the mind and cause a mental breakdown. Mind-control techniques using the human voice are particularly powerful.'

'You mean like brainwashing?' Diane asked.

'It's more sophisticated than that. More like hypnosis.' Ruby jumped to her feet. 'This could explain it!'

Grant was pacing. 'Talking to her inside her own head? Perfectly invisible. Silent. Which would explain why we've nothing concerning an intruder at Moorlands nor at Lin's.'

'If the victims were being coerced psychologically, there would be no trace,' Ruby said.

'It makes sense of why we've no forensics evidence for a perpetrator,' Tom said. 'It makes sense too of the wood dust. Somebody opened that window in advance but it wasn't Phoebe. And we've got the video streaming linking the two cases.'

Diane was nodding. 'Okay.'

'It would be a perfect crime,' Ruby said.

'There's no such thing as a perfect crime. Remember that.' The guv's voice was stern. 'The evidence is going to be very small but it doesn't mean it isn't there. A killer always leaves their mark. The more challenging question is, where to find it. Ruby, have you generated a profile?' Grant thumped his fist on the desk. 'Now we're getting to it.'

Tom's hands prickled with excitement. He ran them through his hair and took a few deep breaths. He and Diane went to make another round of drinks while Ruby sat quietly.

'You and your ghost perp,' Diane whispered in Tom's ear. 'We've bloody well nailed it.'

'For goodness sake someone put these doughnuts out of my reach,' Grant shouted as they left the room.

They came back carrying a tray of mugs, and waited impatiently until Ruby came to the board.

'With two murders and the same modus operandi, we would be looking for a sociopath.' Ruby wrote the word up. 'A killer in hiding who's blending in. Someone with the psychological skill to manipulate. Both Phoebe and Lin were psychologically vulnerable. The killer would have to be someone close, someone who knew their emotional weaknesses.'

'Man or woman?' Grant asked.

'I don't see clues. It could be either. And it doesn't have to be a professional. Patients like Charles and Emma have plenty of psychological insight. To have passed unnoticed, this person has to be likeable. This isn't a psychopath who's awkward and reserved, no. Our sociopath is friendly and good at getting close to others.'

Ruby was writing keywords on the board.

'What about the timeline?' Grant asked. 'It must have been planned in advance.'

'Yes. This can't have been rushed. It takes patience to manipulate and creep close without a victim suspecting. They would have gained Phoebe and Lin's trust. Proven they were genuine. Our killer would have been working on the victims for a while.'

'That's great, Ruby,' Grant said.

'You know how on our first case together the killer collected mementoes? It's a bit of a leap, but the streamed videos could be similar. The videos could be trophies. I'm not sure. It's just an idea.'

'You mean they could be sent by the victim to the killer?' Tom asked. 'That's dark.'

Diane rubbed her arms. 'This is giving me goosebumps.'

'Do you think our killer could have influenced Phoebe and Lin to that degree?' Grant asked. 'That they would switch on their own phones?'

Ruby wrote 'hypnosis' on the board. 'If they're using manipulation and hypnosis, it's possible.'

'We've several potential suspects with psychological insight,' Grant said. 'In fact we're swimming in them.'

Tom crossed his arms. He was working through his ideas. 'We need to narrow it down, guv. Let me think about how we can do that.' He frowned as he swivelled his chair a couple of times. 'Yes! I know. For the professionals maybe I could dig and see if any of them have case anomalies from the past connected to a suicide? That's a massive task. I'd need to cross-reference with some other details.'

'What about a mobile phone at the scene of death?' Ruby asked.

'That's too huge. I know, mobile phone *destruction,* at the scene of death. That might work. It's still going to be a massive amount of data to trawl through.'

'Do it. Make it your priority,' Grant said. 'And Brett Sinclair and Otremba have jumped to the top of the list. They're the only two we already have questions about. If the perp is working on our victims' minds then alibis aren't going to be any use to us. Time to squeeze and see what comes out.'

Chapter 34

Ruby sat in the passenger seat and Grant drove.

'I read the police reports on the White family murders,' Grant said. 'I'd like to hear your take?'

In between finding Lin dead, rushing home to patch it up with his family and wow his new in-laws, and getting up at the crack of dawn with a new focus for the case, when exactly had Grant had the time to read the White files? The chief never ceased to amaze her.

Ruby turned up the air con as she thought through the details. Mrs White's second husband, Smith, had been found dead in his car two days after the murders of his wife and his stepdaughter Juliette. The knife used to slit Juliette's throat was in the car, covered in her blood.

'Smith was presumed to have killed himself from remorse,' she said, 'and the knife was evidence of his guilt. He was known to be jealous of Mrs White's previous husband. Violent arguments had been overheard by neighbours where Smith had threatened his wife. The flashpoint seemed to have been that Mr White had been invited to Emma's sixth birthday party. Smith flew into a rage. It hangs together.'

Grant indicated to turn left. 'Emma has PTSD, correct? Do you think she could be so full of rage it could turn her into a murderer? Into a sociopath?'

'People aren't turned into sociopaths, they're born that way.'

'Right.'

'Basically, what happened to Emma wouldn't turn her into a killer. It might mean she would murder twice, I can't rule that out, but it would not turn her into a sociopath. If she were one of those, it was in her from the beginning.'

'I see.'

Ruby frowned. She felt an urge to come to Emma's defence. 'Emma can be unpolished in how she deals with people, like she was with Mrs Nic. She has an impulsivity – she acts before she thinks, or speaks before she considers if it's wise. Those things don't make her a good fit to be our sociopath. I'd expect our killer to be more outgoing, more polished and smooth. Someone who doesn't make waves. She doesn't fit the profile.'

'I know she's a very likeable young woman and I can see you've built a bridge with her. However, we need to stay professional and stick to the facts. She has the psychological knowledge and she had access to Phoebe and she could have had to Lin too.'

Ruby went quiet.

'Thank you for the profile, it's very helpful.'

They found Emma at the church community centre.

'Hi Ruby. Hello, Inspector. I heard about Naomi and Lin. It's horrible,' Emma said. 'I can't believe Lin would take her own life. I mean, I can imagine her helping Naomi to pass on, yes, and I know it's not allowed and everything. Lin would have been prepared to go to prison for it. She wouldn't run away from what she'd done. She felt it was the right thing. She would stand up for others in the same situation as her sister.'

'Let's go to the garden,' Ruby said. 'It'll be easier to talk privately.'

They found a bench in the shade and Emma sat between them.

'You're investigating Lin's death aren't you? Like you are Phoebe's?'

'That's right. I wanted to find out what you know about Lin,' Grant said.

'Not much about her private life. I can tell you she was a good nurse.'

Grant took out his notebook. 'When we arrived here, someone told us you're making a memorial video?'

'It's for Phoebe. I'm collecting people's memories of her. You know, funny stories and special moments. I'll edit it into a film.'

'Is that your thing? Videos, I mean,' Grant asked.

Was Grant wondering about a possible connection between the streamed videos and Emma? Ruby felt a prickle of unease. Yet she had to admit it was a good line of questioning.

'Yes. I did a film-making course last year and I've been working on it since then. I've set up a site online. I had the idea of making promotional videos and having my own little business. It was my dream.' She shrugged. 'I suppose you think it's silly.'

'I wasn't thinking that at all.'

Emma sniffed. 'I never told Phoebe my plans, you see? And now I regret it. I thought I could earn money and then we could go to Ireland together.'

Ruby felt a prickling at the backs of her eyes. She could see it now, Emma and Phoebe side by side, sitting on an Irish beach.

'Regrets are the hardest to come to terms with,' Ruby said.

'I know. I wish I'd told her. The thing is I wanted to go to Ireland without relying on her funds. I was waiting for the right moment to let her know. And now it's too late.'

Ruby took the girl's hand. 'Oh, Emma.'

'I've got my first client. They're going to pay me quite a lot of money. The guy said if he likes it he'll recommend me to his business contacts. If it works out, I could've supported myself. Moved away.'

'You still can,' Ruby said.

'But it won't be the same.'

It was true. Without Phoebe, it would never be the same.

'You've lost people dear to you once, and now you've lost Phoebe,' Ruby said. 'You're going to have to be strong to see yourself through this.'

'Thanks for listening,' Emma said. 'You're pretty good at it. Both of you. Though I'm sure you're not here for me to cry on your shoulder. I can't tell you much about Lin. How else can I help?'

Grant turned the pages of his notebook. 'Brett Sinclair. What can you tell us about him? We understand he was your sister's boyfriend.'

'Yes. I thought about telling Ruby before then I decided it wasn't relevant. Brett suffered in the past like I did so why drag it up? My stepfather murdered my mother and sister. End of story.'

'What's Brett like?' Ruby asked.

'He's a good therapist. Everyone trusts him. The self-help group can be rough sometimes what with the experiences people come out with, and Brett handles it well. We feel listened to and safe. He runs the coffee mornings and the drop-ins too.'

Ruby nodded. 'And he was Phoebe's counsellor?'

'Yeah, for a while, almost a year actually.' Emma shifted on the bench and shrugged.

'What?' Ruby asked.

'I don't know if I should mention it, the thing is, Phoebe started to get a crush on him. That's not unusual when you're a patient and you're dealing with doctors and therapists and everything, you can sort of start to get in awe of people. You know, put them on a pedestal.'

'Is that what Phoebe did with Brett? I'm getting the impression it made you uncomfortable,' Grant said.

'Sort of, though I felt guilty because when Phoebe told me about it I told her I thought it best if she stopped seeing him for the one-to-ones. It just gave me an icky feeling.'

'An icky feeling?' Ruby said.

'Like he was somehow making her feel that way about him, and now I say it, I know I'm being horrible because he's such a nice person and he wouldn't hurt a fly.' Emma put her face in her hands, shook her head then looked up. 'I shouldn't have told you. Sometimes my mind just thinks the worst of people all on its own. Brett's been nothing but kind to me. He's the one who came to tell me about Phoebe. Later, he even bought me flowers.'

'That was nice of him,' Ruby said.

'I know. And here I am stabbing him in the back.'

Grant frowned. 'Do you have any idea if he was counselling Lin Chen?'

'Not as far as I know. Please ignore everything I've said. I'm just being a horrible person.'

'If what you've told us leads us to Phoebe's killer, then you'll have no reason to be upset,' Grant said as he stood to go. 'And I think you know that as well as we do.'

Ruby stood too. 'Thank you, Emma.'

Grant placed his hand on Emma's shoulder. 'When it comes to murder, everything and anything can be important.'

'Just get them, Inspector. That's all I want. Get them and make them suffer for what they've done.'

Chapter 35

After speaking to Emma, Grant took Ruby for a walk in the community centre's garden.

'Things are moving quickly. What does Brett's profile tell us?' Grant asked.

'Brett's a counsellor, so he's got the expertise to understand the mind and use emotions against people. He knows Phoebe so he would understand which buttons to press and how to weaken her. He facilitates the support group at the church so he had access to her. I need to meet him in person to formulate more than that.'

'As far as we know he didn't have access to Lin,' Grant said. 'Mrs Chen told Diane that Lin had never seen a counsellor. Unless Lin kept that to herself. Let's find out.'

They skirted a small pond and headed back towards the community centre.

'David, I know this isn't a good time to talk but I was thinking about Chrissie.'

Grant smiled. 'What about her?'

'This is her happy time and it's also an important transition. She's going from being your little girl to a married woman.'

He gave her a quizzical look. 'Chrissie has been independent, and independent-minded, for a long time. She doesn't need me.'

'That's the thing. She does. Especially at the moment. It's not only about the arrangements and it all looking nice. Chrissie needs your support. She needs to know you're there for her. Even if this case is messing it up, I hope you can find some special time with her to remind her of those things.'

If she was honest with herself, Ruby had always been a little jealous of Chrissie. Chrissie had a loving father, who was respected and honest. She was going to have a lovely wedding and be walked down the aisle on David's arm. Whereas Ruby had a serial killer father she was ashamed of. A man who had tried to murder her. She refused to feel sorry for herself and she felt terrible for being envious of Chrissie. It was why Ruby had held back from talking with the others about the wedding. It was easier that way. Less painful.

David was frowning and smiling at the same time.

Ruby flapped her arms. 'Please don't take offence. I didn't mean to overstep the boundaries.'

He put his arm around her shoulders. 'What great advice. It's what I needed to hear.'

'It is?'

'Yes. It's the simple things which count, thank you for reminding me. And since we're on the subject, how are things going with you and Tom?'

Ruby felt herself going red. 'They're great. Actually I was going to ask him if maybe he might like us to move in together, and then I thought that would be a bit fast and I should wait. I don't want to put him off.'

Grant laughed. 'I'm certain you're not going to be doing that. I'm sure the two of you will work it out.'

As they neared the building, he dropped his arm from her but she felt the warmth and the fatherliness of it for a long time afterwards, and it made her happy.

They found Brett in the office at the back. When Grant read Brett his rights, Brett didn't seem surprised. He gave them a knowing look. 'Am I under arrest?'

'Not at the moment,' Grant said.

'I wondered when you'd get around to questioning me, what with two girls dead. Three if you count Naomi.'

'Let's save the talk for at Force HQ.'

The three of them went to the car and they drove in silence.

At HQ, Grant got Brett booked in and then took him to an interview room. He switched on the recording equipment and went through the formalities and repeated Brett's rights. Ruby sat down and Grant pulled up another chair.

'So, Mr Sinclair, Phoebe Markham and Lin Chen are dead and you knew them both,' Grant said. 'How about if you start by telling us about Phoebe.'

'I want to cooperate and help in any way I can. I knew Phoebe from the beginning of my work for the community centre. When Anne Markham hired me, she told me her daughter would be one of the clients using the services.'

'And you're Anne Markham's cousin?'

'Yes. Have you found anyone involved in Phoebe's death?'

'Please stick with my questions.'

Brett sighed. 'Anne Markham, yes, she's my cousin. I might as well tell you the full story. Actually I'm surprised Emma didn't fill you in already but I suppose she's been preoccupied the last few days. You see, back when Emma's mother and sister, Juliette, were murdered, I was Juliette's boyfriend. Juliette and I were both nineteen. Emma was six. It was a horrible time. So shocking and I don't remember a lot of it. Anyway, it made me change my career ideas and I decided to train as a therapist. I qualified and worked in Brighton for many years. Then Anne contacted me to say she was setting up a counselling service at the church and would I be interested in applying for the post.'

'You were in close contact with Mrs Markham?'

'Not really. She knew about the tragedy, naturally. It wasn't until her *own* daughter was assaulted Anne became involved in mental health initiatives. That's when she built the extension at the church and funded recreational activities at Moorlands.'

'And did you keep in contact with Emma all that time?'

'We sent Christmas cards and I tried to remember her birthday, though I've got to say I wasn't very good at that one. So it was a surprise Emma ended up a member of the self-help group but not a surprise Phoebe did. As I explained, Anne already told me she wanted Phoebe to be part of it.'

'It must have been a difficult decision coming back to Himlands Heath.'

'A long time had passed. I was in a bit of a rut and running a new service was an attractive proposition.' Brett spoke carefully. He was a studious, serious person and seemed older than his years.

'I understand you were Phoebe's counsellor?'

'I was, for just over a year.'

'Were you aware of any negative influences on Phoebe?'

Brett raised his eyebrows. 'Not that I'm aware of. She was close to Lin, I can say that, and she listened to Lin's advice.'

'Was any of that negative?'

'More disturbing than negative. Disturbing of the status quo. She was talking to Phoebe a lot about independence and finding her own path in life. I'm not sure Phoebe was ready for that.'

'Why did you stop being her counsellor?'

'After her Ireland trip, Phoebe wanted to move on and she stopped one-on-one sessions. She was trying to cut down on the people she relied on. What she wanted was to become more self-sufficient.'

'And that was the only reason?'

'Yes.'

Ruby signalled she wanted to interrupt. 'I was wondering about when Juliette died, how it affected you? You said it was the impetus for you to change careers?'

'It derailed me. I had to redo that year at school. My concentration was shot. I could hardly read words on a page some days. My ambition to be a songwriter went down the plug-hole. How could I continue with music? I'd written a song for Juliette and I learned Juliette had been humming it moments before she died. I couldn't write a note after that. It gave me nightmares.'

'Do you still enjoy music?'

Grant liked the way Ruby was quietly putting her questions. Brett didn't seem defensive and he was giving them plenty of information. Or was he simply feeding them and leading them towards what he wanted them to focus on?

'I slowly got back to playing the piano. Although I don't compose. Not anymore.'

'And what about your own parents?' Ruby asked. 'Can you tell me a little about them?'

'Not much to tell. My mum worked as a receptionist and Dad worked at a bank. They're both retired now. They potter around Eastbourne and do childcare for my sister's two kids. It keeps them occupied.'

'Do you have a partner?'

'Not at the moment. I had a long-term relationship in Brighton. She left me. I suppose that was one of the reasons I wanted to get out. There's been nothing serious since then. Why?'

'Thanks, Brett, that's very helpful,' she said.

Grant sat forward. 'Did you have any knowledge of Phoebe being active on the dark web?'

'What?' Brett gave a small laugh. 'I don't even really know what that is. And Phoebe definitely wouldn't. She wasn't immature, I'm not trying to say that, but she was kind of young for her age.'

'All right, so let's move on to Lin Chen. How well did you know her?'

'I've never met her. I hear about her all the time though, from Phoebe and other people at the church group. I only know of her second hand.'

Brett was so open and seemingly honest, it was unnerving. Was their sociopath sitting right in front of them, giving answers so convincingly?

At the end, Grant took Ruby into another room. He sat on a desk and stretched his shoulders. 'Brett seemed pretty convincing. He's said nothing incriminating. Did you spot any red flags for him being our manipulator?'

'Everything he said pointed to him being Mr Ordinary. Though he did deftly put a question mark over the relationship between Phoebe and Lin.'

'Yes he did, though not so much that it came over as unreasonable.'

'Our perp is going to be very hard to spot and clever at playing our game.'

Grant crossed his arms. 'Yes, and he's given me nothing I can hold him with. We'll have to let him go, though there's one more thing I started to sweat about in there – do you think there's another murder on the horizon?'

'I think you know the answer to that. If this is a sociopath, it's not a matter of if, it's a matter of when.'

Chapter 36

In the video clip, Lin is in her underwear. As she steps into the water I see her lip trembling. Her vulnerability is intoxicating. It makes my breath catch. This is everything I wanted from her and more.

Lin was so blinded by desperation for her sister, she had no idea how I was manipulating her. In fact, Lin had been at breaking point for a long long time.

Why did I have my eye on Lin? Well, it's simple. I hated her. With those doe-like eyes of hers and her sickeningly caring nature, she was one to pull in the admirers. She tugged on heart strings. She invited devotion. And I loathed her for it.

Females like Lin have to be obliterated.

It was me who planted the idea of a pact with her sister. Lin was surprisingly religious and she believed in an afterlife where the two of them would be together and whole forever. What a fool.

In the video, the medication is taking hold and she tells me her final words, just as I instructed her to. Her hair floats in the water as her body softens and glides to its final resting place.

I'm panting with excitement.

First, Phoebe Markham and now Lin Chen. I'm so damn good at what I do.

Two have been ticked off my list. Which leaves one to go.

Chapter 37

Tom was in the office. It was another hot day and he had the blinds down. He wanted a list of deaths in the last five years, in a ten-mile radius of Himlands Heath, in which a mobile phone had been destroyed. He was including drownings and fire as means of death, since mobile phones would be destroyed in those cases too.

The question was, what to cross-reference with – Moorlands? Mental health? Neither of those were possible. He was stuck with trawling through a list of the logs, reading names and ages and places. It was a needle-in-a-haystack task. Especially because he had no idea what he was really looking for.

Lucky for him he had top of the range text-to-speech software. He adjusted his headphones and settled down to a long day of combing through the details.

Several hours later, he was interrupted by Ruby arriving.

'I'm starving. I'm going to get a sandwich. Do you want to come?' she asked.

'Can you bring me one back?'

'Sure.' She smiled. 'You were so concentrated I didn't even know if I should interrupt. Have you got anything?'

'Nada. No links to Moorlands. I've one fatal car accident where a mobile phone was involved. The victim lost control of her car. I'm waiting for a call back with more information.'

'Any links to the Markhams?'

'None so far.'

She put her hands on his chest.

'Hey, we agreed none of that at the office,' he said.

'Why not? Nobody's here.'

'Except they could walk in any minute.'

'Just one little kiss.'

'Ruby!'

'Boring.' She laughed and swept up her bag.

'It's not boring to be professional. If we both stick to the rules we won't create problems.'

She gave him a cheeky look over one shoulder as she left.

He took off his headphones and called after her. 'If you moved in with me, we'd be able to do more of what we want when we want.'

The door banged shut and he was left on his own. Damn, that was not at all the right moment to bring it up. Nor the right way. Talk about doomed to failure. Tom groaned and put his head in his hands.

When Ruby came back she gave him the sandwich without comment. Tom decided it was probably her way of saying no, and his mood dipped a few notches.

A while later he got the call back. The officer on the other end told Tom the woman who died in the car crash had been battling cancer and had recently been diagnosed with an inoperable brain tumour.

Tom thanked his colleague and hung up. He got Ruby's attention. 'Now that's interesting. Fiona Taylor was a cancer survivor who'd recently been told the illness had returned. That's why there was a question about whether she lost control of her car or if she drove into the truck deliberately. The phone was smashed and the truck driver she went head-on with, said he saw her on the phone at the time of the accident.'

Ruby pushed back her chair and came to peer at his screen. 'Did the other driver say anything else?'

Tom checked. 'He thought it could have been why she swerved into his lane. He saw no other explanation. But he didn't say she was filming.'

'Why would he? It's such a strange thing to do. Wouldn't it be usual to assume someone was making a call?'

'I'm going to track down the truck driver.'

'Oh yeah, and about that idea of yours earlier. You know, moving in. When we've got a chance, let's talk about it.'

To hell with his own stupid rules. He whooped with delight, grabbed her and gave her a kiss.

Chapter 38

When Grant requested that Mike Otremba come to Force HQ for an interview, the doctor was not pleased. Grant had decided to back-peddle and bring Otremba in for questioning under caution, rather than arrest him. He was glad he'd taken the more diplomatic route. With a person of standing like Otremba, there could always be fallout if things were not handled well. Not that Grant was concerned about a rollicking from the detective chief superintendent, but one step at a time.

Otremba made it clear he was sacrificing his lunch break.

'I've heard about Lin's death and I'm very, very sorry but why do you want to speak to me? I hardly knew her. Listen, I've a full waiting room this afternoon so this can't take long. Patients have appointments they're entitled to keep. I've got responsibilities.'

'I totally understand and thank you for coming in.'

Grant explained to the doctor that he was not under arrest and was free to leave at any time. Grant had made sure he made Otremba a drink.

Questioning was an art. From what Grant had seen, Mike Otremba enjoyed his stature in the community. He had a showy side to him. He basked in being looked up to.

Grant scraped back a second chair and tossed a file onto the table. 'I know your time is really valuable.'

He took photographs out which showed Phoebe's body where it had landed on the concrete.

'You told me you were Phoebe Markham's general practitioner since she was fourteen years old. So that's for the last seven years.'

'Yes.'

'Here's what I've been wondering about. Did you really care for Phoebe? Or were you more concerned by the kudos you got from your connection to John Markham?'

'How dare you. Let me point out I came here of my own volition to help you with the case. I expect to be treated with respect.'

'The thing is, you came to Himlands Heath shortly after you'd undergone treatment for drug abuse. That's not a very good recommendation, is it? You took a job as a locum probably because it was the only position open to you. Then when one of the doctors at the surgery retired there were four doctors other than yourself who applied for the post. Did you get the job because John put in a good word for you?'

'I got the post based on my performance at interview.'

Grant shook his head. 'I think John vouched for you. Why? Because he wanted a doctor who would care for his daughter. More importantly, he wanted someone who would listen to him, report to him, be answerable to him. It was a question of a shared interest.'

'That's not how it was. I was happy to take over Phoebe's care. There were no strings attached and no favours from John Markham.'

'Isn't it pretty unusual for a locum to get a full-time position, when they're up against four established doctors all of whom have blemish-free records?'

'Listen, whatever you think, there was nothing odd nor dishonest about my appointment.'

'All right, thanks for clearing that up. How about we go back over your last meeting with Phoebe Markham. Another patient overheard you arguing with her. What did you argue about? Was it about Ireland and the fact you sided with the Markhams against Phoebe? Even though she was your patient and, as we both know, she was also an adult.'

'No. We did not argue.'

'That's not what our witness has told us.'

'Why am I feeling I'm under scrutiny? I thought you asked me here to help you make progress?'

Grant consulted his papers. 'I did, please bear with me. People have also told me you didn't support her wish to move away.'

'What people? Anyway, that's not a crime.'

'Then you don't deny it.'

'I already explained. It's because I believed the risks outweighed the benefits. That's the reason I didn't think it was a good idea. Not because I sided with her father.'

'You see this argument you had with Phoebe really interests me. I'd also like to know why you're denying it. Did the argument happen when Phoebe confronted you with evidence of your current addiction?'

'I. Did. Not. Argue. With Phoebe.'

Grant pushed around the photographs, angling them so Otremba would have a better view. 'It was a terrible end to a promising young life, don't you think?'

The doctor pressed his lips together. 'It was tragic. I only wish I could have done something to prevent it.'

'All right. Do you mind if I ask you about Lin Chen? How well did you know her?'

'In passing. I sometimes saw her at Moorlands.'

'Did you like her?'

'What kind of question is that? Not in the way you're implying, of course not.'

'Have you ever been to her apartment?'

'No.'

'You're aware Lin's sister had Motor Neurone Disease? Did Lin ever seek your advice about that? Did she confide in you?'

'Absolutely not.'

'All right, this is really helpful, thank you.'

'If you've finished, Inspector. I think it's time for me to leave.'

'Of course, I appreciate your cooperation. Oh yes, one last point. At the group practice where you work, a member of staff told me she has questions about your behaviour. I advised her to put her concerns in writing.'

The confidence went out of Mike Otremba like air from a punctured balloon. 'What are you talking about?'

'This person has smelled alcohol on your breath on more than one occasion. They were very troubled about it and didn't know what to do for the best, until they spoke to me. Naturally, I told them the best course of action is to contact the General Medical Council. I took a formal statement too.'

The member of staff had been the one-in-a-million secretary. She had been sitting on her concerns for some time. First, as she explained to Grant, because there had been no concerns raised by patients. Second, because she would rather dismiss her suspicions as being unfounded and silliness, rather than accuse a respected doctor of malpractice. Why shouldn't a doctor have a drink from time to time? And third, because she felt a great loyalty to Mike Otremba.

'I believe you argued with Phoebe two days before her death, because she confronted you about your addiction. You risked losing your licence. You are in a relationship with the hospital manager, are you not? It would, theoretically, have been feasible for you to get the window key from her office, take Phoebe to the top and push her off.'

'Now you're going too far. Are you looking to get a reprimand from your superiors?'

'I'm sorry, sometimes I get carried away.'

'Listen, we argued. Phoebe showed me pills which she said had dropped from my pocket. Believe me I had nothing to do with her death. Nothing.'

Grant sat back. The doctor was sweating. He was unbuttoning his collar and yanking aside his tie.

'Was Mrs Nicholson in on it?'

'Let me repeat. She had nothing to do with Phoebe's death and neither did I.'

'Did she know you took the key?'

'I didn't touch it. Please, leave Wendy out of this.'

'I'll be bringing her in for questioning too, doctor. Informally, of course.'

Taking his time, Grant gathered the photos from the table.

'Please, no.'

Grant ignored the man and stacked the pictures neatly, sliding them back in the envelope. Perspiration glistened on Otremba's brow as Grant pushed back his chair and made to leave the room.

'Wait!' Otremba said. 'There's something else.'

'What is it you want to tell me? Are you using again?'

'Yes! But I didn't kill Phoebe.'

'Did you argue that day?'

'Okay. She showed me a packet. I flipped.'

'You flipped. I see. Did you threaten her?'

'No. I was angry. I didn't threaten her, I swear it. It's true I was scared. I've been in denial. Trying to make like I wasn't hooked again when I knew I was. I didn't go near that window key and Wendy never would either.'

'Where were you when Phoebe fell?'

'I was at home. I told you that.'

'Yes, and Wendy Nicholson was conveniently stuck in traffic.'

'Listen, you can track my phone, can't you?'

'Perhaps.'

'I took a call from a patient whose little boy was very ill. She was worried about his temperature rising and she phoned me just before I got the call from Moorlands. Can't you track it? It'll show I was at home.'

Now he felt under threat, Mike Otremba was bleeding information. It was the moment to squeeze him for everything he'd got.

'Did Lin seek your advice about her sister's illness?'

'I already told you, she did not.'

'Do you have a home computer?'

'What? Yes.'

'I'd really appreciate if you gave in your home and office computer, and your mobile. An officer could accompany you and collect them.'

'If it will clear this up in your mind, then yes. I don't have anything to hide. Though I don't understand. I took the call from the patient on my mobile.'

It would be very useful to have the man's technical equipment to check for dark web activity. The technical team had already briefed Grant and told him any perpetrator could have a hidden device, or they could try to delete records of their activity except traces would always remain and could be dug out by an expert. However, on Grant's reading of the doctor under pressure, it was likely the man was actually innocent.

Yet in Grant's eyes Otremba would never be completely free from blame. If the doctor had not been an addict, if he had a better connection with Phoebe, if he been more vigilant – he could have realised something was wrong.

Grant led the way to the door. 'Thank you again for your cooperation.'

And he fervently hoped the doctor would be tortured by his own conscience.

Chapter 39

Tom was already in the incident room. Ruby was the next to arrive for the briefing and though he had the urge to kiss her, he stopped himself just in time.

She slung her bag on the table. 'What's been happening?'

'Plenty. I served the Production Order on Hunt's bank and the information on his accounts has come in. Five thousand pounds was transferred to Hunt soon after his release. Then another five thousand a few days later. You're not going to believe this – it came from John Markham.'

'What!'

'That's not all. The DCs have identified Hunt on camera in Himlands Heath the afternoon Phoebe died. I just texted Grant with it.'

'Tom, that's great.'

'I know.'

'What's that funny look on your face? Is there something else?'

'Did you hear about Charles?'

'Charles? What about him?'

'I got a message from the nurse on his ward. Charles has been transferred to the Secure wing.'

'Oh no.'

'Imagine. Me and him are pretty much the same age but his bipolar disorder is sucking all his energy. She told me he's become too depressed to talk. Catatonic, she called it. Apparently, it's happened to him before. I really feel for the guy. The nurse told me some patients become so depressed they stay catatonic for months.'

'It must have been really weighing on him how he couldn't save Phoebe.'

'I know. It made me feel like shit when I heard the news.'

Diane and Grant arrived together. The boss went straight to the front, rolling up his shirt sleeves as he went.

'Thank goodness for air conditioning. Right, we've got a lot to get through. First, Mike Otremba admitted he has an addiction. He's going to refer himself to the General Medical Council. He also told me he took a call from a patient which proves he was at home when Phoebe fell. The DCs are looking into getting triangulation data from the phone company to see if they can prove or disprove what he says. If that doesn't work we'll be sending the techies around to Otremba's house to check signal strength – to see if they can pinpoint his exact location when he took that call. As soon as the result comes in, Tom, I want to know.'

'Right, guv,' Tom said.

'Second, Brett. He came out squeaky clean on questioning.'

'As we'd expect our killer to,' Diane said. 'Ruby told us they'd be blending in, likeable and all that.'

'We've nothing to move Brett further into the frame,' Grant said. 'And Ruby and I talked to Emma. It didn't throw up anything new.'

'I've been thinking about her,' Diane said. 'Emma White probably knows the door code. She'd know how to take the window key from Mrs Nic's office. She was close to Phoebe.'

Ruby crossed her arms. 'She wasn't close to Lin. And would she kill her best friend so she could get a nice apartment? I doubt it.'

'I like Emma too, but we've known people who've killed for far less,' Diane said.

Ruby wasn't convinced. 'Those two girls depended on each other.'

Grant tapped the board. 'She stays on the suspect list. What about Lin's postmortem?'

Tom consulted his screen. 'She had significant levels of sedative in her bloodstream. Cause of death was by drowning. There were no unusual markings on the body to indicate a struggle.'

'You mean she took an overdose and then got in the bath?' Diane said. 'Could a killer really have manipulated her to go that far?'

Ruby went to the whiteboards. 'Yes. Remember, Lin was in a fragile emotional state. She could, hypothetically, have assisted Naomi and then been persuaded by our third party to take her own life. She was known to be a fighter but could that have been turned against her? What if she believed her parents might be blamed for assisting Naomi? Protecting them would be a very strong motivator.'

'Then why not simply confess to assisting Naomi herself?' Diane asked.

'True. But we don't know how Lin felt being the sister who was not ill. The sister who didn't have MND. The one who got to lead her life while her sister has suffered for years. Survivor's guilt could have been used against Lin. It's incredibly powerful. It all sounds so logical when we talk about it here except emotions don't work like that. They overpower logic. This person was trusted by Phoebe and Lin. Our victims may have relied on them, spilled their hearts out to them. I think it's completely possible Lin could have been manipulated to take those pills and get into the water.'

'Shit,' Diane said.

'Right,' Grant said. 'Thanks for that clarification, Ruby. Tom, I got your message about Hunt. Give us the headlines.'

'Two five-thousand deposits were made into Hunt's account. It came from an offshore fund registered in the name of John Markham.'

'That's a bombshell,' Diane said. 'Well done.'

'There's more. The DCs have been checking through the surveillance footage in Himlands Heath the afternoon before Phoebe's death. They spotted Hunt in the crowds at Himlands Heath train station.'

'Once this is over, I'm going to be buying that person a drink,' Diane said.

'Me too,' Tom said. He sent the surveillance shot to the big screen. It's incriminating. More than enough to bring him in.'

The guv's grey eyes seemed to have got darker. Tom had seen it before when they were honing in on suspects. He really hoped Grant would be sending him down to Brighton to grill Hunt.

'Ruby, I'd like you there when we break the news to Emma about her windfall. Tom, get down to Brighton and arrest Hunt.'

'Right, boss.'

'Go get him, Tom,' Diane whispered.

Grant ran a hand through his hair. 'We don't have the one vital piece of information which will crack this case wide open. Yet.' He looked at them in turn. 'We're getting close. Diane, you and I will question John Markham.'

Tom exchanged a glance with Diane. She gave him a small nod. Being a local lad, he'd heard rumours about what happened in the past involving Grant's ill-fated school trip. Tom had the impression she was as relieved as he was that Grant was doing the right thing and bringing her in on the Markhams.

Chapter 40

Phoebe's apartment was top of the range, with a walk-through lounge diner, two enormous bedrooms and a balcony with an amazing view of the distant green hills of the Sussex Downs. The Markhams had spent substantial money on the apartment itself and on what Grant supposed was arty, minimalist and ultramodern décor and furniture.

Grant had Ruby and Diane with him. He wanted Ruby to observe Emma when John broke the news of Phoebe's bequest. John Markham was already there and he explained that his wife was not feeling well enough to come. Emma was to arrive later, and did not know why she had been invited over.

Grant and Diane put on protective gloves and they systematically sifted through Phoebe's papers and letters. It had all been searched already.

'This is where you found the letter?'

Grant was finding it difficult to not question John concerning the money transfer to Hunt. It would be better to ask John to come in for an interview. If he was honest with himself, perhaps he should not even be handling this case at all.

'It was in that drawer, about halfway down the pile. The rest is to do with her health and her medical appointments.

There are a few bank statements and such like. Phoebe was haphazard about her affairs.'

Grant gritted his teeth. The payment to Hunt had made him question everything about John. Even the man's voice was grating on him. He had read through the notes of the original investigation into Hunt's crimes. Right from the beginning, had there been some liaison between Hunt and John Markham? How could that be possible? It was monstrous.

Yet Grant had heard of crimes where parents pimped their children, or had been aware of criminal intentions towards their children and ignored them. It made him sick. Surely that could not have been the case with John Markham? Or was Grant so blind, he had badly misjudged his old school friend?

He was looking at papers and not properly reading the words. It was no good, he couldn't keep it in. 'My inspector's informed me you transferred two large sums of money to Hunt.'

He said it icily, in the same way he would skewer any potential suspect in a murder case. He saw Diane stifle her surprise. The shock on John's face was textbook. His eyebrows arched upwards. He opened his mouth to say something but for a few moments nothing came out.

'Excuse me? I have no idea what you're talking about.'

'Then let me make it clearer.' He knew he'd raised his voice and he didn't care. 'You transferred five thousand pounds to Hunt's account three weeks ago and then one week later you transferred another five thousand.'

'David, please, I did no such thing. Why would I ever, ever! After what he did!'

Grant's anger spiked. He had to clench his jaw. My god, had John been manipulating them from the beginning? Two girls were dead, one of them Markham's daughter, and Markham had the nerve to lie.

'That's enough! Don't stand there and lie to my face. After we've had our conversation with Emma, you and I will be discussing this at HQ.'

'Please don't shout. You've got it wrong.'

John was pressing his hands to his cheeks, then rubbing them up and down his chest, then back to his cheeks, pacing right next to Grant and beseeching him with wide eyes. Grant could hear the man panting.

'There must have been a mistake. Please listen, David, you've got to believe me. I'm sure we can sort this out.'

'There will be no sorting it out. There will be a formal statement taken in an investigation room.'

Diane would be interviewing Hunt and they would get to the bottom of whatever sordid transaction had taken place.

'Mr Markham,' Diane said, her voice stern with authority. 'Emma will be arriving soon. As the DCI has said, we'll discuss this later.'

Diane shot Grant a warning look and Grant took the hint and pressed his lips together.

He left the room abruptly and went on a tour of the flat.

Diane was right, he needed to calm down before Emma arrived.

Ruby trailed Grant around Phoebe's apartment, while Diane stayed with Markham in the living room.

'He had the gall to wish Chrissie well for her wedding. How dare he,' Grant said. 'His own daughter dead on the concrete. Lin in the bath. And he twisted my guts with guilt. Is he our manipulator?'

It was a rhetorical question yet Ruby felt compelled to answer. 'I don't know.'

Grant didn't know either. Had Markham been involved in Phoebe's death? The man had been distraught, hadn't he? He still was. He and his wife were broken.

Grant ran his hands through his hair. 'My god, what a bloody case this is.'

Ruby knew better than most how offenders could use all means to fool those around them. Her father had done the same. The collateral damage to people who found out later they had believed, or loved, or stood up for a killer, could destroy people. Murderers could be more devious than anyone could imagine, though she could not see how John Markham could have got to Lin.

'Like you always say, we have to suspect everyone,' she said. 'No exceptions.'

Grant tugged at his collar to loosen it. 'The more distance between me and Markham right now, the better.'

Ruby stayed with Grant. A few minutes later, the intercom buzzed and it was Diane who answered. 'Please come straight up, Ms White.'

Emma was wearing one of her flowery blouses. 'Hi Ruby, I didn't expect to see you here. Hello Mr Markham. Hello Inspector.'

Grant shook her hand. 'Come in please. I'm sure you're wondering why Mr Markham has invited you.'

'I suppose I am.'

'You've been here before?' Grant asked.

'Lots of times. It was our safe place. And it's much nicer than my flat, so we usually came here.'

'To do what?' Grant asked.

Emma shrugged. 'Hang out. Eat pizza. You're making me uncomfortable. Why are you here?'

Ruby gave Emma a smile of encouragement. Emma definitely had a strength about her. It wasn't easy to be assertive with someone like Grant. In this kind of surprise situation, lots of people would not have managed to ask straight questions.

Grant handed over Phoebe's letter. 'Mr Markham invited you here because he'd like you to read this.'

Emma unfolded it slowly, checking each of their faces before she started reading. A few moments later she gave a gasp. 'I can't believe it.'

'Phoebe wanted you to have her apartment and her car. My wife and I want you to have them too,' John said.

A tear rolled down Emma's cheek. 'This is incredible. Are you sure?'

'You meant a lot to our daughter. Please, we want you to accept the gift.'

'Did you know about the contents of this letter?' Grant asked. 'Did Phoebe show it to you? Or did you discuss it?'

Emma blew her nose. 'I had no idea. We never talked about stuff like money.'

'Why not?' Grant asked.

'It's obvious, isn't it? Because I have nothing to give. Phoebe had an allowance and I have my social benefits. She knew I worked at a fast-food place and that it's hard for me to afford. Have you seen my flat? At least it's mine but it's a dump. This is incredible.'

John Markham took something from his pocket and he handed it to Emma. 'These are for the car, which is outside. My wife and I need time to prepare the apartment. We'll let you know when we're ready to hand it over.'

Emma inspected the keys. 'This is her fob. She bought it when the self-help group went to the seaside. Of course, take your time. However long you need.'

Emma went to the window and gazed at the distant countryside. 'I always loved this place and Phoebe knew it. I don't mean I was jealous or anything because I wasn't. It's just Phoebe was very… fortunate.'

Emma was crying. She looked around at the furniture and the artwork, then she seemed to sway a little. Ruby followed Emma's gaze. She was staring at the coffee table and a pile of books stacked next to a decorative bowl.

Emma walked over and picked up the one on the top of the pile. It was a much-worn notebook, purple, with a gold elastic holding it together.

'Do you recognise it?' Ruby asked.

'This is mine,' Emma whispered.

Perhaps the revelation that the apartment was now hers, was sinking in. Emma seemed to be in shock. She stood in a daze, the notebook in her hands.

'What's wrong?' Ruby asked. 'Is it something to do with your notebook?'

Emma shook her head. 'It's nothing. I was just thinking of the last time Phoebe and I were here, you know.'

'If the book is yours, please take it,' John Markham said. 'Are you all right? I appreciate this has come as a surprise. I hope it's a positive one. Given the circumstances, Anne and I are glad something good can come of it.'

As she clutched the book and the keys to her chest, Emma looked like she wanted to run away.

'If you don't feel up to driving today, you can come and collect the car later. I can take you back if you like.' Markham glanced at Grant. 'Actually, that might be difficult.'

'We can drop Emma on our way,' Grant said.

Everyone headed for the door. Grant went first and Ruby made sure she stayed close to Emma. The girl was behaving strangely. It was as if she was trying to act like nothing had happened, although Ruby felt sure that something had. Something mysterious and very significant.

Chapter 41

A few hours before, Emma had been lying in bed when she received the message from John Markham, asking if she could meet him at Phoebe's apartment.

The previous evening, she had started editing the clips she'd taken for the memorial video and she had recorded her own tribute to her friend. She would need much more material, and she planned to go back to the church in the afternoon. Mr Markham's message was unexpected. She hoped he did not need help going through Phoebe's things. Doing that would make her too sad. Surely Phoebe's mother would be the best person for such a terrible task.

She wanted to ignore him except for her sense of loyalty. The Markhams had always been kind to her. She didn't want to let them down.

I'll be there. She texted back.

Rolling out of bed, she pulled the curtain and put the kettle on to boil. Opening the fridge, she groaned. One yoghurt pot sat on its own. She had no butter and no cheese, and no bread either. She'd not had the presence of mind to think about food. The store on the corner would be open, except she didn't have the energy to go there. She promised she would pass by on the way home. She had to look after herself. It was her number one rule. She grabbed the yoghurt and a spoon.

She got lukewarm water for her shower. Goddamit, sometimes she hated this place. It was even worse to think she might be stuck here forever. How wonderful it would be to live somewhere calm and peaceful, not where she could hear the neighbour's arguments and his drunkenness and the names he called his partner.

She didn't want to end up like the woman at the end of the corridor either, who had lived there for fifteen years. That was a promise Emma had made to herself – that she would get out, no matter how, and live in a nice place. She had a dream of a little cottage and a lawn dotted with buttercups. She had a plan.

She browsed her rail of shirts and picked out a blouse splashed with giant poppies, and headed across town.

Emma's legs felt wobbly as she walked up the stairs to Phoebe's apartment. They had shared so many happy times there.

It was one of the police detectives who opened the door. It was a surprise to find two of them there and Ruby as well. Emma read the letter. She had to go through it a second time, pausing on each word to make sure she had not misunderstood. This could not be true.

That was when the inspector grilled her. It was uncomfortable to pass under his scrutiny. His eyes rested on her and didn't move away. She felt the weight of every word he said and it made her feel guilty. But why should she? Phoebe had made her own choice.

Emma tried not to squirm. She'd had nothing but bad luck in her life. Why shouldn't she have good fortune? Yet it had come at the cost of her best friend and Inspector Grant was not going to let her off lightly.

She managed to hold her ground and not disintegrate in front of them. Mr Markham was kind. There were no accusations from him, which was a relief. And that's when the world had turned and threatened to go black – because Emma spotted her journal sitting on Phoebe's table.

At first she wondered if she were hallucinating. She was frightened to reach out and find nothing there, but she made herself do it anyway and yes, it was real. She dare not open it. She dare not give it too much of her attention.

'What's wrong?' Ruby asked. 'Is it something to do with your notebook?'

Emma clutched the journal and swallowed hard. She shook her head. 'It's nothing. I was just thinking of the last time Phoebe and I were here, you know.'

The conversation between the others turned to buzzing in her ears.

This was impossible. Phoebe certainly would never have touched it. Emma was certain she'd not brought it there herself. What was going on?

Chapter 42

Tom sped to Brighton. He had set the interview up at Brighton police station and patrol officers had collected Hunt. A uniformed officer stood in the corner of the room and Tom switched on the video and recorded the date and time. They each stated their name and rank for the camera. Tom went through the rest of the formalities and then sat back and gave Hunt a cool stare.

Hunt was in a surly mood. 'What am I doing here? This is police harassment. You've no grounds for arresting me.'

'Please give your name,' Tom said to Hunt.

'Adam Hunt.'

'I have questions to ask about sums of money transferred to your bank account. If you would look at the statements in front of you, please.'

The statements were exhibits in plastic bags, catalogued and coded for reference. The two transfers had been highlighted in yellow. Hunt took his glasses out of his pocket and peered at the papers. 'What of it?'

'Ten thousand pounds was sent to you by Mr Markham. What was it for?'

Hunt leaned back and gave a nasty smile. 'It wasn't John who gave it, it was his wife.'

'Anne Markham? For what reason?'

'Is it a crime?'

'Please answer the question.'

'You're fishing, aren't you? You've got no idea why that girl threw herself off. Or if she was murdered or what this is about. How funny.'

The man's smug answers got to Tom. *What a bastard.* 'Perhaps you can enlighten me.' He heard the cold professionalism in his own voice. 'And bear in mind the decision of the parole board. We both know they wouldn't like you denying your previous crimes again. Perhaps it might cause them to review the decision they made to release you.'

Hunt scowled.

'Also, I remember you told me your brother works long hours. I'm sure owning a restaurant is demanding. I don't suppose he uses cannabis to help him with stress, does he? I noticed the odour when you and I talked last time. Perhaps I should mention to my Brighton colleagues they should take a closer look? Maybe they'll consider getting a search warrant for his house, his car. Even his restaurant.'

Hunt held up his hand. 'There's no need for that.'

'Then I'm going to ask you one more time and once only. For what reason did Anne Markham give you this money? How about you explain it to me from the beginning and don't skip anything.'

It turned out Hunt owned a house in Himlands Heath. It had been unoccupied while Hunt was in prison, apart from his brother occasionally checking on it. Hunt had intended to move back.

Hunt knew John Markham had spoken to the parole board and tried to get the early release overturned. It had made Hunt furious. So when Anne Markham contacted him and asked him, in fact, as Hunt described it, *begged him*, to not return to Himlands Heath, Hunt had refused.

Tom didn't like the self-satisfied look on Hunt's face when he said that. The man pushed forward his shoulders and puffed out his cheeks, making like he was king of the hill. King of the dirt hill, more like.

'You decided to profit from their distress and their desire to protect their daughter by extorting money?'

'I didn't extort anything. Anne offered it to me and I generously accepted. They owed it me. I was their friend. They threw me under the bus. At trial, they refused to testify on my behalf.'

Of course they did, because you sexually assaulted their daughter. Tom prevented cutting words escaping his lips. 'What did Anne Markham want in return?'

'She wanted me to stay out of Himlands Heath. She wanted me to sell my house and never come back.'

'And you agreed?'

'For ten thou? Course I did. I never liked that town anyway.'

Anne Markham had, at the very least, made questionable decisions. The poor woman, she must have been desperate to prevent Phoebe ever seeing Hunt again. She had given away vast sums to a known criminal. Yet she had no way of enforcing her will on Hunt.

'I imagine that must have irked. Having to toe the line and do what Anne Markham wanted? Why should she get to decide what you do? You're a free man, aren't you?'

Tom slapped a photograph on the desk. 'This was taken at the train station at 4.20pm on the day of Phoebe's death.'

'It slipped my mind.'

The man did his best at a sneer but the swagger had gone.

'You told me you weren't in Himlands Heath that day. What were you doing? Were you so bitter you couldn't wait to get your revenge on Phoebe Markham?'

'I don't know what you're talking about.'

'You came to Himlands Heath. You frightened Phoebe. Either you followed her back to the hospital, and later that evening, you took your chance and dragged her to the top floor, where you pushed her to her death.' Tom paused. 'Or–'

'That's rubbish! I never went to Moorlands.'

'You came to Himlands Heath. You told me Anne Markham paid you a lot of money to stay away. Now why would you do exactly what you'd agreed not to do, if it wasn't to kill Phoebe?'

'You think I'd risk going back inside?'

'You blamed Phoebe for putting you away.'

'Yes. But I didn't kill her.'

'Then why come to town?'

'To serve them right! That snobby bitch thought she could pay me off.'

'So you want me to believe you came to town, coincidentally on the day Phoebe died, simply to spite Mrs Markham? You're going to have to do better than that. You came to kill.'

'No.'

'You wanted revenge. You must have enjoyed seeing the terror on Phoebe's face when she spotted you in the high street.'

Hunt smirked. 'The little bitch shit her pants. Except it wasn't me who killed her.'

It was confirmation Phoebe had seen him.

'Did it get you excited to see her scared? Like the day you assaulted her in the showers?'

Hunt was shaking his head.

Another thought occurred to Tom. 'How did you know when Phoebe would be in town?'

Right day, right time, right location. Phoebe said she saw him outside the post office which was around the corner from her apartment. She came to do a home visit with the OT. How many people knew about that visit? Not many. One of them must have tipped Hunt off. So he knew exactly where to be and when, in order to frighten Phoebe.

The obvious answer would be Kate or Viktor, the OTs. There were other hospital personnel who knew of the visit – Mrs Nicholson, Doctor Hargreaves, the nurse on duty on Phoebe's ward, who had been Lin. Or perhaps Phoebe's parents.

Hunt was breathing heavily. His lip was curled like a dog about to throw itself into a fight. He leaned across the table. 'I didn't. It was chance.'

'Someone told you. Who was it?'

Hunt laughed. 'You think you're clever, don't you. Wouldn't you like to know?'

It was times like these it was a great shame you couldn't act like in the movies and bust open your suspect's face, or smash their nose down on the table. Hunt was never going to willingly assist the police. What a disgusting example of a human being.

When Tom left Hunt, he phoned Grant.

'It was Anne Markham who gave Hunt the money, not John. She paid him to stay away from their daughter.'

'He admitted to being in town that afternoon?'

'Yes and he admitted to seeing Phoebe. And her seeing him.'

'Did you get his phone?'

'I'm bringing it back with me.'

'There's a chance it'll give us what we need.'

'There's one more thing, boss. The way he talked about it, I'm pretty certain Hunt came back to frighten her. And like Ruby would say, that would have pushed Phoebe more under the control of the killer. I think whoever tipped off Hunt is our murderer.'

Tom was on the outskirts of Himlands Heath when he received a call. It was the truck driver from the cold case.

'Thanks for getting back to me. I wanted to ask about the collision you were involved in.'

'That was ages ago.'

'I know and I know there was no blame on you. In your statement you said Fiona Taylor was using her phone at the time of the accident. Do you remember?'

'Yeah. She was.'

'I suppose you assumed she was making a call. What I'd like to know is, do you think it's possible she was filming?'

Silence. Tom could hear traffic noises in the background. 'Are you still there?'

'Yeah. I'm in the cab on a long-haul. Don't worry, I'm using hands-free. You mean making a video with her phone?'

'Something like that.'

'It happened fast and it was such a long time ago. I dunno. I always assumed she was talking to someone.'

'Think back. Is it possible she was using the camera?'

'She was holding it up, that's all I can tell you. I could see it clear as day. I always thought it was odd she held it sort of highish. Like it was in front of her face almost, rather than in front of her mouth. She wouldn't have been able to see the road properly.'

'Thank you, sir. You've been very helpful.'

Tom felt a buzz of excitement. The conversation wasn't a total confirmation but it told him the lead was worth pursuing.

Chapter 43

The next morning, Emma sat cross-legged on her sofa bed and did a meditation. She'd learned it from Viktor in one of his relaxation classes. When she opened her eyes, the sun was casting a golden glow across the living room wall.

She glanced at Phoebe's keys. The news about the apartment was incredible. How could Phoebe have been so generous. How could she even have planned ahead like that.

Today, she wanted to spend time at the church talking to the rest of their friends so she could finish the memorial in time for Phoebe's service. The Markhams would be holding Phoebe's official service later, meanwhile Brett had organised a time for the self-help group's informal goodbye. Emma's video needed to be ready.

Brett was there when Emma arrived at the church.

'How are you doing today?' he asked.

She didn't feel ready to share the news about the apartment. 'Not so good. But I could be worse.'

Brett rearranged some flowers which were in a vase on top of the piano. 'I'm always here if you need to talk.'

'Thanks. I really want to do a good job with the video. People have been supportive and I don't want to let them down.'

'Have a bit more confidence in yourself, Emma, and yes word has got around. There are quite a few people coming in today because they want to take part in it.'

'Cool. I thought I might do the filming in the garden, if that's all right with you.' And then she would have much less chance to blank out because it generally happened when she was on her own.

'That's a nice idea. There are plenty of shady areas.'

'Yes. And Phoebe loved the garden.'

'She did, didn't she.'

'I'll get started then.'

She went outside and picked a bench under a tree. Leaves overhead filtered the sunlight and gave the space the feeling of a little haven.

There were people milling about the community hall and one by one they came over. Emma recorded their anecdotes. Some also shared photographs taken on group outings. The previous year they had gone to Brighton for the day, the Christmas before they'd cooked a lunch together, and when one of the self-help group members had a baby, they had held a baby shower. They all had special moments they'd shared with Phoebe.

Emma became absorbed in her project. It was enjoyable to draw people out. Amazing too, how everybody reacted differently to the camera.

It wasn't until mid-afternoon she realised how much time had gone by. She'd interviewed more than fifteen people. She stretched her arms. It would be good to head back and get started on the editing.

She sat for a few minutes and let the emotions of the day wash over her. How she regretted not telling Phoebe about her secret plan for them to move to Ireland together. She hadn't told about her first video client either, who was an estate agent, because she'd been scared they would drop out or turn into a dud. On the contrary, they liked her ideas for a humorous promotional clip featuring their staff. In fact, if this assignment went well, she might even land a contract to produce promos for the whole chain of estate agents.

One of Emma's friends had left a sandwich for her. She had just taken a huge bite, when the sound of the piano filtered out to the garden. She choked. A horrible cold sensation raced up her spine. The sandwich fell from her hand, landing in the dirt.

Clutching at the edge of the bench, she willed herself to fight off the panic.

Stay in the present. You're strong. You can do it.

The melody was unmistakable. It was Juliette's song. Her worst trigger.

No. She was shaking and as she clutched at the bench fury raced through her. How dare he. How dare Brett play that song.

She forced herself to her feet and stalked inside. 'What the hell are you doing!'

Brett looked up, astonishment plastered across his face. There were a few people over by the coffee bar and they stared at her.

'I'm picking out some songs for Phoebe,' Brett said. 'Would you like to help?'

'No, I bloody well wouldn't. How dare you play Juliette's song! Nobody has the right. Not now, not ever.'

Nudging his glasses up his nose, Brett squinted. 'I wasn't. I wasn't doing that one. I never would.'

'Liar.' She was hoarse with anger.

Brett pushed back the piano stool and walked across. 'Why don't we talk about this in my office?' There was a calm and reassuring tone in his voice. He appeared concerned and so did other people.

'Don't think you can pretend. I wasn't imagining it. I heard my sister's song.'

'Come on, Emma. Let's talk somewhere private.'

She allowed him to lead her down the hall to his office. It was large with two comfortable chairs by a small table. Brett indicated for her to sit, and he did the same, his arms resting on his knees as he leaned towards her.

'I assure you. I was not playing your sister's song.'

'I heard it.'

'You're mistaken, I was going through a few I thought might be suitable for the ceremony.'

'You told me you never played it again! Not since Murder Day.'

'It's the truth. I never have. Emma, believe me, I wasn't playing your sister's song.'

Her breathing was out of control, as if she were about to have an anxiety attack. And that's when she realised her hands were slippery. She stared at them. They were covered in her sister's blood.

'Emma? Emma, what's going on? You're safe. You're at the church with me and you're safe.'

They were slick and red. She could smell blood and death.

Brett's words faded to a buzz and all she could hear were Juliette's gurgling breaths and the final rasps as life left her.

She was once again in her childhood living room. Her mother was lying dead in the kitchen doorway. Her sister's neck was gashed and no matter how hard she tried she couldn't get it to go back together.

Blood was running over her hands.

Tumbling to the floor, she curled into a ball, and she knew she was screaming her sister's name.

Chapter 44

Grant was bringing John Markham in for questioning when he received a call from Tom. Tom had found out it was Anne Markham who'd transferred the money.

As Grant made eye contact with John in the rear-view mirror he saw the man try not to flinch. In all these years of being fellow survivors Grant always imagined nothing could threaten that bond. Now he knew he was wrong and it gave him an acid taste of disappointment and dismay. 'Is your wife at home?'

'She's not doing well. Please leave her out of this, in the name of all that's holy,' John said, his voice breaking.

'I want to call by your house and pick her up.'

When he made a u-turn, a sobbing escaped John's lips. Grant felt like something inside himself was ripping.

'Please don't drag her along. Surely you can have some compassion. We're friends aren't we? Anne's got more than enough to deal with.'

From behind, John grabbed Grant's shoulder and Diane, who was in the passenger seat, turned and gave a sharp order. 'Take your hand off the DCI immediately or I will place you in handcuffs.'

'I'm begging you, David. I can answer any questions you've got.'

'Unfortunately, I don't think you can,' Grant said. 'No more discussion. We're picking up your wife.'

John caved, bending in half as if he were a shattered man who was trying to hold himself together. He moaned.

'I'd better get in the back,' Diane said. 'Check he's all right.'

Grant pulled over and he gripped the steering wheel as sounds from the back seat brought a memory of the tragedy they'd faced together. John had moaned in the same way back then when they had huddled together. He remembered it so clearly. A few survivors swathed in blankets, so confused, so shocked. One moment they had been many and then they were less.

He shuddered and said a small prayer for the lost and for the remaining, as he always did when he thought of that day. Then he pushed it aside and focused on the present – on Phoebe and Lin and finding who murdered them. That was his priority and his only priority. Not any kinship he might feel for John Markham.

'He's okay. Let's go get Mrs Markham,' Diane said.

Grant stared straight ahead and did all he could to block out the distress coming from the back.

Anne Markham pulled her cardigan around her. The interview room was several degrees cooler than outside and Grant was glad Diane had reminded her to bring something warmer.

'Can I get you a coffee, or a water?' he asked.

'No thank you, David.'

'Detective Inspector Collins is going to be leading the interview,' Grant said.

Diane started the recording and went through the formalities. Then she pushed copies of the bank statements across the table.

'I understand you paid Mr Hunt ten thousand pounds, split into two separate deposits, into his account. I'd like to understand why you did that. Please could you explain it to me.'

'Oh. You know about that, do you? I suppose it was bound to come out. John doesn't know.'

Diane tapped the papers. 'Mrs Markham, you need to explain this. We have to understand what's been going on between you and Hunt.'

'Nothing has been going on. I paid him to stay away.'

'From what?'

'From my daughter. From Himlands Heath.' Anne turned to Grant. 'Don't you see? I did it for her.'

Grant shook his head. 'You should have told me before. This doesn't look good.'

'I don't care how it looks. Hunt was getting out. We were horrified and John did his best to influence the parole board. But that monster managed to manipulate them. They let him out for good behaviour. Can you believe it! He assaulted four girls and he gets out for good behaviour. It's a travesty.'

Diane ran her finger over the figures on the statement. 'And so?'

'I had to protect my daughter. I contacted Hunt and offered to pay him if he never came back here. At first he refused. Or at least, he pretended to refuse although he was simply negotiating. If I had more courage I would have killed him. Taken a gun and–'

'Stop right there,' Diane said. 'Let's focus on what actually happened.'

'We agreed on five thousand. Then he asked for double and I paid it. He said he would live with his brother. That I'd never see or hear from him again.'

Grant's heart sank. How naïve Anne Markham had been. A mother desperate to protect her child. Or was there more at play? The evidence could very well point to a different conclusion. The fact was, Anne Markham could have paid

Hunt to carry out any kind of deed and both she and Hunt could be lying.

'And how did you communicate with Hunt?' Diane asked.

'At the beginning by email and after by phone.'

'Do you have any records of your conversations?'

'I think so. I definitely still have the first email I sent.'

'I need you to hand over your computer and your phone so our technical staff can verify your statement.'

'What? You mean you don't believe me? David, tell her. This is the truth.'

'It's not a question of belief or trust,' Diane said. 'What we need are facts to corroborate what you've told us. If you cooperate and allow us to get what evidence we can from your devices, that can only help the investigation.'

'I don't see how this is going to find Phoebe's killer. Or Lin's.'

'Because it will allow us to eliminate certain lines of enquiry. And by a process of elimination, we get to focus on the ones which matter.'

It was a relief when the interview was over. Grant avoided speaking to Anne or John. He simply led Anne to her husband and then watched from the window as the two of them walked arm in arm across the car park, Anne Markham being supported by her husband.

Some days, he really hated what he had to do. But you didn't get to pick and choose. If you went down that road, before long you looked at yourself in the mirror and saw a dirty cop who bent the rules to suit himself – the sort of officer Grant had made it his job in the past to root out. At the end of the day it was all about justice for the victims. And only about that.

It was another reason Grant had recruited a chunk of his old team for the MIT, because they were the ones who had stood by him when he had gone up against corrupt officers, and senior ones at that.

In a case like this you needed to lean in hard. It caused guilty people to make mistakes. They could expose themselves by their lies and their errors. Diane had done well. They both knew that rather than paying Hunt to stay away, the mother could have paid Hunt to turn up.

'Are you okay?' Diane asked Grant.

'Not really. I feel sorry for them and then the next minute I have to remind myself they might be the ones manipulating us.'

'Yeah, I know what you mean. Let's see what her emails and texts tell us.' Diane sighed. 'How's it going with your daughter, have you patched it up yet?'

'I haven't had the time though Ruby gave me a brilliant idea. I'm going to invite Chrissie to a little tea shop we used to go to when she was small. It's by the river. We used to go for a walk and then have tea and cake. I want to do the same again and we can talk and connect. Ruby reminded me it's the simple things which matter.'

'She's right. Ruby's got a wise head on young shoulders. One thing though, and you're not going to like it – if we haven't got our killer, you're going to have to break the habit of a lifetime and put the case second to fit in that tea shop, you know that don't you.'

'I do. Are you and Tom going to gang up on me again?'

She shrugged. 'Oh yes. If that's what it takes.'

'There's also a massive risk I'll miss the wedding rehearsal. It's in a few days.' Grant raised his hands in surrender. 'Don't worry, I've a contingency plan. My son's come home early and he's ready to stand in for me, not for the ceremony itself, only for the rehearsal. He's going to video the whole thing.'

Diane shook her head. 'You're cutting this one fine.'

'I can't help it. As long as I can fit in the river walk and the cake, that's all Chrissie and I need.' Grant rubbed his forehead. 'John Markham's done my head in. At the end of today, meet me at the office and bring the others please. There's something I need to tell you.'

Chapter 45

I hear Lin's parents are struggling to cope. Good. Don't they realise she deserved to die?

'What do you think of the video, Mother?'

Mother is lying in bed. Grey and shell-like, she has prolonged periods where she refuses to eat or drink. My mother hasn't spoken for years. She's not physically incapable of speech – she still possesses her tongue – but she's sunk into such a severe depressed state she's what they call catatonic. They say it runs in families. Is this what I have to look forward to? If so, even more reason to crack on with the fun.

'I said, what do you think of Lin's death, Mother?'

Her eyes are glistening as she stares into space. I know she can hear me. I know she's in there somewhere. When I show her the videos, I see the flicker in her eyes. Oh Mother, you will respond to me, one way or another. You and I are alike, we enjoy the same things.

'All right if you're going to spoil it for me, have it your own way, don't respond. I won't tell you who my next target is then.'

I huff my shoulders and turn away.

She liked the one of Phoebe but it seems Lin's death hasn't caught her attention. Still, I'll be showing her a new video soon because the third on my list is close to her breaking point. That girl is an elastic band stretched over taut. One more millimetre and she'll snap.

I can judge these things. Because while some people know how to make people better. I know how to make them worse.

Chapter 46

It was coming to the end of a long day. Grant took a detour to pass by the cemetery. In a sheltered spot, a plaque listing the names of the lost had been set into the wall. In front of it was a patch of garden, planted with pansies and in the centre of the flowers sat a stone teddy bear. It always made Grant's heart ache.

He had been there many times since he was a boy. At first, often, though he told nobody. As the years passed, his visits became less frequent, falling mostly on the anniversary or at New Year, or the beginning of the school term.

It was time to tell his team. It was only fair for them to know the link between him and John Markham and how, when they were both seven, they had gone on a school trip which had ended in disaster. Sixteen children had left. Three of them had been lost and one had been scarred beyond recognition.

Grant lay a small bouquet of roses on the lap of the teddy bear. The tragedy was one of the reasons he had decided to become a police officer. Grant had been helped from the wreckage by a uniformed constable. They'd kept in contact and many years later when Grant completed his training at police college, the man had come to Grant's passing out parade. Grant remembered how they had both cried.

Having to treat John Markham so cold-heartedly had gone against every instinct in him yet that was his job and he was at peace with it.

Sending a message to Diane saying he'd be there in five minutes, he left the graveyard.

Tom received a message from the Crime Scene Manager, Sejal, saying she had an update. Could this be the golden nugget that would break the case? *Chances are slim to nothing. So don't fool yourself, Delaney. Just do your job and do it well. There are no miracles in detective work.*

He rushed back to headquarters and found the CSM waiting for him.

'You've got a nice set-up here,' Sejal said. 'Lucky for some, isn't it.'

Tom gave her a good-natured smile. He didn't know if the white streak in Sejal's hair was natural or if she had bleached it, but it suited her. He sensed a bit of a combative manner, or maybe she was used to having to defend her corner. She was probably about the same age as him. Either way, all he was interested in was the information, not a sparring match.

'It's a step up from our old office, that's for sure. What have you got for us?'

'It's about the dark web. The techies confirm Phoebe Markham and Lin Chen posted to the same place.'

'Great.'

'They've been all-out on this one. They've made up identities and created false accounts. They wanted to find out what kind of site it was and their first guess was a chat site. Then they thought maybe an auction where people paid to buy or view a video.'

Tom realised he'd forgotten to offer Sejal a drink, which was probably a mistake. But this was important stuff and he wanted to hear it all. He nodded, to keep her talking.

'Yeah well, their final conclusion was it's not a chat nor an auction site.'

'What is it then?'

'They think it's a secure messaging service. Given it's housed on the dark web, it means people can exchange in secret. They're fairly certain Phoebe and Lin streamed their last videos to only one person. And it was the same person.'

'Who?'

'That's the bummer. They don't know and there's no way they can find out. Believe me, they've had their top hackers on it, trying to get more info and trying to recover the videos themselves. They were gutted they couldn't make it. That's why I thought I should come over and tell you myself. It's the end of the road. No identity and no videos.'

Tom rested his forehead on the wall. 'Shit.'

'Before the team briefing, there's something I need to tell you,' Grant said.

Tom sat with the others in the office. He'd told them the bad news from Sejal. Everyone was as disappointed as he had been. Now Grant had something personal he wanted to tell them before the briefing. Tom looked straight at Grant, to prevent himself exchanging glances with Ruby and Diane.

'Like I told you, John and I have known each other since we were children. It's not unusual in a town like Himlands Heath although the link I have with John is more uncommon than most. I thought it's time I explain rather than you speculating and relying on gossip.'

Grant went on to tell them about the trip to a remote hostel. Of the fire which started in the night. How the children were trapped in their dormitories. Of the flames and the smoke and the panic, and how three children perished and one was so badly burned they thought he would not survive. Grant said he and John had been together when the fire started. Their part of the building had partially collapsed.

'Ironically, it was the collapse which saved us from the worst of it,' Grant said. 'It took them a long time to get us out of the wreckage. Perhaps I was wrong to have taken on the investigation into Phoebe's death. When I saw Phoebe's body and the first details were coming to light, I couldn't let it go.'

'You couldn't let it go because you felt a loyalty to John Markham,' Ruby said.

'Yes. At the beginning it was wrong of me to question the Markhams on my own.'

'You didn't know it would get so tangled,' Diane said. 'Or Anne Markham would pay Hunt off.'

'No, but it would've been better if I'd kept the lines clearer and told you everything from the beginning. I've always stressed how vital it is to be professional at all times. I didn't follow my own rules.'

'You are now,' Diane said. 'The fact is we need to keep the case. We're too far in to pull out.'

Tom gave his tea a stir. 'I knew there was a story, I just didn't know what it was. I'm glad you told us.'

'Diane's right,' Ruby said. 'We have to carry on.'

'Are there any other questions?' Grant asked. 'No? Then let's head to the incident room and get on with it.'

Chapter 47

Tom slurped from his mug.

'The cause of death for the mother was blunt force trauma to the head,' Grant said. 'Basically, she was bludgeoned to death. Juliette's throat was slashed and she bled to death from a severed jugular.'

Grant thumped the board. 'As you know, two days later Mrs White's second husband, Smith, was found dead. Cause of death carbon monoxide poisoning. The knife used to kill Juliette was with him.'

Grant recapped how the police investigation uncovered a number of arguments, overheard by the neighbours. Smith was jealous of his wife's ex-husband and when Mr White was invited to Emma's sixth birthday party, this was thought to have been the ignition point for Smith's murderous rampage.

'What about Emma?' Diane asked. 'How was it she survived?'

'Good question,' Tom said. 'I was wondering that.'

Ruby came forward. 'There was no explanation for why Emma was spared. After the body of Smith was found, the police closed the case. There's no similarity between the vicious killings of the White family and the death of Phoebe and Lin. The only common link is Brett Sinclair. He has a relationship with Phoebe which he could have used. But his link to Lin was flimsy.'

Diane nodded. 'At the time of the White family murders, how could a nineteen-year-old have subdued Smith, a grown man who was known to be violent, and then staged Smith's death and presented Smith as the murderer? I don't see it.'

'Me neither. Right, let's move on. And I know it's a damn blow we won't get the videos nor the ID of the person they were sent to. It means it's going to be down to detective work,' Grant said. 'What else have we got?'

'I've come up with more details to add to the picture of our killer,' Ruby said.

Grant pointed to the board. 'All yours.'

'I've been looking for patterns,' Ruby said. 'A video was streamed from both victims. This has to mean something to the killer. Like I said, is it symbolic? A memento? What's its purpose? The killer risked the phone being analysed. They knew we'd find out about the dark web and they weren't bothered. Which means they know about hacking and technology. They knew they would be safe. It tells us they're intelligent, organised, able to plan over a long timespan to achieve their desired goal. Also, able to put other pieces of the picture into place, such as Hunt spooking Phoebe that afternoon and Lin's sister dying hours beforehand.'

Grant wrote up the keywords for Ruby.

'Next, geographical information. This person knows Himlands Heath and Moorlands. We have to assume they know the location of Phoebe's apartment, or at least, knew the route Phoebe would take on the day of her home visit.'

'Do you still stick by your conclusion this doesn't have to be a professional?' Grant asked.

'Absolutely. Long-term patients have as much insight into the mind as staff. They might not have the theoretical framework but that's not as important. Here, it's the practical side they have to be master of. Plenty of patients know exactly how words and suggestions can be used against someone and can be planted powerfully in their mind. They understand how to break someone's resolve. How to foster dependence. Those are the foundation of mind control and hypnosis.'

'Right.'

'The victims are both young women. I think this is significant too.'

'You mean the killer likes messing with girls?' Tom asked.

'There's no evidence of a sexual motive,' Grant said.

'Though remember, Lin was wearing only her underwear in the bath,' Diane said. 'And Phoebe had on a flimsy nightdress. Not sexual, but there could be a voyeuristic element to the murders.'

'You're right.' Grant was studying the bullet points. 'One other thing – we've got to presume the killer is planning another murder.'

'If this is a sociopath, it's a certainty,' Ruby said.

Grant took a drink from his mug. 'You know what I'm thinking about the White murders? It's a bit of a shot in the dark, but who else might have been involved? Who is around today who would have been around fifteen years ago? What about the idea of Brett having been involved in the White murders and working with an accomplice? I can't help feeling there could be something in that.'

Tom stared at Grant. It was an interesting idea. Had the boss done it again? Come up with a leap which would propel them forward?

'Someone who was around then who's also around today?' Diane said. 'Maybe.'

'One person we can eliminate from the list is Mike Otremba. The signal strength data from the phone call places him close to his home,' Tom said.

'Anything from the cold cases, Tom?'

'I've one which might be interesting. Three years ago, a woman was killed near here in a car accident. She was using her mobile at the time of the crash. There was a question about whether she killed herself deliberately or lost control of the car. That question came up because she'd recently been told her cancer had returned and was now inoperable. I spoke to the driver and he said it's possible she could have been filming. I'm digging into her case to find out everything I can.'

'All right. Keep at it. Meanwhile, dig for somebody who could have been around fifteen years ago. A person who might have tipped off Hunt. Who fits our profile.'

'It would be worth speaking to Anne Markham again,' Diane said. 'Find out if she knew the Whites.'

'Agreed, take Ruby with you. For now, everyone go home and get some sleep.'

They went next door to pack up their things.

'Boss,' Tom said. 'What about the rehearsal for Chrissie's wedding? I've set an alarm thirty minutes before.'

Diane tapped her phone. 'Me too.'

'Right. Well, we'll see how that pans out. Thanks. Have a good night everyone.' Grant swept up his jacket and left.

'What are the odds he doesn't make it,' Tom said under his breath. It wasn't that Tom wanted the boss to miss it, he was simply being realistic.

'I hope he does this time,' Diane said.

Tom held the door open for Diane while Ruby switched off the lights. 'I bet you a lunch he won't,' he said.

'Don't be so sure of yourself,' Diane said. 'You're on.'

'Tom, you're a hypocrite,' Ruby said. 'You're going to be just the same as Grant. You'd probably even miss your own wedding if a case was coming to a head at the wrong time.'

'Who says I'm going to get married?'

'I do. You're the marrying type.'

'And what about you?'

'Not so much. Though I might come around.'

What did that mean? Was she teasing him?

Ruby and Diane laughed then walked along the corridor together, leaving Tom shaking his head.

Chapter 48

The memorial service at the community hall had been planned for the self-help group. However, so many centre users asked if they could come that Brett made it open house. Emma didn't mind because she'd already interviewed lots of people outside their group for the video. She spotted Grant sitting in the back row. Ruby was there too.

Emma went to find Brett. Did she feel embarrassed? A little. She had known Brett for so long, and he had known her in her darkest days. Although now, Emma wanted to be better. Brett being a counsellor didn't mean she could collapse all over him and not feel bad about it. Screaming on the floor and accusing him of playing Juliette's song had been going too far.

Brett had brought her down from her panic attack, he had consoled her and accompanied her home safely. He had offered to set up an emergency appointment with her psychiatrist, which Emma refused. They both knew the anniversary of Murder Day was coming up.

She found Brett in the kitchen where he was fussing with plates. People had brought food for sharing after the gathering.

'We're never going to be able to eat this lot. Hi.'

'Hello,' Brett said. 'You look nice.'

She had chosen a dress for the occasion. One which Phoebe had picked out from the Oxfam shop. 'Thanks, you too.'

He was wearing a colourful shirt, which was unusual. They had agreed today would be an occasion for bright colours.

Emma shifted uncomfortably. 'I'm sorry about yesterday. You know, all the screaming and everything.'

'No need. Let's concentrate on the ceremony, shall we? How are you doing?'

'I'm good. I'm so nervous about the video. I hope our friends like it.'

'I know they will.'

'Thank you for the gift.' He had sent chocolates which had been unexpected and very touching.

Brett blushed. 'You deserve it.'

'This is a mountain of food.' She pushed a plate of sausage rolls away from the edge of the table. 'Shall I load the video onto the laptop?'

'Yes please. The projection is set up.'

Emma went next door. Their friends had given their favourite photographs of Phoebe, and Brett had printed them off and created a wall of pictures. The room looked lovely. Candles and flowers were dotted about, as well as a number of Phoebe's paintings.

Chairs were arranged in a semi-circle. Emma passed along the row, exchanging hugs with her friends. She took her place towards the middle.

The memorial was informal. One of their friends had brought his guitar and they sang together. Another person read a poem they had written in memory of Phoebe and then Brett played an Elton John song on the piano. Then it was time for the video.

Emma was hot and sticky from stress. She knew every word of it by heart and she scrutinised the faces around her as they sat through the film. To her astonishment, people laughed in the right places, they oohed and aahed at the right moments, and there was plenty of dabbing at the eyes and sobbing as they listened to each other's memories of the girl they had lost.

At the end, everybody was tearful. They congratulated Emma and she felt so relieved. Thank goodness. Her very first video had been a success.

It was a strange truth that mourning a loss in company could bring about a feeling of jubilation. Life suddenly felt more precious and more carefree. The plates of food were carried in and they helped themselves. Everyone was chatting loudly, talking in an uninhibited way which they seldom did.

Emma felt a nudge at her shoulder and she turned.

Ruby had found the ceremony very moving. 'It was a lovely occasion,' she said. 'You did a great job with the video.'

'Thanks. It's been a rough twenty-four hours getting it finished. I wouldn't have managed it without Brett.'

Grant looked in Ruby's direction. He was asking her to probe.

'Brett seemed to be nicely in control without making himself centre stage,' Ruby said.

'I had a bit of a collapse yesterday, with the strain of it all. He looked after me. Again. He even bought me a gift.'

'More flowers?'

'Chocolates. Expensive ones too.'

'That was nice of him. Maybe he was being a bit romantic?'

'You kidding me? Of course not. He's like a big brother to me, nothing slimy. If I didn't have him shoring me up I'd be in pieces by now.'

'We were wondering,' Grant said. 'Apart from Brett, is there anyone you know today who your mother knew? Did she know the Markhams?'

'No way. Phoebe went to some posh school. We moved in very different circles.'

'What about people at the hospital?'

'I don't think so.' She shrugged. 'I was so young. No one's talked about knowing my mum if that's what you mean. Why?'

Grant didn't answer the question. 'We'll let you go now. It was a touching video.'

Ruby put her arm around Emma's shoulders. 'Yes, it was. You did well today, Emma, really well.'

Chapter 49

Emma awoke feeling groggy. Her tongue was stuck to the roof of her mouth and the air was stuffy and stale. She rolled off the sofa bed, rubbed her eyes, and got dressed slowly.

She knew today would be hard to get through. The anniversary of Murder Day was coming up and she owed her father a visit. She had been putting it off. On the anniversary itself, she preferred to be on her own, which was why she always went to her father's nursing home a few days beforehand.

Taking a banana, she ate it while she waited for her piece of toast to be done. This was always a bad time of year but this year it was so much worse.

The care home was a bus ride away. She had not yet had the heart to collect Phoebe's car. It would remind her too painfully of what had been lost. Would the seats hold the scent of Phoebe? She wasn't ready for it. She'd got through the memorial. Now she must get through the anniversary.

Her father was sitting by the window in the communal lounge. He had diminished since she last saw him. His white, wispy hair had not been washed. He wore slippers and baggy trousers and a shirt she did not recognise. Mixing up of the residents' laundry happened all the time.

She placed her hand over his and kissed his cheek.

He was thin and the nurses often told her he did not eat well, and she had the impression he was fading away. It wasn't just his body which was growing weak, his mind was too, because her father had dementia. It was the reason he lived in a care home.

'Hello my darling,' he said.

It was a good sign. He didn't always recognise her.

Pulling a chair alongside, she ignored an elderly woman who was sitting in the corner. The woman called out every few minutes, 'Marion! Marion!' She had dementia too, they all did there, and who Marion was, or had been, was anyone's guess. A carer came in and put on some classical music, and the woman calmed a little and waved her hands in the air as if she were conducting the music.

'I'm so glad to see you,' her father said. 'Do you like your new bicycle?'

Emma's heart plummeted. It wasn't a good day for him after all. He was talking about the bicycle he had bought for her sixth birthday and had intended to give her on Murder Day. It was sky-blue with silver handlebars, just as she'd always wanted.

'I love it, Dad.'

He squeezed her hand. 'You'll be able to ride it anywhere you want. I'll teach you.'

Emma had gone to live with her father after her mother's death. A long time after Murder Day, he had taught her to ride. When he first became confused, Emma had cared for him but the dementia kept progressing and by the time Emma was sixteen he had moved into a care home. Since then, he had gone downhill.

She wondered if a part of him knew the anniversary approached, since he never asked about the bicycle except at this time of year. She settled down and started telling her father a long story about the video contract. He smiled, and oohed and aahed and congratulated her. And for those few minutes time stood still, and everything seemed right with the world.

When she left, Emma promised herself she would try to hold on to the feeling. It might help her to get through the next few days.

Chapter 50

I'd been working on Lin for a while.

It's been a tragic journey for her family, caring for Naomi. Still, it was wonderfully convenient for me because the sister was a valuable lever.

When the blow came from Dignitas, I sensed my moment of triumph was close.

'How could they turn Naomi down?' I shouted. 'She's exactly the sort of person they're supposed to help.'

It devastated Lin. It was fun to see her despair. With Naomi nearing the end of life, there was no way another doctor was going to overturn Naomi's depression diagnosis. Lin knew it, I knew it, and so did Naomi – of which fact I reminded Lin on several, well-timed, occasions. When someone is drowning in anguish, I enjoy pushing their head under.

What about Phoebe? Well, as for her, I capitalised on Phoebe being eyeballed by Hunt. It was masterly how I orchestrated that encounter. It's what pushed Phoebe over the edge.

To be honest, I feel my real forte, apart from ridding the world of vermin, is knowing how to play with someone. Knowing the words which go deep and burrow into their wounds causing agony.

When a person's resistance has been beaten out of them by the injustices of life, it's easy to slyly slip in suggestions. With Lin, I told her the things she wanted to hear – your parents will understand, Naomi deserves a dignified death, you're the one who can do it. Then I moved to the next stage – the pact with her sister and the only way the two of them could find peace.

Peace was what they craved. A silence to their crippling pain.

Lin had always tortured herself for being the lucky one. The one born disease-free. Why do you think she worked herself into the ground for her sister? It wasn't love. It was the torment of guilt.

Lucky for me Lin felt it was her fault what happened to Phoebe. If she had been more vigilant that night, if she had realised something was wrong, if she had seen, if she had heard, and on and on. It was the final straw I used to inch Lin right to the edge.

I tell them it's okay. I tell them it's the only way. And having battled with their despair, and worked with it, and fought with it and lost, they know I'm right.

Chapter 51

When Emma returned from visiting her father, she felt as if all the strength had been sucked out of her. She lay down. Would the nightmare about her sister return that night? She had a horrible premonition it would. She had no resistance left. Her life was shit and it always would be – just one long battle against the inevitable torture of standing by and seeing the people she loved die.

You can make it. Once Murder Day is gone, you must carry on living. Life goes on.

But what kind of life? Was it worth it? Just so she could get ripped apart again and again.

She knew that despairing voice inside her from the dark days of her PTSD.

Don't listen to it. This will pass.

Sunlight dappled the ceiling and its patterns danced around the lamp and shimmered off the wall and the corner of Phoebe's painting. Suddenly she sat bolt upright, her breath trapped in her throat. The apartment seemed to close in on her and the darkness rushed in, threatening to tip her world.

It's not real.

She swallowed. Sunlight glanced off the waves of Phoebe's painting and they also reflected off a thread of silver hanging from the corner of the frame. A necklace. One Emma knew well.

You'll see. When you go there it won't be real.

She forced herself to her feet. She could hear her own raspy breaths. Taking tiny steps, she kept her hand stretched out in front, shuffling forward like someone from her father's nursing home.

When her fingers contacted the string of three freshwater pearls, she let out a strangled cry.

It was real. The pearls were misshapen and there was no mistaking it.

It was Juliette's necklace, the one Emma had wanted to borrow for the party.

When Emma came to, she was lying on the floor with the necklace clutched in her hand. Her mind was reeling as she picked up her mobile. She needed help. The question was, who to ask? Brett would have been her first choice except the police had been asking questions about him. Who would be her next best bet?

A while later, the intercom buzzed and she crawled to it.

'Emma, it's Ruby.'

'Please come up,' she croaked.

When Ruby arrived she found Emma on her knees. 'Thank you for coming. I didn't know who else to call.'

'What's wrong?' Ruby put her arms around Emma. 'What's happened?'

She held up the necklace, as if would explain everything.

They sat for a while on the floor and then Ruby helped her up. 'Let's sit and you can tell me what's going on.'

Emma felt as cold as if it were a winter's day. She was shaking so much, Ruby searched for a jumper to put around her shoulders. Then Ruby made a hot tea. Emma was still clutching the necklace.

'Tell me about the necklace, was it Phoebe's?'

'Juliette's.'

'It belonged to your sister. Okay.'

'On Murder Day, I was going to ask Juliette if I could borrow it. Minutes before she was killed. My dad kept it and when I was sixteen he gave it to me. Ever since, it's been stored with my special thing–'

Emma stumbled to the kitchen, banging into a cupboard on the way. She yanked open a drawer. It was full of cutlery, and at the back was a keepsake box. She opened the lid and feverishly raked through the contents. It was impossible to tell if anything was missing, so she tipped it upside down on the bed and laid out the precious items one by one.

'Is everything there? This is your special box, right?'

'Yes. Nothing else is gone.' She sagged. 'Juliette's necklace was inside. Somebody hung it on Phoebe's painting. I found it when I got home.'

'How is that possible? Are you saying you didn't take it out yourself?'

'Of course I didn't!'

'Who else knows about the box?'

'No one.'

Ruby went to check the windows. 'We're four floors up. Nobody can get in except by the front door. Does anyone have a key to your place?'

'No. Unless...'

Would Ruby judge her? Most people would be scared, or think she was mad, although Emma had the impression Ruby might understand.

'I don't know. I've not been doing good. My PTSD has got worse since Phoebe died. It's always worse this time of year because it's the anniversary of when my mother and Juliette were killed. I get hallucinations. I get memory blanks and then I don't remember what I've been doing or how I got to places.'

'Are you saying you *could have* taken out the necklace and not realised it?'

'That's the thing. I don't know for sure. Though I don't *feel* I did it. It's not what I'd do. It's difficult to explain but when I have memory blanks I end up in a place I don't remember going to, but I've never done odd things. I don't see why I would put up Juliette's necklace. Part of me would know it would freak me out.'

Except there had been one other time recently when another odd thing had happened, hadn't there – when her journal had ended up at Phoebe's apartment.

She'd always thought the pearls were beautiful. She fingered them.

'It's scary not knowing if my mind is playing tricks. Do you think I'm going mad?'

'You were never mad, Emma. You lived through a traumatic experience and it took you time to recover. Those memories are still there even though you've worked to dilute them. It's natural they get stirred up. They've not got the same hold over you they once did.'

'Sometimes I feel they have.'

'That's normal. Remember, you're much stronger than you think.' Ruby smoothed out the sofa cover. 'Do you mind if I ask about when Mr Markham told you Phoebe left you her apartment?'

'What about it?'

'There was a notebook and you said it was yours. I got the feeling you were acting… I don't know, strangely. Like something was going on and you didn't want anyone to know.'

Emma almost laughed. This woman was too perceptive for her own good. 'If you must know, it was my journal. It'd gone missing. I never take it outside my apartment and then it turned up at Phoebe's. It threw me.'

'First your journal turns up at Phoebe's. Now your sister's necklace has been moved. I'm glad you talked to me.'

'There's something else. Sometimes I see my hands dripping in my sister's blood. I can smell it. I feel it, slippery and warm. I hear the horrible noises she made as she died. To be perfectly honest my whole life is falling apart. The other day, I even heard Juliette's song playing at the church. It was the one she hummed the afternoon she died.'

Ruby put her arm around Emma's shoulders. 'Perhaps your mind is playing tricks although I can't help thinking there might be a different explanation.'

'Which is?'

'Someone is playing with you.'

Chapter 52

I'm too smart for those doltish detectives. The journal was a masterly touch and now the necklace – I'm so brilliant, sometimes I surpass myself. Of course, I know the ins and outs of the White family saga. I've spoken to Emma about her fears and her struggles. We've discussed her nightmares and hallucinations. I know the right buttons to press to nudge her to the precipice.

With the anniversary of the White murders coming up, the timing is ideal.

Do I think she's ready? To be honest, she's more of the challenge than the others.

Can I be the one to break her? Can I use her own weakness against her?

I have a way to take that girl so close to the edge she'll never come back.

I'm so glad I kept all the props for Murder Day.

Chapter 53

Emma had lost track of the time. The necklace had unhinged her. If she believed in herself and she wasn't actually losing it, then like Ruby said, the only other explanation was someone was playing with her mind.

How could that be possible? Yet Emma knew enough about psychology to realise an adept person could unpick you piece by piece. They could break down your resistance and build up your fears and paranoia.

After Ruby left, and Emma sat turning events over in her mind, a horrible thought occurred to her. Was that what they'd done to Phoebe? Was that why the police hadn't yet got someone behind bars? The idea enraged her. Phoebe was often anxious and frightened. Only a truly evil person would toy with someone in such a vulnerable state. And what about Lin? Could the same thing have happened to her?

Emma pressed her fists to her temples. No, it could not be true. She was letting her imagination get the better of her. Except the more she thought about it, the more it made sense.

She would kill them. She would literally kill them with her bare hands. Who the hell could it be?

Ruby had been asking about Brett. It couldn't be him, or could it? What about him playing Juliette's song and then denying it? Or had that in fact been her own mind tricking her? She beat her fists into the cushions.

When she recovered from the fit of fury, she stared at the patterns made by the sun and let them calm her. If someone had broken Phoebe's mind it was the perfect crime. It would be done in secret and the police would never find out.

She gazed at her friend's painting. Wait. There was one way to expose the killer. Play along. Play into their hands. If someone was toying *with her* by using her journal and her necklace then she would go along with it and flush them out. Perhaps spread the idea she had suspicions who the killer might be.

The question was, could she do it? Was she strong enough to withstand their games?

Do it for Phoebe. You can get evidence and take it to the police.

The idea frightened her because she knew how weak she had become.

Find the bastard.

She could drop a few hints with members of the self-help group. Maybe speak to patients at Moorlands. Word would soon get around and it might bring the killer back to her.

How else could she dangle herself like bait? Phoebe and Lin had been at a low ebb and she must make it known she was too. She stared at the ceiling. What would she do if she feared for her own sanity? That was easy, because she had already considered it several times in the last few days – she would go to see her psychiatrist, Doctor Hargreaves.

Brett had been trying to encourage her to do exactly that. The only reason Emma had resisted was because the thought of going back to Moorlands terrified her and she had vowed she'd never take medication again. But no, that was wrong thinking because the killer might be watching. She shouldn't be staying away from Moorlands she should be going there.

Do it for Phoebe.

Emma picked up her mobile and made the call.

Chapter 54

Emma was sweating so much her shirt stuck to her back. Doctor Hargreaves was sitting opposite in a summer dress with a deep v-neck. She looked so cool and collected. Sometimes, Emma hated her psychiatrist.

'Thank you for fitting me in at short notice,' Emma said, and she was ashamed how pathetic her voice sounded. It was always the same at Moorlands – she regressed to a child.

'It must have been hard for you after we lost Phoebe. I'm glad you've come in.'

Emma bit her lip and nodded.

'I hear you've been talking to the patients. We've spoken before haven't we, about how you should bring your troubles to me and not to them.'

'I'm sorry. I came a bit early for my appointment so I went by the ward to see friends. It's been such a sad time.'

'It's a sad time and a struggle not just for you. Other patients have their own difficulties to deal with. Stirring up fear and suspicion doesn't help anybody.'

'That's not what I was doing.'

Doctor Hargreaves pressed her lips together and sighed loudly, making it clear she was annoyed. 'Do you have a suspicion about who Phoebe's murderer might be?'

'No.'

'Because if you do, you should tell me.'

Emma wiped perspiration from her temple. 'I really don't have any idea.'

'All right.'

It didn't sound like it was all right. Doctor Hargreaves seemed angry. Emma wriggled in her seat and avoided the doctor's gaze.

'Of course, with the anniversary being so close, it must be a struggle for you. Would you like to talk a little about it? Did you go to see your father?'

'Yes. He was in good spirits but it's been hard,' she muttered.

There was a long and awkward silence.

'And have you been hallucinating again?'

It was like having your deepest wounds exposed for discussion. This was the reason she had wanted to avoid coming here because there was nothing private. All her failures were out in the open, instead of being sheltered and protected.

'Yes. Of my sister's blood on my hands. I had that once or twice. And then I thought I heard Juliette's song playing. And I blanked out, I think only once.'

'Anything else?'

As if that were not enough? Emma fidgeted. Should she tell about the journal and the necklace? She didn't want to. She sat on her hands and stared at the doctor's shiny bracelets.

'As I said, I know the anniversary is hard. You are the girl who survived. We've talked before about survivor's guilt and how you blame yourself. You once believed it was your fault your mother and sister were killed. Let's talk a little about that, shall we? Is that how you feel today?'

Well, she *was* to blame, wasn't she? She was the one who'd wanted to invite her father in the first place. It had triggered horrible friction between her mother and stepfather. She was the one who started the whole tragedy. And then she survived.

She had been upstairs while her mother and her sister were dying.

'Uh huh.'

'Could you say more? You're not very talkative today, Emma.'

'It's like everything's coming undone. I can't hold myself together.'

'That's understandable. I think it would be best if you spend a short time at Moorlands. I know you're resistant to the idea. But I think that's why you've come to see me today, isn't it? Because you know you need help. In this difficult period it's important to have professional support. I can prescribe a course of medication.'

Her whole body was shaking and she wanted to run.

'Thank you, doctor. I don't want to come to Moorlands. I want to try to see myself through this on my own.'

Doctor Hargreaves frowned and tapped her fingers on the arm of her chair. 'From everything you've said today, I think it's clear you're not able to manage.'

Emma swallowed. She understood the Mental Health Act enough to know Doctor Hargreaves didn't have enough to section her and keep her in hospital against her will. She was not a risk to herself. Not yet anyway. Was Hargreaves the killer? Emma knew she must make the murderer come to her, not walk like a lamb into a trap.

'Please let me try. If I have pills it might take the edge off.'

'If that's what you prefer I'll write you a prescription. Though you really must ask yourself, is this the wisest choice?'

The doctor's tone was clipped. She was annoyed again. Emma braced herself and put up with being chastised as if she were a naughty schoolgirl. Hargreaves knew how to exert authority over patients in subtle ways, such as acidic disapproval. In fact, she was known for it.

Emma clutched at the arms of her chair. Had Hargreaves somehow planted the journal and the necklace to try to unhinge her? Was Phoebe's murderer right in front of her?

'If you change your mind, you can contact reception and we'll see if there's a bed free. The problem is I can't make any promises.'

'Thank you,' she muttered, and she couldn't wait to get out the door and into the fresh air.

Was it Hargreaves? What was going to be the doctor's next move?

Emma knew she must be ready, for whatever was sprung on her.

Chapter 55

'I wanted to check, there were no gifts found at Phoebe's, nor at Lin's, am I right?' Grant asked.

Grant was driving to Moorlands and he had Sejal on speakerphone.

'Nothing which was identified as a gift, no,' Sejal said. 'There were a few jewellery items at Lin's which might have been gifts in the past. Did you have anything specific in mind?'

'Were there any flowers or chocolates? Or the remains or signs of them?'

'Definitely not.'

The SOCOs had forensically scoured Lin's place. Search officers had methodically searched both Lin's and Phoebe's apartments.

'There's nothing which stood out,' Sejal said. 'If there was anything, it would have been flagged already.'

'It's unusual for a killer to leave no trace. There was nothing on CCTV cameras either to show any of our potential suspects coming or going.'

'Don't get disheartened,' Sejal said.

'I'm not.'

'I've heard you're not exactly a second-rate DCI.'

'You're big on the compliments then,' he said, wryly.

Her laugh was unexpected, and very nice to hear. 'Keep me posted. This is your first MIT case. It can't beat us,' she said.

It didn't escape his notice Sejal used the word 'us'. At least something was going right – he'd pulled her onboard.

'That's a promise,' he said.

Grant believed what he had told his team, that there was no such thing as a perfect crime – but where the hell were they going to find it.

Tom was checking through the background searches on their suspects. Who had tipped off Hunt about Phoebe's home visit? It was the OT department which had organised it, though as he checked through the team's initial searches it didn't seem anything had been missed – Kate and Viktor had no convictions, no cautions, no blemishes on their careers.

He was about to throw his headphones down in frustration when the phone rang. It was the doctor who had treated the crash victim.

A few moments later Tom punched the air and put in a call to Grant.

'Guv, I've got something!'

He heard traffic in the background and Grant indicating to pull over.

'What?'

'It's the cold case. Viktor is our man. The car crash victim was under the care of the hospice and at that time, Viktor was part of their team.'

Chapter 56

Emma was sitting at home clutching her knees. She was trembling as if she had taken the pills Hargreaves gave her, yet she had thrown them in the bin. Why was she shaking so much? Was she plain terrified?

She sniffed at her clothes. Moorlands had left the same stink it always did. It brought all the bad memories of being out of control and of being treated like a failure.

Her thoughts ping-ponged between Phoebe and Lin. Had somebody manipulated them? Used their own pain against them? Were they doing the same to her now? Emma clasped her hands between her knees.

Remember you went to Moorlands for a reason. If someone's coming for you, you'd better be ready.

Closing her eyes, she concentrated on her video project and the plans which the buyer had praised.

You've made something of your own. You've got a life worth living.

The negative thoughts tried to overpower her. They were like a swarm cutting off the light. Was this how Phoebe felt, after she'd seen Hunt? Trying to convince herself to keep going. Trying to hold onto self-belief as it slipped through her fingers?

All Emma wanted to do was get into bed and stay there. Yet she was waiting. For what? For a sign. For the killer to show themselves.

She must have zoned out, because she was dragged back to consciousness by a banging on the door.

It was her neighbour – the one who had been there for fifteen years.

Emma pushed her hair out of her eyes. Who cared if she looked a mess? There was no need to make excuses in front of a neighbour who pretty much always had bad days.

'This came for you while you were out.'

It was a package, about shoe box size.

'Oh right, thanks. Who delivered it?'

'Some courier guy.'

The neighbour shuffled off and Emma slammed the door. She never received parcels. Turning it over, she found no sender name or address.

Could this be from the killer? If she wanted to find out, she had to open it, right?

Grabbing a corner she stripped away the wrapping and tore off the lid. As she caught a glimpse of what was inside her stomach heaved. She moved as fast as she could and threw up in the toilet.

The journal. The necklace. And now this.

The world went black and her head thumped against the bathroom tiles.

When the room stopped spinning, she dragged herself up. *Don't cry,* she commanded herself. *You can do this.*

She crawled back to the box.

Whoever sent this, they killed your friend. You have to see this through.

With one shaking hand, she reached inside and gingerly touched the fabric. It was a red tartan miniskirt. She stroked the pattern and then lifted it out. It was a perfect match for the one Juliette had worn. Although it could not be the exact one from Murder Day because it was not stained.

She took out the second item. It was a t-shirt with two palm trees on the front. Juliette's had been faded and much loved. This version was brand new.

Emma's pulse was thumping. Someone had sent her the same outfit as her sister's. She gritted her teeth.

A typed note lay in the bottom of the box – *Get dressed for the occasion! Meet me at the church.*

Meet at the church? Did it mean it was Brett? Emma tried not to cry. Brett had been her friend and he had been Phoebe's too. They had trusted him.

A rage flared inside her. It burned in her chest and she clutched the t-shirt, wanting to scream. The bastard. He had tricked Phoebe. He had murdered her. Well, two can play that game.

I'm going to finish this, Phoebe. For you.

Chapter 57

Diane pulled into Anne Markham's drive and turned off the engine. With Ruby by her side Diane crunched across the gravel and rang the bell. Anne answered the door.

'Hello officers. How can I help you?'

'Good afternoon, Mrs Markham. May we come in? We've a couple of questions to run by you.'

Perched on the edge of a sumptuous armchair, Diane took out her notebook and began by asking about Brett Sinclair. Anne repeated what they already knew – Brett was her cousin and Anne knew about the White family murders because she'd lived in Himlands Heath at the time. She knew Brett had been friends with Juliette.

'Brett wasn't only friends with Juliette, was he? They were going out together,' Diane said.

'Yes, that's right.'

'How well did you know Mrs White?'

'I didn't know her at all.'

'And Mrs White's husband, Mr Smith?'

Anne was wringing her hands. 'I had no connection to Mr Smith personally. I know he was Juliette's stepfather and I know what he did, and he killed himself afterwards.'

'I see.' Diane flicked through some pages of her notebook. 'And how often did you see Brett at that time?'

'Hardly ever. He was a lot younger than me. Maybe we met once a year at a family event like a wedding or a christening.'

'Then years later you offered Brett a job as a counsellor at the community centre,' Diane said. 'Can you explain how that came about?'

'I didn't offer him the post. There was the vacancy and I told him about it. There were other candidates who applied and Brett was appointed because he was the most suitable. There was no favouritism. I wouldn't even have remembered he was a counsellor if Kate hadn't reminded me.'

Diane's pen hovered mid-air. 'Kate, the OT? She reminded you Brett was a counsellor?'

'Yes. She sits on the advisory panel for the church. She was very helpful when it came to setting up the services we wanted to run.'

'How did she know about his qualifications?'

Anne shrugged. 'I assumed they kept friendly contact. She, Brett and Juliette were at school together.'

Diane stifled a gasp. How she loved detective work. The art of following the trail to the bitter end. The three of them had known each other! Why had that not come up in the searches? My god, was Kate their hidden sociopath?

After the call from Tom about Viktor, Grant sped the rest of the way to Moorlands. It was a blisteringly hot afternoon and the grounds were deserted as he ran to the OT department.

The OTs were having a cosy meeting, sitting in the kitchen at the back of the art workshop, eating strawberry tart.

Kate ushered him in. 'Come in, Inspector. Vik and I are going through the planning for next week.'

She was wearing a pale blue frilly dress, of a similar style to the previous one. Viktor had just crammed his mouth full and he was about to shake Grant's hand when Grant told him he was under arrest. The young man choked.

Kate shrieked. She banged Viktor on the back.

'Please step out of the way,' Grant said.

'You can't arrest Vik! What's going on?'

Grant read Viktor his rights while Kate backed up against the wall, her hand over her mouth.

Diane and Ruby left the Markham house. Outside at the car, Diane called it in. It was Tom who answered.

'Kate knew Brett and Juliette?' he said. 'That's strange. I found a link in the cold case to Viktor and it looks like he could be our murderer. Grant's bringing Viktor in for questioning.'

'But it could be Kate,' Diane said. 'We've grounds to arrest her too. Can you contact Grant? I'm going to Moorlands to find her.'

She told Ruby what had happened and started the engine.

'Wait,' Ruby said.

Ruby had been making a call of her own.

'This is urgent.' Diane tapped the passenger seat. 'We're closing the net.'

'It's Emma. I can't get a hold of her. She promised she'd keep in touch. We've got to call by her apartment. I'm worried she's being lined up as the next victim. She told me weird things have been happening to her and the more I think about it, the more it seems to me the killer could be setting her up for a breakdown. Every time I see her she's more fragile. We've got to hurry. I think our murderer has turned their attention to Emma.'

Chapter 58

When Diane told Tom her new priority was to search for Emma, Tom put in a request for patrol officers to pick up Kate at Moorlands. It was too late for Grant to return to the hospital because he was five minutes from HQ.

When Grant walked into the office, Tom was on his mobile. 'I just had patrol on the phone, guv. They've arrived at Moorlands and Kate's not there. She told colleagues she had a headache and was going home.'

Grant didn't miss a beat. 'We need to find Kate as a priority and I need to question Viktor. Circulate her description to patrol so they can search for her. Ask officers to join you at Kate's house. Get a search warrant.'

'I'm on it,' Tom said.

Everything was happening at once and the team needed to stay focused. Grant hurried to the interview room. He could trust Diane to find Emma, and Tom to track down Kate. Meanwhile he needed to grill Viktor for more information.

Viktor was sitting with his large hands resting on the table. As Grant went through the formalities the OT had a bemused look on his face.

'Right, with that out of the way, let's get on with it,' Grant said.

'I don't understand,' Viktor said. 'Why am I under arrest?'

Grant stared at Viktor and the young man flinched. 'Let's start with Lin Chen shall we? I understand you were in a relationship and then you split up?'

'Yes.'

'When did the split happen?'

'About six months ago.'

'Did it make you angry she left you?'

'I wasn't angry, I was hurt. I cared about Lin and my feelings for her didn't stop once we'd split up. I knew she wanted to devote herself to her family. She told me she didn't have the emotional space to be in a relationship. That's why she broke it off. I knew it wasn't because she didn't want to be with me.'

'After the split, how often did you speak?'

'Maybe three or four times a week in private. We were good friends. And we saw each other at work.'

'And you continued those private chats?'

'Yes. Like I told you, I cared for her. I wanted to give her my support.'

'And what about after Phoebe died? You've been talking to Lin since then too?'

'After that terrible night we talked every day.'

'In these frequent conversations of yours, what did you speak about?'

Grant was watching Viktor like a hawk. He wasn't defensive, as many suspects would be. When he spoke about Lin he had an air of regret and deep sadness, even though he was confused about why he was being questioned.

'How she was doing, if there was any way I could help her, stuff like that. Of course we talked a lot about Lin's sister.'

'Did you discuss suicide?'

'I knew Naomi's application to Dignitas had been turned down and we talked about that, yes.'

'What about in relation to Lin? Did she confide in you she felt suicidal?'

'Absolutely not. I loved her. I would have done anything for her and if she'd felt that way I'd have made sure she got help.'

'You're sure? She didn't speak about it even after Phoebe?'

'She talked about her sister's wish to die. Nothing more.'

'Lin didn't tell you she considered taking her own life?'

'I already told you. No!'

'All right. What about Phoebe? You were her art teacher, weren't you. How much time did you spend with her?'

'Quite a lot. We hold art sessions three times a week and Phoebe never missed them. She often worked in the studio on her own too, and if I had five minutes here and there I'd pop in to see her.'

'You'd pop in to see her. Why was that?'

Viktor snorted. 'To encourage her, of course. It's my job.'

'But you liked her didn't you?'

'Yeah, and? You can't seriously think I've got anything to do with her death. Or Lin's.'

'Did you know Emma White's family?'

'What? No.'

Grant rested his forearms on the table and Viktor hastily withdrew his.

'What I'm thinking is that the person who orchestrated Phoebe's death and Lin's is very clever. It seems to me that person was able to manipulate those young women when they were at a low ebb. We believe the killer was a person they trusted. Someone who knew them intimately. Someone who understood how to break them down and control them. Someone, for instance, like you.'

Viktor started to laugh but stopped himself. Instead, he went an odd colour. 'That's ridiculous.'

Viktor was sweating. It was around this time people started wondering if they needed a lawyer. It was one of the oddities of interrogation – you could make someone tell you things they didn't need to, by implying you knew more than you did. Though if Viktor were their sociopath, he might also be well versed in the law. Ruby had told Grant many sociopaths made it their business to learn all they could about police procedures so they could stay one step ahead.

'I'd like to ask you some questions about Fiona Taylor.'

'I'm not sure who that is,' Viktor said.

'Shall I jog your memory? Fiona Taylor was one of your patients. She was a cancer survivor who suffered a relapse. Unfortunately, the second time around she was diagnosed with an inoperable brain tumour. A few weeks after she received the bad news, she was killed in a car crash.'

Grant waited while the information sank in. 'Ring any bells?'

Viktor nodded slowly. 'I remember. Before I worked at Moorlands I was at the hospice. It was a while ago.'

'Although the verdict of the coroner was accidental death, I'm beginning to think Fiona Taylor was murdered. Possibly by the same means as Phoebe and Lin by which I mean psychological manipulation from someone close to her. I believe she may have been manipulated into taking her own life.'

Viktor pointed to himself. 'And you're looking at me as the one who did it? That's... that's ridiculous.'

Grant placed photographs of Fiona, Phoebe and then Lin on the desk and lined them up, facing his suspect. 'Strange how you knew them all.'

'Wait, you've got this wrong.'

Grant's phone vibrated and he took it from his pocket and checked the screen. Tom had arrived at Kate's house and there was nobody home. They were about to force the door.

'Listen, I think it might be a good idea if I take up that offer of a lawyer.'

As Viktor wiped the sweat from his face, Grant pushed Fiona Taylor's photograph closer. He didn't feel any mercy for the man. Strange how Kate had told her colleagues she was leaving early because she had a headache, yet she was not at home. Grant felt a cold focus as he ran through the possibilities. The seconds ticked by and beads of sweat rolled down Viktor's temple.

'Now Viktor, when you worked at the hospice, did you have any contact with your current colleague, Kate?'

'Actually, yes. We met on a training course. Kate was much more experienced and she kind of took me under her wing. She became my mentor and I learned a lot from her. It's because of her I knew about the job coming up at Moorlands.'

According to Diane, Kate knew Brett at school. She knew Juliette. Plus she had known Viktor at the time he worked at the hospice. Could she be the link, not Viktor?

'How much did you talk to Kate about your work at the hospice?'

'Quite a bit though nothing unprofessional. She often asked about my clients and she gave me advice. She wanted to help me.'

'Did you talk to Kate about Fiona Taylor?'

'I think so. I was rather fond of Fiona. She was a lovely person and one of my first clients.'

'Did your relationship with Ms Taylor stretch beyond professional boundaries?' Grant asked.

'Absolutely not!'

'Did Kate show a particular interest in Fiona Taylor?'

'Only like I told you. Kate offered advice.'

'What about your relationship with Kate, has *that* ever gone beyond professional boundaries?'

'Of course it hasn't. Kate's old enough to be my mother. She sometimes acts like my mother too. I guess you've realised she's like that with everybody.'

'Why do you think she wanted to help you?'

'How should I know? She always talks about how she doesn't have family. I wondered if maybe mentoring filled a gap in her life.'

'And has her interest in you always been platonic? Please be honest. It's not going to help anyone if you don't tell the truth.'

Viktor blushed. 'I suppose I got the idea she liked me more than she should. I never played up to it and don't get me wrong, nothing has ever happened. Sometimes I catch her gazing at me and it makes me pretty uncomfortable. If you must know I've been thinking of moving on because of it. Though I haven't told Kate yet.'

Grant clenched his fists. Viktor hadn't given anything away which incriminated himself.

Yet what about Kate?

Had a woman in a frilly dress murdered Phoebe and Lin, fooled Grant, and almost got away with it?

Chapter 59

Emma got dressed. It was grotesque to put on the clothes. She made herself do it. *These aren't Juliette's, they're only a copy.*

Catching sight of her reflection, she looked so much like her sister she almost had a panic attack. She knew her emotions were wrecked and her system was on overload.

Night was falling by the time she left her apartment, although it wasn't darkness which frightened her, it was the memories from the past which were crowding in. She wished she had a friend by her side except that was impossible wasn't it, because Phoebe and Juliette were the only real friends she'd ever had.

She clutched her denim jacket close to her. As she neared the church, her legs were shaking so badly she had to slow down.

The church was in darkness but she could make out flickering lights coming from the community centre.

You can do this. Brett is trying to bring you down. Don't let him.

As she followed the path around the building, she could hear the piano playing. It was Juliette's song. Emma clutched at the wall to steady herself. She wanted to put her hands over her ears, though instead she pushed herself forward.

The hallway was dark. Taking tottering steps, she went towards the music.

The community room was lit by candles which threw shadows on the walls.

The piano stool was empty.

It must be a recording, she told herself. *Or is it in my head?*

Next to the piano stool was a low table. At first she didn't recognise what was placed on top. Only once she leaned close did she realise it was a hedgehog cake. 'Happy Birthday. Six Today' was written in icing. It was a perfect match of the one her mother had made for her.

The shock ripped through her, making her vision go fuzzy. The blood drained from her head and she had to fight to stay upright. It took a while for her to get a hold of herself. She couldn't handle this. She should get out of there.

The hairs on her arms were standing on end, as if she were being watched. Turning slowly in a circle she checked around her.

'Who's there?' she called.

A shadow detached itself from the wall and the candles lit the face of a person she knew only too well. Her knees went weak.

'It can't be.'

Chapter 60

I've been in love with Brett Sinclair since I set eyes on him. From that day, I decided he would be mine.

At first, I contented myself with admiring him from afar. I decided I was going to be his first and his only love. I had it planned out. He would be devoted to me. We would be married. I knew which dress I would wear and which church we would marry in. We would have two children, one girl and one boy. Brett would come home every night and play the piano for me. One day, when we were old and grey, he would die in my arms. 'You are so beautiful,' would be his last words.

Brett and I were fused in love and I was determined to protect what was mine. So when Juliette White moved to our neighbourhood and *she made him invite her* to the end of term gala, I cracked. She was trying to steal him. How dare she. Brett belonged to me.

What did I do? I went around to her house. When Mrs White tried to get in my way, I smashed a brick again and again into the stupid woman's head. Then I slit Juliette's throat.

It was surprisingly easy. I remember the triumph of standing over that little bitch and I suppose that's when I got hooked.

I felt no remorse, which was a bonus. I suppose I'd always known I was different. Yet this was the proof. Murderous intentions – yes I'd felt them. The desire to kill – yes. But it had all been kept under wraps until that glorious day when I was free. Free to be myself.

It made me happy. Especially when my mother understood my impulses. Because when I came home plastered in the blood of murder and with elation shining on my face, she didn't condemn me. No, she covered it up for me.

It made me wonder if she had killed people herself, though I never dared ask. We had a silent understanding, is the best way to explain it. And who cared if she had, anyway? Not me. Like mother, like daughter, I suppose. Why shouldn't sociopathic traits run in families just as much as any other tendencies?

You see, my mother was friendly with Mrs White and with Mrs White's new husband, Smith. When the police were looking for Smith to question him about the murders, my mother warned him and hid him in a garage. When he finally decided it would be best if he turned himself in, she gave him pills and suffocated him with fumes from his own car. Then she planted the knife I'd used to kill Juliette on the passenger seat. It was the cherry on the cake. She was clever, my mum.

Now here I am with Emma. Emma has made the same mistake as Juliette. She has attracted the care of Brett Sinclair, like her sister did. She made him give her flowers and chocolates. I saw them in her apartment. Oh yes, I have keys to her place and to Phoebe's. When they were in hospital, I took the precaution of making copies.

Next door is the church I was going to marry Brett in. It seems fitting I've chosen it for my little masquerade and it's lovely how Emma has come dressed as Juliette. I didn't know if she would. Though Emma was the next on my list I've had to escalate things a little, in case as rumour has it, she does have a suspicion about Phoebe's killer. Though now I see the shock lancing through her, I realise she had no idea it was me.

'Hello, Emma. I'm so glad you came.' I use the cheery voice I use at Moorlands.

She's confused and more than a tad wobbly on her feet. I don't think she can speak.

'Would you like to blow out the candles? And then we can have a little chat.'

I take a box of matches from my pocket and light the six candles on top of the cake. 'There you go, dearie, remember to make a wish.'

She doesn't move and I feel my rage stirring.

'Did you kill Phoebe?' she asks.

Emma's voice is croaky and strained.

'Now, now, let's not get ahead of ourselves. First the candles and then the chat. All these years of blaming yourself, don't you crave knowing the real reason your mother and sister died? I'm the only one who can tell you.'

Somewhere deep in those shocked eyes of hers, I catch a flicker of interest. And I know this is going to end the way I want it to.

Chapter 61

Kate's house was a two-bedroom property in a quiet cul-de-sac. After banging at the front and the back, Tom and two patrol officers used an enforcer to gain entry. It was a torpedo-like ramming device. One swing and *crunch,* the lock splintered away from the frame.

'Search the ground floor,' Tom directed, 'I'll check the top.'

Tom took the stairs two at a time.

Along the hallway, the walls were adorned with little pictures of cats and kittens, which seemed to fit in with Kate's image.

The main bedroom smelled of her perfume and it caught at the back of his throat as he quickly checked the room. Nothing seemed out of place or suspicious. Next, he scanned the bathroom, which was neat and decorated with more cute kitten pictures.

'Anything?' he shouted out.

'Not here,' the officers called back.

When Tom turned the doorknob of the second bedroom, he found it locked. Taking one step back, he threw out a solid kick. The lock splintered and with one more shove the door opened.

As he stepped inside a disgusting musty smell engulfed him. It was dark and Tom held his breath as he fumbled for the light switch.

'What the hell!'

His exclamation brought the others pounding up the stairs.

'What's this supposed to be?' Tom's male colleague said, gagging. 'What a… Is she demented?'

It was a surreal scene, as if they'd walked into a horror show.

Tom put on protective shoe coverings. 'Looks like it to me.'

In the middle was a round dinner table and two upright chairs. A wedding dress was draped over the back of one chair, with a bridal veil placed on top. The other chair was the shocker. On it sat a life-sized doll of a man. It was very realistic, the face painted with a smile and fringed by dark hair, the features lifelike and a replica of Viktor. The Viktor mannequin was dressed in a dinner jacket and bow tie and it sat facing the chair with the wedding dress.

The female officer, Hilary, pointed to a piano in the corner of the room. 'There's another one of them over there.'

Tom crossed to the piano. The second mannequin was a replica of Brett Sinclair. It was sitting with its hands resting on the keys as if it was playing.

Hilary put her hand over her mouth and looked at the table. 'That's disgusting.'

It was covered in old food, including an elaborate wedding cake and Hilary was right, everything was rotting.

'That dress and veil, was somebody planning on getting married?' she said. 'How long has this stuff been here? All this decay, it reminds me of that Charles Dickens book, you know the one? Great Expectations. Where Miss Haversham was stood up by the man she loved and she never got over it.'

Tom had never read any Dickens. He grunted a reply and inspected the one photograph sitting on the table. It was Kate in the wedding dress. She had her arm around an elderly woman who was lying in a hospital bed. He peered more closely. Right by the woman's bedside was a cabinet, and on it was a notepad with the logo of Moorlands.

Tom stabbed at his mobile phone, deftly taking pictures of the mannequins and the table and the photograph, as he put in a call to Grant.

'You think Kate's your killer?' the male officer asked.

The wedding dress and mannequins said it all. 'Hell yes.'

Chapter 62

Ruby was glad to be with Diane who was always calm under pressure. They were standing outside Emma's apartment.

'She's not answering,' Ruby said. 'And she's not picking up her phone, it's going to voicemail!'

Diane nodded. 'Okay we need to think this one through. Uniform are on their way and we're going to get inside. Think about other places Emma might be. You know her best. Did you manage to get hold of Brett?'

'Yes, Brett's meeting us here. Look, here come patrol now.'

'Brett had better make it fast. Then we can get some answers about Kate. Tom said she's not at her house.'

Tom had passed information to them about the mannequins. It made sense to Ruby. The killer had an obsession with Brett and with Viktor, most likely a sociopathic obsession which she would protect by all means.

The uniformed officers had brought 'the enforcer' and they were soon inside Emma's apartment. They quickly checked the main room and the bathroom.

'No one home,' Diane said. 'What's this?' She put on gloves and inspected the package. 'No return address and whatever was in it, doesn't seem to be lying around.'

One of the uniformed officers called from the doorway. 'There's a guy downstairs says he's here to speak to you. A Brett Sinclair.'

'Right. We're coming.'

Ruby followed Diane down to street level. Brett's sandy hair was flopping in his eyes.

'What's going on? Have you broken into Emma's place?'

'No time to explain,' Diane said. 'Talk to me about Kate. Tell me exactly how you know her, starting from the beginning and make it fast.'

'Er, we went to school together.'

'At what age?'

'From when we were small.'

'And Juliette White knew you both too, am I correct?'

'Juliette came to Himlands Heath later when we started secondary school.'

Ruby moved closer to Brett. 'Were you and Kate friends?'

'Not really. Why are you asking?'

'I think Emma's in danger. You say "not really", but is it possible Kate had feelings for you? Perhaps intense feelings or inappropriate ones? Please think hard.'

Brett pushed his glasses up his nose. 'Kate and I were never close. If you must know, when we were young, Kate did this weird thing where she invited me to the church. It was when we were nine. She said she wanted to marry me. After that, I avoided her as much as I could.'

'The church? Wait, the same one with the community centre?' Ruby asked.

'Yes.'

'When Kate invited you to the church, describe it to me.'

'This is really embarrassing. If you must know, she was in a fancy dress outfit making herself look like a bride. She had a ring she wanted me to put on her finger. I freaked out. I ran away as fast as I could.'

Ruby started pacing. Kate inviting Brett to marry her fitted in with the mannequins and the scenario Tom had described at Kate's house. The wedding dresses and the church connection were important. 'Diane, it's possible Kate's taken Emma to the church. We need to check.'

'Brett, get in the car,' Diane ordered.

Ruby fastened her seatbelt. 'Hurry.'

Brett was wide-eyed as they pulled away from the kerb. 'What's going on?'

'Brett, why do you think Kate helped you move back to town by reminding Anne Markham you were suited for the job at the church?' Ruby asked.

Brett was in the rear seat and he grabbed on as Diane took a corner at speed. 'I don't know. Because Kate's thoughtful? Because she knew I was in a dead end. That thing at the church was when we were kids. It was a game.'

'And since you've been working here, how would you describe your relationship with her?'

'If you must know, she can be cloying. Although I feel really mean saying it.'

'In what way is she cloying?'

'The way she fusses around me. She's always checking I'm okay. She does it with everyone, doesn't she? But sometimes all those bits of attention sort of add up and become, I don't know...'

'An infringement?'

'That kind of thing, yes.'

'Now it makes sense.' Ruby wiped perspiration from her brow. The pieces of the puzzle were flying into place. 'She more than liked you, she was obsessed by you. Asking someone to marry you when you're nine and inviting them to the church isn't normal behaviour. It wasn't a kid's game. It was real for her.'

Diane didn't take her eyes of the road. 'Oh god.'

'I'm thinking Kate has learned to hide her murderous impulses underneath her fussy mother image. I think Kate's motive is sociopathic obsession.'

Brett shook his head. 'This can't be right.'

'It is. Kate thinks of you and Viktor as her possessions. The two of you belong to her. Any interest you show in other women means those women have to be eliminated. It makes me even more sure Emma is Kate's next target. Brett, you've been worried about Emma ever since Phoebe died. You got her gifts and you keep a special eye on her. I think the care you've been showing towards Emma would have driven Kate to a frenzy.'

'Shit,' Diane said. 'If you're right, Kate could already have Emma. We've got to assume she plans to kill her.'

Chapter 63

Kate had to be tracked down as a priority. With an alert out for patrol to bring Kate in, Grant returned to the hospital. He hurried to Mrs Nicholson's office. She looked as glamorous as usual, in a crisp white dress, with her hair artfully framing her face. She was not pleased to see him, though she made a small effort to hide it.

'DCI Grant, how nice. I imagine your team's enquiries will be over soon?'

She was too professional to mention that thanks to him, her partner Mike Otremba, was currently under scrutiny by the GMC, on permanent leave, and on a waiting list for a rehab clinic. Grant didn't mention it either.

'Not yet. Things are moving fast,' he said. 'I need to find your OT, Kate. Have you any idea where she might be?'

'Uniformed officers were here not five minutes ago asking me the same thing.' Mrs Nic patted at her hair. 'I've no idea. She reported as being sick and left the premises. That's all I can tell you.'

Grant took out his phone. 'I need to urgently identify the woman in this photograph. It seems she may be a patient, past or present.'

He showed the photograph Tom had found at Kate's house.

'Well, that's Kate.'

'I know that.' It was hard for Grant to keep his irritation under control.

'I don't know who the other person is. From the background, I'd say it was taken on the Secure ward. I suggest you go over there and I'll call ahead and warn them you're on your way.'

'Can you speed up the process by circulating this to staff?'

'I suppose so.'

'Then do it. A young woman could be in danger.'

All the evidence was pointing to Kate. Did it mean she was also implicated in the past murders of Juliette and Mrs White? While it was possible, though improbable, for nineteen-year-old Kate to have carried out the murders of Mrs White and Juliette, Grant did not see how Kate could have killed the stepfather. The woman in the photograph was important to Kate, might she have answers?

As they crossed town to get to the church, Diane received a text message. 'Read it out, Ruby, what does it say?'

'He's asking about Kate. Brett, do you know who this person is?'

Ruby showed Brett the photograph found at Kate's house.

'No idea.'

'What about Kate's parents?' Diane asked. 'Do you know what happened to them?'

'I think Kate's father left when Kate was small. I've no idea what happened to her mother. While I was in Brighton, Kate changed her name to Kate Phillips, which was her father's name.'

'You didn't think to mention this before?' Diane said. 'Now I understand why we didn't know Kate was at school with you and Juliette. If she changed her name, it wouldn't have shown in the cross searches.'

'Sorry. I didn't think it was important.'

Diane sped through a yellow light. 'Didn't you think it was odd she changed her name?'

'Not really. She said she did it to stop people asking her about the White murders. I could understand that.'

Diane rolled her eyes. 'Call it in, Ruby. Grant needs to know. What was her name before she changed it?'

'Kate Davies.'

'Davies, Davies, why is that sounding familiar?' Diane said. 'It's common enough, but… wait, wasn't the Whites' neighbour Mrs Davies? She was the one who gave testimony about Emma's stepfather's violent behaviour!'

When Grant got the call from Ruby, he was running and had to stop to catch his breath. Was the elderly woman at Moorlands the neighbour of the White family? The one who gave testimony against the stepfather. Was she Kate's mother?

By the time Grant arrived at the Secure ward, staff had already identified the woman in the photograph. When they confirmed the woman's name was Ivy Davies, Grant felt sweat prickling his brow. Ruby was in a panic because she couldn't get hold of Emma and that made Grant worried for Emma too.

Grant turned to the nurse. 'It's urgent I speak to Ivy Davies.'

'Ivy's a long-term patient here. She's suffering from catatonic depression. In layman's terms it means she's so depressed she isn't able to speak or communicate. It might be urgent for you, but I don't think you're going to get much from her. She won't respond.'

'Charles told us that when he has periods of catatonic depression he can hear and understand everything which is said to him,' Grant said. 'Even though he can't speak.'

The nurse sighed. 'Even if that's the case with Ivy, she hasn't spoken a word for months. She's been highly resistant to treatments.'

'I have to try.'

'All right. I'll take you to see her.'

They arrived at Ivy's room where the woman was sitting in bed, staring straight ahead.

'Can she write?' Grant asked.

'There's nothing physically stopping her. However, she doesn't do that or any other movement. Her depression is so profound, she has withdrawn from the everyday world.'

'Then how does she eat?'

'We feed her. When food is put in her mouth, she swallows it although she'd not make the movements to feed herself. Obedience is one of the symptoms of Ivy's condition. She doesn't resist when we give her food or drink.'

'Can you tell me if she has any visitors?'

'Ivy has no family who come to see her, I'm sad to say.'

Diane had told him Kate started her career at Moorlands under the name of Kate Phillips and that she had changed her name from Kate Davies. She'd been clever to hide her identity as Ivy's daughter.

'What about the occupational therapists, do they come to this ward?'

'Oh yes, both Kate and Viktor. I've heard from colleagues Ivy's been known to laugh when Kate does a session with her, though I've not heard it myself. It's the only response Ivy is known to give, so Kate somehow works a miracle.'

A miracle, Grant thought sarcastically, no not that, something far more sinister and evil. He was ready with his phone. He had also come up with a theory. Had Ivy Davies played a part in killing Emma's stepfather?

He brought up crime scene photos from the White murders, holding his screen in front of Ivy's eyes. 'Are you seeing this, Ivy? Do you recognise what I'm showing you?'

The nurse looked uncomfortable. 'Is this necessary?'

'It absolutely is,' Grant said.

He talked Ivy through the photos, describing the murders and then how the body of the stepfather had been found, together with the weapon used to kill Juliette.

'This is a photograph of Mr Smith in his car,' Grant said.

'This is too much. It's unethical,' the nurse said. 'I'm getting my supervisor.'

'You do that,' Grant said. He was sure this woman was not an innocent. She was as guilty as her daughter.

When the nurse left the room, Grant continued. 'We know Kate is your daughter. Did she murder Juliette and Mrs White? Did you know about this and help her cover up her crimes? You testified against Smith. Were you the one who led Smith to that garage, Mrs Davies? Did you kill him?'

There was no way to know if Ivy Davies heard or understood a word he said.

Grant leaned towards her. 'You were the one who gave testimony to the police saying Smith was violent. I believe you were your daughter's accomplice.'

The nurse and the supervisor walked in. 'This is totally inappropriate,' the supervisor said. 'I must ask you to stop.'

Grant ignored them. 'We believe Kate murdered Phoebe Markham and nurse Lin Chen. I think you're aware of those killings too, Mrs Davies. What does your daughter do which makes you laugh? Does she show you the videos of their deaths?'

There was an ungodly sound from the bed as the old woman opened her mouth to reveal toothless gums and emitted a horrible piercing screech.

The supervisor dropped the clipboard she'd been carrying.

Ivy Davies was laughing.

Chapter 64

Emma's plan had been simple. Go to the meeting and confront Brett. Punish him and injure him, or worse. If she couldn't manage that, then get him to confess and record it.

It was probably a stupid plan, a ridiculous plan. But it was all she'd got.

She had not thought beyond that. Now she was faced with a situation she could not handle. It wasn't Brett it was Kate. Kate knew the details of Murder Day and she spoke as if she had been there. How could that be?

Emma had gone there to find the truth about Phoebe and now she was being given the chance of finding the truth about Juliette? Her mind teetered on the edge.

'Well dear, make a decision. Do you want me to tell you or not? If so, all you've got to do is blow out the candles.'

Kate giggled. She was dressed as she usually was, in an old-fashioned dress with frills. She was soaked in her habitual perfume. How could she know about the cutting of Juliette's throat and the caving in of their mother's face? Had she witnessed Smith in the act?

Yet Kate had dangled a bait so enticing, Emma could not resist. Could knowing the truth absolve her from blame? Might it lift the curse of guilt which crippled her life?

Emma leaned forward. She had no breath, and it took many attempts to blow out the six little candles.

Kate clapped her hands. 'Bravo. Here's a drink for you. It's lemon fizz, like you had for your birthday.'

She passed a glass and waited until Emma drank it.

'Good girl. And now, I'd like you to take off your jacket and hand it to me.'

Emma's phone was recording from one of the pockets. Slowly, she slipped it off her shoulders. She could only hope the woman wouldn't check.

Kate patted the pockets and tutted as she pulled out Emma's mobile. Dropping it to the floor, she smashed it and ground her shoe into the remains.

'That's enough of that. Don't look so disappointed because I'll be recording this myself. My mother will enjoy watching the replay. Shall I cut the cake, or would you like to?'

Emma's knees finally buckled and she landed in a heap. 'I want to know about Phoebe. What did you do to her?'

'Ah now there's a story. If you must know it all started with Viktor.'

Kate cut into the birthday cake and put a slice on a plate. She passed it to Emma.

'Sit straight now, there's a good girl, and eat up. You see, when I met Viktor, he made me breathless. He was perfect and so beautiful like an angel. That's why I suggested I become his mentor and that's when we fell in love.'

'You're in love with Viktor? You can't be serious.'

'Don't be rude, dear. Viktor adores me. He couldn't wait to join me at Moorlands and he's so attentive and thoughtful. His smile lights up my day.'

'You're mad.'

'No, Emma. I think you'll find you're the one who has lost your mind. You see, Viktor and I are inseparable. The mistake Lin and Phoebe made was to try to take him away from me.'

Chapter 65

Emma looks nice in her tartan miniskirt. It's ridden up her thighs as she slumped to the ground, but I'm not one to pick fault.

'Viktor and I met on a training course. Him being new to OT and me being experienced, I figured he'd appreciate help climbing the ladder. I was right. He fell for it and he fell head over heels in love with me too.'

Emma makes a scornful noise. I don't like her lack of respect. She'll regret that later.

'Back then, Viktor was working with cancer survivors. A lot of them adored him and one liked him far too much. I soon got rid of her. Then I found him a job alongside me. Our Moorlands honeymoon was like a dream until Lin got her claws into him.'

'Honeymoon!'

'Yes dear, our honeymoon. I've got to say, I had to work hard to worm my way into Lin's confidence. She was a tough cookie. I worked the Naomi angle. Little by little, without her realising it, Lin came to depend on me. I was the one who made suggestions about how to make her sister's life more bearable. I was the one who supported her through the Dignitas application, and through the Dignitas failure. I was the one willing to listen to whatever feelings she needed to vent, and believe me she was boiling in rage and self-hatred and anguish.'

I'm walking in a circle around Emma. I like the fear in her eyes.

'Meanwhile, I got another side of Lin's story because Viktor confided in me. He told me he had feelings for Lin. I can tell you it was hard to control myself. But my days of rushing in with a knife were over. I'd learned to be stealthy – to find my victim's weaknesses and use them to my own ends. It's much more fun.'

I lean in to take a smear of chocolate. 'Same with Phoebe. She spent far too much time in Viktor's company. He was the art specialist and my goodness she capitalised on it. She had him twisted around her little finger. My poor Viktor, he saw Phoebe as the successful artist he could never be, while in reality she was nothing but a scheming parasite trying to suck his love.'

'That's sick,' Emma says. 'Phoebe was no threat to anyone.'

'She was vermin!'

Emma is crying. She's been stupid enough to drink the drugged lemonade I gave her. This is child's play. Soon she'll be begging me to send her to oblivion.

'How do you know about my family? Were you there? Did you kill them too?'

'As I said, all these years of blaming yourself, I'm the only one who can tell you what really happened. Let's get started shall we? You can play Juliette. I've a doll which can be your mother. And how about if I play the part of the killer.'

I collect my props.

'You lay down here.' I take Emma's shoulders and guide her. 'And we'll put your mother over here in the kitchen.' I place the doll on the floor. 'And now I'll explain exactly what happened and why.'

Emma does as she's told. She lies on the ground and I push her legs together, her arms by her side.

'This is how your sister lay as she died. You see, I grabbed Juliette from behind when I slit her throat, and there was no struggle. She fell like a log.'

'*You* killed them!'

'Let me tell you how it went. First, I tapped on the kitchen door and your mother saw it was me through the glass panel and she let me in. That was a big mistake.'

I like the flickering lights. It gives atmosphere. I mimic the actions, rapping on an imaginary door and smiling, then stepping through as Mrs White invites me in. I have one hand behind my back.

'I had a brick in my hand which I'd taken from the garden, and I smashed it into your mum's head.'

Emma is motionless. She's in shock. Plus the medication I added to the drink is whizzing through her.

I swing my arm in an arc. *Bam,* I say, as I cave the doll's head in. 'She didn't see it coming.' My voice is chatty and conversational. I pride myself on how well I can keep up my façade.

'Why?' Emma says, her voice cracking.

'Your mother was in my way. Your sister was the one I was after. Juliette was trying to steal my Brett. He and I were going to be married.'

As rage invades me, my mask falls away and I tilt my head to scream at the rafters. 'I was to be his *first and only love.* His entire being was to be devoted *to me*!'

Chapter 66

Emma's head was spinning. She should never have come. Kate was psychotic.

Kate pulled out a knife.

'I used a knife just like this one, to cut your sister's throat. Then I watched as the blood pumped out. The elation I felt defies words. But you've always been right, it was your fault.'

Emma felt the last of the fight draining from her. 'Wh-what?'

'*You are* the one to blame. You see, I knew you were in the house and I was wondering what I'd do if you showed up. Probably it would have stopped me.'

Emma's heart shattered into thousands of pieces. Those words did more damage than any knife. They were the ones she had dreaded hearing all her life. She'd always believed if she had come downstairs sooner, she could have saved her sister. It was true.

'No,' Emma whispered.

'Oh yes, dearie. You're responsible for your sister's death. An innocent child witnessing such a horrific act, no I could not have accepted it. And on your birthday too? Impossible. Juliette would have lived if you'd only shown your face a tad earlier.'

Dry sobs wracked her body. She flapped her arms hopelessly like a fish out of water as the self-hatred surged to monstrous proportions and swallowed her whole.

'There, there. Ever since Murder Day you've wanted to know the truth. Now you do. And as for little Phoebe and loathsome Lin, they deserved what they got. They were just as toxic as your sister. They should never have tried to steal what wasn't theirs. I enjoyed taking their lives. Brett and Viktor are mine.'

Chapter 67

Ruby gripped the edge of the seat as Diane drove as fast as she could. Grant arrived at the church the same time they did.

Tom came running from a side street. 'I circled the place and spotted Kate's car,' he said breathlessly. 'She's here.'

All eyes were on Grant.

'I want a stealth approach,' Grant said. 'Whatever's going on in there, our priority is to calm it down. We're assuming she has Emma with her. I'm going in as a negotiator. Tom, find a quiet way in around the back. Ruby, what's your take on the situation?'

'If Emma is here, Kate intends to murder her. Kate broke down Phoebe and Lin's resistance. She's been doing the same with Emma. Emma is going to be fragile. She's likely on the verge of a nervous breakdown. I don't know what Kate's saying to her or how she'll try to manipulate her for the final step, but Emma may no longer value her own life. We mustn't underestimate Kate. She's formidable.'

'Jesus,' Diane said. 'Then what's David's way in?'

'I don't know. And I don't know how Kate will react to us. I need to come with you,' Ruby said. 'Until I see and hear it, I can't guess how best to advise you.'

'All right. Diane, I want you to stay at the front entrance. Make sure all officers know this is a potential hostage situation and don't let anyone come crashing in.'

Chapter 68

Emma's hands felt slippery. If she looked at them, she knew they'd be covered in her sister's blood. She never deserved to survive. She was the guilty one, responsible for Juliette's death. Kate had confirmed it.

The knife glinted in Kate's hand. 'You wanted to know. Now you've got to live with the guilt for the rest of your life.'

Emma didn't want to. It was too much. It had always been too much to bear. It was time to stop fighting. How lovely it would be to give up. But a little voice inside her battled on because Kate had also killed Phoebe.

'You win,' Emma said.

'How about the same ending as your sister? Wouldn't that be nice.'

Kate was walking towards her when a man's voice called from the distance.

Emma squinted. Who the hell was that?

While Kate was distracted, Emma tried to get her legs under her except they had gone numb and wouldn't move. It was like the air was thick and she couldn't get it into her lungs. The only thing she could do was reach out to the table with the cake. Several large candles were alight around the edge and there was a tablecloth hanging down fringed with tassels. Stretching out, she grabbed a handful of tassels and yanked as hard as she could. Down came the cake and the candles. With a *whump* the cloth caught fire.

If she was going, she was damn well taking Kate with her.

Chapter 69

Emma's a fighter. She always has been. I've watched her long and painful path. She's chiselled out a way to live with what happened. Not many do. Now isn't that a thing? And I've just kicked her legs from under her, figurately and psychologically. I've destroyed what she's taken years to build. I really am brilliant at what I do.

This time, I'm the one recording Emma's ending to show to my mother. Mother will enjoy it as much as I do. It will make her laugh. It's the least I can do for the woman who made me who I am.

When a man's voice calls from the doorway, I twist in his direction. My heart leaps thinking it's Brett. Has my first love come to find me and pledge himself to me once more? But it isn't, it's the nasty detective. And that's when there's a *whoosh* and flames leap across the floor.

I screech in rage, the muscles in my neck straining and my mouth agape. Fire surrounds Emma making it impossible to reach her. I would so have enjoyed slitting her throat, although now I'll have to hope she burns in agony.

Within seconds, the curtains are alight.

As I run for the rear exit, black smoke billows from them and Emma is screaming for help.

Chapter 70

'Go back!' Grant shouted to Ruby. 'Crawl to the wall. If you can find an extinguisher, use it. If the fire gets hold, get out.'

Grant dropped to all fours. In a building fire, toxic gases and hot smoke were your worst enemy. They poisoned your system, overwhelmed you and made you disorientated. In a worst case scenario your lungs would be burned from the inside. As a survivor, Grant had made it his business to learn everything about fire. He knew how they started. He knew how they spread. He had studied how building structures became unstable and collapsed.

Fires terrified him. For years after, he had nightmares where he heard the screams of his friends caught in the blaze. And it played on his mind, how he had done nothing to stop what had started out as a prank.

Emma's cries for help tore through him. In a few moments it would be impossible to reach her. Was he already too late?

Heat seared Grant's face and neck, the pain of it making him cower. The energy of the fire was trapped and superheating the room. An enclosed fire could reach one hundred degrees Celsius within minutes. Soon his clothing would be burned to his skin.

Goddam it, move, man.

The crackling of the flames stoked his fear. There was no way round, which meant the only way to Emma was through. Grant took off his jacket and wrapped his arm as a barrier to shield his face. He would be burned as he ran through the fire. His only chance was speed. *Do it! Run!*

Emma suddenly stopped screaming which meant she had been overcome. He remembered that horrible moment from the past when his friends had stopped too, and he and John Markham, huddled together, had instinctively understood why.

Grant bent his head low. He let out a war cry as he charged to cross the ring of fire.

Chapter 71

Diane and Ruby were in the hallway halted by the ferocity of the fire. They used extinguishers to try to keep the doorway clear. It was a losing battle. The heat and smoke were overwhelming. Diane could no longer see inside the room and fumes were choking her and Ruby.

'We have to pull back,' Diane yelled. 'If the fire gets behind us we'll be trapped.'

'No! Grant's in there. And Emma!' Ruby shouted.

'That's an order! Fall back.'

The fire was already a deadly, deafening inferno. Diane pushed Ruby ahead of her towards the exit. Moments later they stumbled into the churchyard and Diane fell to her knees, retching.

Ruby was face down on the grass and she was crying. Diane was too weak and dizzy to go to her. Sirens were getting closer. The firefighters would have specialised equipment and breathing apparatus, there was still a chance.

Her head was spinning as a figure came around the side of the church. Diane's spirits leapt except it wasn't Grant, it was Tom. He had Kate in handcuffs.

'Are you okay, Ruby? Diane? Where's the boss?'

'Still inside,' Diane said. 'We couldn't get to him. I hoped he might have come out your way.'

Kate laughed. 'Doesn't look like it.'

'Stay quiet,' Tom ordered, 'you're coming with me.' He turned to Diane. 'I'm putting her in the car.'

By the time Tom came back, the firefighters had arrived. Black smoke was billowing from a side window as Diane explained there were two people trapped inside the building.

Chapter 72

Grant had reached Emma. She was unresponsive and he took her in his arms and ran to the rear of the room. Kate had left at the back and his only chance was to use the same exit. The smoke was thick and blinding and he kept his shoulder to the wall as he searched for a way out. There didn't seem to be one. The panic mounted like a live thing, mixing up his thoughts, making him doubt himself. Was he going in the wrong direction? Had he missed it?

Grant put Emma down.

Get a grip, man!

The air was more breathable at floor level but he was getting woozy from the fumes. Soon he'd pass out. And that's when a memory popped into his mind from all those years ago – a glimpse of a face lit by the flames, of a person who wasn't supposed to be there.

He slumped against the wall.

Get up! Retrace your steps!

He couldn't breathe. There was no oxygen. His lungs were burning as he tried to get to his knees. He wasn't going to make it. He was going to let Emma down and they were both going to die. He would never walk Chrissie down the aisle, he'd never even take her on their special outing.

Emma was a slight build. He took her arms and leaned backwards, dragging her along the floor after him.

One step. Now another.

It should have been easy except he had no strength left. The pain in his chest was unbearable.

One more step! Come on!

He staggered and she almost slipped from his grasp.

Emma's hands were in Grant's as consciousness was leaving him.

No! Don't give up. Just one more step.

Chapter 73

Tom was kneeling beside Diane and Ruby. Part of him felt like crying, as Ruby was. Instead, he struggled to keep it together. 'They haven't found the chief or Emma yet.'

'They will. They'll get to them in time.' Diane sounded sure, although Tom felt certain she was as desperate as they were.

'There was no way I could get in from the back,' he said. 'Not unless I let Kate get away.'

'You did the right thing,' Diane said. 'Don't think about it.' And then she had a coughing fit.

The glass of the windows shattered and flames leapt into the night.

'No!' Tom shouted.

Ruby's face was streaked with tears. She stared at the firefighters who were attacking the blaze. 'Do you think it's too late?'

'Don't give up yet.' Diane wiped at her mouth with the back of her hand, smearing soot everywhere. 'Focus, Tom. Did Kate say anything?'

'Sorry, yes, I have her mobile. The video was still running when I took it from her. It seems she was recording events inside the church.'

'Why the hell didn't you say? Let's see,' Diane said.

The three of them huddled together. Tom put his arms around them both and he started the replay. The got close to the screen to try to block out the sound of the fire behind them, and to give each other support. Tom took a few deep breaths. Surely this wasn't how the chief was going to go? Burned to death in a building, just like the horrible event he'd escaped as a child. No, Tom refused to believe it.

'This is incredible,' Ruby said.

Tom squeezed them both close.

'She must have felt so confident,' Diane said. 'She never suspected she wouldn't get away with it. This is all the evidence we need.'

Tom wiped at his eyes. 'I can hardly believe it. We can convict Kate for Phoebe and Lin. And for Juliette and Mrs White. She's confessed to the lot.'

'Well done for grabbing her. Grant's not here and I'm not well enough to lead this. You're in charge. Get Kate into custody.'

Tom gave a grim nod. 'You've got it. Wait! Looks like they've found someone.'

Diane shoved Tom on the shoulder to make him go and see what was happening. He ran across the grass. There was only one body. He could see the firefighters carrying it out. Paramedics were already there with a stretcher and equipment. Tom held his breath as he got closer.

'It's Emma!' he shouted to Diane and Ruby. 'They've got Emma!'

Tom craned to see around the side of the building. No more firefighters were emerging and a frisson of fear ran up his spine. Where was the chief? This was taking too long. The building was an inferno. Nobody could survive in there.

'If you would step back please,' one of the firefighters told him.

'Of course, yes, sorry.'

And that's when two firefighters appeared carrying a second body. Tom dreaded the worst. Then a shout went out and somebody came running with oxygen equipment and a mask was fitted to the face. Relief shot through him. Grant had survived.

'They've got him. He's alive,' Tom yelled across the lawn. Ruby gave a small wave.

Emma and Grant were taken away by the paramedics and Tom jogged back to his colleagues.

'I couldn't see much of what was going on and I didn't want to bother the ambulance crew,' Tom said. 'They've headed off to the hospital. Looked like the boss was unconscious. Emma too.'

Diane put her hand on Tom's shoulder. 'They've survived, that's what matters. Now let's concentrate on Kate and the conviction.'

Chapter 74

Ruby waited at the hospital while Emma was treated for smoke inhalation. When Emma was able to talk, Ruby came to her bedside.

'Hi,' Emma said. Her eyes were bloodshot and puffy and her voice sounded hoarse.

'I'm so happy to see you. For a moment there, I didn't think you'd make it out.'

'Me neither.'

'I want you to know that without you we wouldn't have hard evidence against Kate.'

'You've got her then?'

'Yes. Tom arrested her when she tried to escape. She's in custody.'

Emma smiled. 'Without you and your inspector, I wouldn't be alive.'

'Going in there on your own, you were brave though a little foolish.'

'I know. That's what we do for our friends, isn't it? Phoebe deserved it. I thought it through and I got this idea I could flush out the killer. So I followed the instructions. She sent me an outfit and she told me to meet her at the church.'

'And you did.'

'Yeah. For Phoebe.'

A knot formed in Ruby's throat and she swallowed hard. Emma had put herself in danger for her friend.

Ruby poured them both some water. 'We have a recording of Kate admitting to killing Juliette and your mother. She also confessed to murdering Phoebe and Lin. It's enough to put her away. She had her phone video running the whole time.'

'That was stupid of her.'

'She didn't expect to be caught. Kate wanted to show the video to her mother. We think her mother was the one who framed Smith for murdering your family.'

'Her mother? I mean, how sick is that. Will she go to prison too?'

'No. Kate's mother is a patient on the Secure ward at Moorlands.'

'Wow.'

'I know. We weren't expecting that.'

'I can't believe I trusted Kate all this time. She was lovely. Fussy and frilly and mothering everyone. She's the last person I'd have suspected.'

'That's how she got away with it. Kate is a sociopath. We'll be questioning her to find out more but it's pretty clear she was obsessed with Brett and then with Viktor. In her mind, they belonged to her. When they showed love and care towards other women, Kate murdered those women.'

'All Juliette did was go out with Brett.'

'Kate spun a scenario in her mind. One which had to come true. In which she was Brett's only love. That's why she murdered Juliette.'

'And my mother was collateral damage. I can't believe it.'

'Later, Kate turned her attention to Viktor. Both Phoebe and Lin were women Viktor cared for a great deal. That's why they became Kate's targets. There's a third woman we know about too from Viktor's past, that was likely a victim. Kate was clever. She changed her habits to become stealthy and silent.

She used her knowledge of psychology to push people over the edge.'

Emma sighed. 'She almost managed it with me too. Inside the church she wormed her way into my mind. The way she blamed me for the death of my family was so convincing. I was ready to give up.'

Ruby put her hand over Emma's. 'Except you didn't. Like I said, I'm glad you made it.'

They sat quietly for a while. What a courageous young woman. Emma really should be proud of herself.

'Thanks for coming to see me,' Emma said. 'How's your inspector doing?'

'His arms were burned and he's still being treated. But the doctor says he'll recover.'

'Please thank him for me.'

'How about you do that yourself a bit later. I know he'll want to see you, he's that kind of person.'

Chapter 75

When Grant was well enough and Tom could hand over to Diane and slip away for half an hour, Tom went to the hospital. The medics said it would take a while for Grant's voice to recover.

'I hear you secured Kate's phone. Well done,' Grant said in a whisper.

'News travels fast.'

'While I was on the ambulance trolley I overheard the paramedics talking. I've been waiting for one of you to come by. I'd like to see the video.'

Tom shook his head in exasperation. Even when he'd suffered severe burns, didn't the guv give himself a moment off?

'I thought you might,' Tom said. 'Which is why I took the precaution of bringing a copy.'

'Good man.'

Tom took out his phone and they both watched as the scene inside the church played out. After, Grant hitched himself further up the bed.

'I didn't realise Emma started the fire,' Grant said.

'She wanted to bring Kate down. Emma told Ruby it was the only way she could think of. This video is all the evidence we need for a conviction.'

'It bloody well is. So what are you doing hanging around here? Get on with questioning her.'

'You're not going to be making it for Chrissie's rehearsal tomorrow then?'

Grant indicated his arms which were bandaged from shoulder to wrist. Tom felt sure the burns were painful despite the morphine.

'Not with this lot I'm not. Still, my son's ready to step in and take my place. Though I've told him he's got no chance for the actual ceremony. At least Chrissie is talking to me now.'

'I suppose a brush with death might have helped.'

'You won the bet then.'

Tom blushed and Grant laughed. 'How did you know about that, guv?'

'I have my sources, and by the way, when I'm not around, I'm looking to you to take the lead.'

Tom wondered if he'd heard wrong. Diane was the senior member of the team, not him.

'I won't always be here. The MIT needs great detective work and leadership. You're the right person. Get used to stepping up, Tom. One day, I hope you'll lead an MIT of your own.'

Tom felt himself going red again. 'If you say so, guv.'

'I do say so. It's about time you understood your own worth. Have you informed Anne and John we've a suspect in custody? What about Mr and Mrs Chen? They deserve to know.'

'It's under control. Diane called by to see Mrs Chen. We didn't know if you'd prefer to be the one to tell the Markhams.'

Grant held out his hand. 'I appreciate that. Pass me my phone, will you? Yes, I'd like to make that call.'

Chapter 76

Back at HQ, Tom and Diane spent half the night questioning Kate. For the last session, Tom had Ruby in the room with him which turned out to be a good decision. They joined Diane in the office afterwards.

'I thought you were tying up the loose ends? You've been hours,' Diane said. 'I haven't been able to concentrate on anything.'

'I'm exhausted,' Ruby said.

Diane pulled out two chairs. 'Sit down, you two, and let me make you a drink. It must mean it went well. You wouldn't have been in there so long if she'd clammed up.'

Tom stretched his shoulders. 'She realised it was over. She wanted to talk about what she'd done and get it off her chest. I think she felt Ruby was a kindred spirit.'

'I'm definitely not that. Although I do understand her motivations and why she acted the way she did.'

'Yeah, well she explained her acts pretty clearly,' Tom said. 'Brett was hers. So was Viktor. Other women attracting their attention drove her to a murderous frenzy.'

Diane handed a mug to Ruby. 'Like you thought, then. It's shocking how the attack on Juliette happened at such an early age. Kate was only nineteen. I find that incredible.'

'Most psychopaths lie low until they're much older, although the signs would have been there from the beginning. It's interesting Kate lived alone with her mother. Maybe it meant she didn't have to hide her killer tendencies.'

'Are you calling her a psychopath now, rather than a sociopath?' Diane asked.

Ruby nodded. 'I am. Though I'll leave the final diagnosis to the psychiatrists.'

'Right to the end she denied her mother had any role in killing Smith. That was the only part we didn't manage to get out of her, though I'm betting Ivy was involved,' Tom said.

Diane pursed her lips. 'Me too.'

Tom smiled at Ruby. 'You did great in there. I think she enjoyed showing off to you.'

Ruby shrugged. 'They often do. It's one of their traits.'

'I'm glad criminal profiling is your specialism and not mine,' Diane said. 'Give me good old-fashioned detective work any day.'

Tom laughed. 'I'll give Grant a call to let him know it's wrapped up. Who knows, we might get home before daylight.'

Chapter 77

One week later, Grant walked his daughter down the aisle. Miraculously, his suit fitted well, most likely, he thought, due to a diet of hospital food.

By the time Grant returned to work, all the MIT office furniture was in place.

'Welcome back, David,' Diane said.

Tom looked up. 'Nice to see you, boss. I just made you a mug of tea. Piping hot.' He passed it over.

'This place is looking good,' Sejal said, as she clonked her mug against Grant's. 'I heard you were coming in today. I thought I'd call by.'

'I'm glad you did. You ready for our next case?' Grant asked.

Sejal smiled. 'Always.'

Ruby came to join them. 'Emma sends her best wishes. She's got a video assignment this afternoon.'

'Has she now,' Grant said. 'That's good news. She told me her business is taking off.'

'I know. She sounds excited.'

Sejal tucked the white streak of hair behind her ear. 'Did you know there's a rumour going round about you and Tom moving in together?'

Ruby rolled her eyes. 'How did that get out? Yes, we're looking for a place, and before anyone asks, it was me who asked Tom, not the other way around.'

Tom waved his hand in the air. 'I admit she's right. She took me by surprise.'

Grant smiled to himself and made no comment. Ruby and Tom had already run that one by him individually. They made a great couple. Grant took Ruby aside as he headed for his desk.

'I wanted to let you know, that idea of yours to have a special moment with my daughter, it worked. It brought us back together as close as we've always been.'

Ruby crossed her arms. 'That's nice. It must have been special giving her away at the church.'

'It was. She looked so beautiful and happy. Who knows, maybe one day that'll be you.'

'I doubt it.'

'You never know.' He leaned to whisper in her ear. 'And for the record, if you're ever looking for someone to be the father of the bride, I hope I might stand a chance.'

Grant smiled to himself as she walked away. He glanced around the room. He was surrounded by his top team. Roll on the next case.

Epilogue

A long time after, Grant happened to see John Markham in the high street. Grant's relationship with John had gone back to being occasional. The conviction and imprisonment of Phoebe's killer had passed, but not the pain of the bereaved parents.

The burns on Grant's arms had healed. John stared at the puckered skin and Grant felt sure it reminded him of their mutual friend, now a man, who had been scarred that night long ago, and had undergone years of reconstruction treatments.

'How's it healing up?' John asked.

'Not too bad. How about you and Anne? I hear Anne's been helping Emma redecorate the apartment.'

John nodded. 'We wanted to give the girl the chance of a fresh start. Keeping in touch with Emma is helping Anne, actually it's helping all three of us.'

That was nice to hear.

'There was something I wanted to mention to you,' Grant said. 'When I was trapped in the fire at the church, I remembered something, John, something I'd buried, something from when we were caught by the flames.'

John rubbed his hands over his face. 'What can there be to remember, except being trapped in hell?'

'What I remembered was a glimpse of a face lit by the light of the fire. It was someone who shouldn't have been there.'

John shook his head in bemusement.

John had no recall of it though now Grant had a suspicion that what happened to his classmates might not have been an accident.

He didn't know how and he didn't know when, but he vowed one day, he would find out the truth.

****

Hello Dear Reader,

Thanks so much for supporting my books!

If you're an avid reader and you'd like to receive news and updates, I'd love you to join my Reader's Group. Don't worry, no spam. I'll only get in touch when I have something I think you might genuinely be interested in, like the release of a new book. I offer a free gift to new members and you can find details on my website – www.girdharry.com

Though it took a while to tap it out on the keyboard, the idea for Deadly Silent came to me towards the end of lockdown. I kept seeing news stories about people experiencing difficulties with depression and mental health and this especially struck me because a few of the stories I read were from young people. That's where I got the inspiration for the friendship between Emma and Phoebe.

I hope you enjoyed Deadly Silent. Please feel free to get in touch with comments or feedback, or if you've any questions. I always like to hear from readers 😊

Wishing you Happy Reading,
Ann Girdharry
Email – ann@girdharry.com

Acknowledgements

Huge thanks to my wonderful beta reader, Shalini Gopal (Digital Reads Media) and my editor, Morgen Bailey.

Special appreciation to Mark Romain for his comments on the police procedural elements. Mark was a Metropolitan Police officer for thirty years. He spent two stints on homicide, the last one spanning ten years. It's always a pleasure to work with him.

You might also like…

Deadly Motives (Grant and Ruby Book 1)

Secrets never stay buried forever…

The Detective
When a nurse is brutally strangled, Detective Grant recognises the work of a killer called Travis.
Grant's a respected detective but early in his career he caught Travis for the murder of five women and Travis has been incarcerated ever since. The problem is, Travis was at the hospital when the nurse was murdered.

The Profiler
Young and talented, Ruby is a criminal profiler. Grant takes her under his wing to work this case. It could make her career or it could break her, because Ruby's been in hiding for a reason.

Deadly Twists
When a second woman is murdered, they realise all is not as it seems.
Why is their suspect always one step ahead? Why does Travis keep talking about mistakes Grant made in the past? And most shocking of all, why is this case so personal to Ruby and what is she hiding from her colleagues?

Praise for Deadly Motives-

'A truly phenomenal story'

'Superb read. A must for all crime readers.'

'One that will really keep you guessing until the end.'

'Killer novel. Five Stars.'

Deadly Motives has over 1500 Five Star Ratings on Amazon and Goodreads.
Grab your copy today!

You might also like,

Deadly Secrets (Grant and Ruby Book 2)

How long can you get away with murder?

Mr Quinn whispers a terrible secret on his death bed. Hours later, the person he spoke to is viciously murdered. Detective Grant, Ruby, and the team, rush to the scene.

Himlands Heath is an idyllic Sussex town but two children disappeared many years ago and they were never found. Quinn knew them.

Then another person who knew the children dies.

What about the rich Watson family? Benefactors of the town and admired by many, are they victims? How did Sir Paul Watson's wife drown on the night of the children's disappearance?

The team track a suspect who got away with it for years. But when Grant realises senior police officers withheld information, the investigation takes a darker turn.
Sergeant Tom Delaney's father knew the children too, and corruption and secrets from the past will be used against Tom, as the killer turns their attention to one of Grant's own...

What readers are saying –

'Oh my! It just gets better and better! Loved it'

'Just finished this. It was amazing!!!'

'Loved this one'

'Fast becoming my 'go to' author when it comes to psychological crime thrillers!'

Deadly Secrets hit the Top 50 Hot New Release Chart in both Amazon USA and Amazon UK.

Get your copy today!

You might also like,

The Couple Upstairs

The perfect home…. or the perfect nightmare?

The Couple
Ellie Mitchell is a writer and her husband, Rob, is a surgeon. They met after a whirlwind romance and everyone sees them as the ideal couple – happy, successful and in love.

The Lodger
Sabrina is mother to a five-year-old daughter.
A single mum who's going through a messy divorce, Sabrina is looking for a place to stay and when the Mitchell's offer her their downstairs apartment, it's the perfect place to lie low and heal from her wounds.

A shocking secret…
The three of them form a friendship but all is not as it seems. Lies and terrible secrets lurk beneath the surface. As their lives become entwined, who can be trusted?
Someone has a sinister agenda and one of them must discover the truth, before the only way out is murder…

What readers are saying –

'Tense and thrilling'

'Nothing is as it seems'

'This was excellent, the best psychological thriller I have read for a long time.'

'A real page turner.'

'Highly recommended.'

'A fantastic thriller that keeps you guessing…lots of twists and turns.'

Grab your copy today!

My Titles

Grant and Ruby

Deadly Motives
Deadly Secrets
Deadly Lies
Deadly Silent

Kal and Marty

Good Girl Bad Girl
London Noir
The Beauty Killers

Psychological thrillers

The Couple Upstairs
The Woman in Room 19

Printed in Great Britain
by Amazon